P9-ECR-830

ZOMBIE APOCALYPSE RUNNING CLUB

ALSO BY CARRIE MAC

10 Things I Can See from Here

Wildfire

ZOMBIE APOCALYPSE RUNNING CLUB

CARRIE MAC

CROWN
NEW YORK

This is a work of fiction. Names, characters, places, and incidents either are the product of the author's imagination or are used fictitiously. Any resemblance to actual persons, living or dead, events, or locales is entirely coincidental.

Visit us on the Web! GetUnderlined.com

Educators and librarians, for a variety of teaching tools, visit us at RHTeachersLibrarians.com

Library of Congress Cataloging-in-Publication Data is available upon request.
ISBN 978-1-5247-7104-1 (trade) — ISBN 978-1-5247-7106-5 (ebook)

The text of this book is set in 11-point Warnock Pro Light.

Editor: Kelly Delaney
Cover Designer: Trisha Previte
Interior Designer: Cathy Bobak
Production Editor: Melinda Ackell
Managing Editor: Tisha Paul
Production Managers: Nathan Kinney and CJ Han

Printed in the United States of America
10 9 8 7 6 5 4 3 2 1
First Edition

For Hawk, Esmé, and Elena

July 20, 2030

According to Racer's beloved training guide, the *Coachpotato*, a person can go from not running at all to comfortably running three miles at a stretch in thirty days of training. We are three weeks into it. I suggested that maybe we wouldn't be able to train every single day for thirty days, what with the brutal heat, dwindling food supply, and constant threat of zombies taking us down. Racer says we practice, no matter what. It's fitness *science,* he says, and because he's a three-time Special Olympics gold-medalist triathlete, and a World Down Syndrome Games track-and-field rock star, and the one who taught running clinics for the Special Olympics, the Seniors Center, and the entire staff of Dicky's Pizza one spring when they wanted a chance at winning Marion Gap's annual Toilet Trot, he is our final authority. On running, and zombies.

If they're gray and their skin is falling off, he says, *they've been zombies a long time. If they look like people, they are fresh.*

Racer is the head (and only) coach of the Zombie Apocalypse Running Club—note my club shirt in his favorite powder blue—membership of three. Or four, if you include his brother, Eddie, who made the shirts and is probably dead, but we haven't gotten into that with Racer yet. The chicken I'm gripping so hard by the feet squawks and thrashes, slapping me with her wings and pecking my leg. Behind me, the first two zombies—I'd call them fresh, sort of—run down the middle of the road, gaining ground. The third one is gray and broken; a dangling foot attached by a thin ribbon of ligament slows him down. My thighs burn and my bones protest each time my sneakers hit the pavement. I feel like I'm running the fastest I've ever run in my life—and at the same time like I cannot move fast enough, no matter what's at stake.

The damn chicken slows me down, but there is no way I'm going to let her go. She is supper, and we all really, really need *supper.* I pause just long enough to wring her neck, add the tiniest second to bask in her new and blissful stillness, and then start running again.

I'm mad that Racer made us train this morning, because that used up the tiny bit of energy I started the day with, and now I don't have any at all to run from these zees. I'm hungry. So hungry. I want a huge meal that will fuel my giantess body. If I was a tiny thing, like Soren or Racer, maybe our tiny so-called meals would be enough. But they are not. I did not start out in this zombie apocalypse with stamina worth shit. I thought I was a fit person, hauling hay bales and wrangling sheep my entire life. It's only now I realize that the only thing that matters is if you can run faster than the zombies. My lungs burn as I suck in the hot summer air. And then, all of a sudden, I am entirely out of breath.

My vision narrows with each bounding heartbeat. My head thumps toward blackness. I feel my grip on the chicken slipping, so I focus all my brain power to command my fingers to squeeze her dry, scaly legs so hard that I feel one crack like a twig. Supper secured, I teeter and fix my sight on the moving truck jackknifed across the road just ahead of me. I take a couple of very precious seconds to check on the zombies; the first two are close enough that I can hear their low warbling, like they're chewing on the language they used to have. I have about the same number of seconds left to reach the cab, swing up, open the door—it will *have* to be unlocked—and get inside and out of their reach. My body wants none of it. *Conditioning,* Racer says. *Very important,* he says. *You need it,* he says. *You are not a strong person, Eira Helvig.* So he says.

But that's not true.

I am the *strongest* person I know. At six and a half feet tall, 270 pounds, I can carry three fifty-pound sacks of horse feed at a time without thinking about it. I'm just not a good runner.

In this moment, I have to run. It's not an option to stop. I will not be turned or killed by those wretched human remnants. Those garbage skin sacks of infection and filth. I haul myself up, fumble with the door handle for a second that I cannot afford, and collapse into the stifling heat of the cab, which reeks of—it takes me a second to place it—*bananas.* The smell is so pungent that I can taste the fruit I haven't had in over a year, but it's sour too, and rotten, and I cannot catch my breath in this oven. I let the chicken drop onto the gas pedal and then retch and retch, my head hung over the passenger seat floor. When nothing more comes out, I sit up.

The two fresher zombies bang on the truck with their dirt-and-blood-blackened hands. When I put my face to the window, they don't even look up, and as much as their fingers scramble across the door as if they're reading braille and they touch the handle over and over, they obviously don't know what to do with it. They still look like people from up here, recent turns, filthy people whose clothes are in tatters and with only one work boot for footwear among them, even now that the one with the broken foot has caught up. That one looks up just now; his cloudy eyes vibrate back and forth. The bite-shaped gash that turned him has rotted away that entire cheek, leaving his teeth as two clacking rows. It makes it easy to think of him as a monster that needs to be slayed rather than someone's once-beloved.

I hear the *pfft* of a flare coming from down the block. There's Soren on the roof of the library, another flare in hand. The one he threw has landed in the back of a pickup truck filled with leaves from last fall, which are now on fire. The zombies circle the truck, not at all interested in me anymore, but they are now positioned exactly where I need to go, and moving past will surely get their interest again.

The stench of bananas is from what used to be two paper sacks of them but is now a dehydrated puddle of rot, the peels split and dried up like long beans, curling and hard. There is also a paper sack full of plastic bags of what used to be chewy, whole sun-dried bananas—Liv's favorite—which have been demolished by rats and mice, leaving only the packaging.

But, *but,* this banana aficionado—or desperate looter of a banana shop?—also had several containers of dried bananas, from the bulk section, it looks like. They've mostly been raided by vermin too, except there are two jars that have fallen in the wheel well, out of the splash of my vomit, and these two jars are full of those creamy-colored crunchy discs of heavenly goodness.

I grab the chicken, pry the jars out of the well, and then scramble over the banana mess. I open the door as quietly and slowly as I can and only hop down when the door is wide open and won't slam shut behind me.

Run, Eira.

Run!

You can do it. You're a stronger runner now than you have ever been in your life. Move your glorious self *forward* with your legs—legs that have more muscle in them than Soren does in his whole body.

RUN.

One and a half blocks to make it back to the others. One and a half blocks of running in the exact same direction the zombies went. Not great apocalypse logic, but going any other way would mean taking longer, and I wouldn't know what I was getting into. At least this way, it's the devils I know.

I cut through the maze of cars and trucks and abandoned and looted suitcases and duffel bags and leathery corpses and bodies held together by bones and fraying clothes. I grip the chicken's feet so tight that I can feel a talon digging into my palm. I hold the jars of banana chips to my chest as if they are jars brimming with actual gold coins. Soren and Racer keep waving me over from the library roof.

"Go, go, go, Eira Helvig!" Racer shouts down as I approach the door. "Go!"

I take the turn around the edge of the building and scurry

over the makeshift barrier that I now realize *will* actually keep the zombies (if not intruders) at bay and jump down the steps to the basement door, which Racer opens just in time for me to fall in.

"So proud!" He hugs my waist, smashing his cheek against my sweaty shirt. "You did it!"

I drop the banana chips. When I hear the breaking glass, I roll onto my back, cover my face with my hands, and cry.

PART I

CHAPTER 1

393 days earlier

With Mom and Liv looking after the homestead, Dad, Soren, and I are on our way to the annual Midsommar Renaissance Festival at the Sigurdsons' apple farm in the Yakima valley. Blessed Are These Orchards—BATO—is made up of four hundred acres with thousands of apple trees and is about a four-hour drive from our place in the mountains. Our homestead is called Gefjunland, named after the Norse goddess of fertility and abundance. Dad regrets not putting *God* in the name, but he and Mom named our land back when they were more into Viking stuff as a lifestyle than they are now. We still dress up for all the faires, but we're less fanatic about it. Dad saves all his fanaticism for God now.

I like being the Viking Giantess of the event circuit, but this is probably the last time I will put on my Viking Giantess costume. No one except Soren knows this, and not because I announced it or anything, but because he's my twin, and we've been two halves of an escape plan that is finally going to happen, after several botched attempts.

This is the year we're going to do it.

We have jobs lined up at the blueberry farm, where we can stay in the bunks with the other workers until the season ends. By then, we'll come up with what to do next. So, this might be the last Renaissance faire either of us goes to for a very long time. The last time Soren will sell the wares from our homestead—honey and candles, vegetables, Dad's knives and horseshoes and candelabras, his leather goods, Mom's linen aprons and pinafores—while Dad "drums up orders for the coming year" (drinks mead and plays liar's dice with his friends), and I conquer whoever dares compete against me in a sword fight or take teenage boys' and drunk men's five-dollar bills in exchange for selfies with their heads by my boobs, which is where they end up when I stand beside most men. *Giantess* is a bit of an overstatement—the tallest woman ever was Sandra Elaine Allen, born in 1955, seven feet, seven inches—but my height plus an elaborate and historically accurate Viking-era warrior costume is still enough of a curiosity to bring in at least two hundred dollars in selfie profits over a Ren faire weekend.

I can take anyone in a sword fight and win the pot. I can drape an arm over the shoulder of whatever loser wants to hand over five bucks. I can flirt with the girls who come on to me—there are always several confident and out and adorable queer sweethearts for every Ren faire—and even make out with a few.

But when it comes to seeing Lola today, my hands shake and my guts churn just thinking about laying eyes on her in person for the first time since New Year's, when we came to see the new house and when we came *this close* to kissing in the tree house before we were interrupted by several of her younger siblings.

"You still going to do it?" Soren asks under the voices of the commentators on Dad's favorite radio station, CRN—Christian Radio Network. I'm too distracted by the men arguing to reply. They spar over an outbreak of toxoplasmosis in Russia that is turning people into zombies. Well, it sounds like zombies: infected people suddenly attacking other people, biting them, which is causing the parasite to . . . What? What is even happening, really?

These men say things like *unprecedented aggression, the infected, not enough facts yet, remains to be seen, containable, unexplained,* but the fact is that the ones that have either been caught alive or shot dead have all been infected by *Toxoplasma gondii.* Which is a parasite. Which sounds like a whole lot of zombie potential.

"The question is, what started this?" the first man says. *"What is different about the toxoplasmosis* now?"

"The Russians," the other man says. *"That's what. That's* who. *We're just going to pretend that* where *this is happening has nothing to do with it?"*

"Simmer down there, Daniel. Forty million Americans already have asymptomatic toxoplasmosis." This man sounds very sure of himself, probably because he spent thirty seconds on Google and now considers himself an expert. *"It can be dormant, and reactivated over time."*

"Not like this," Daniel says. *"This is not your standard kitty-poop toxoplasmosis."*

"The woke folk will blame it on climate change," the other one says. *"Melting polar ice caps. You wait. They will. Mark my words."*

"Digging in their recycling for some cardboard to make their signs and march in the street," Daniel says. *"Or maybe just hiding out until the Next Great Vaccine That Hardly Works."*

This "developing health emergency" was on CRN news for the first time when we were not even an hour from home. It mentioned a research station in the Arctic Circle, then the Kamchatka Peninsula in Russia. But when we pull off the highway and our horse trailer bumps along behind our beat-up old truck as we kick up dust on the dirt road that leads to the faire, they say the *Toxoplasma*-spurred violent infection is in Alaska now, via a fishing boat that crashed into a pier and the crew of fifteen men who spilled onto the streets and started attacking people.

"Alaska is a great place for this to happen," Dad says. "Every good man will take up their ample arms and hunt them down before they get a chance to get to Anchorage. Alaska is filled with good men."

I think of what's happening up north in some ways like I thought about the Ebola outbreak in Africa in 2027. Terrible, but hard to be that scared of because transmission requires direct contact, and it was happening so far away. Not like COVID, which made its way to our town so easily. I was only seven, but I remember the library shutting down for months and Dad refusing to put a mask on to go into the stores. But this is isolated. Bizarre. Never heard of in humans. Like Dad said, the Alaskans will take care of it, no matter how many bodies it takes. By the time we drive under the iron BLESSED ARE THESE ORCHARDS sign and through the gate, I'm back to thinking about Lola and what will be our first kiss. I try not to think about the fact that our kisses will be numbered because I don't know when, or *if,* I'll ever be back here. The Sigurdsons are my parents' friends first. Bersi and my dad are best friends, with that competitive edge that preppers like to sharpen on each other. Lola won't be allowed to see me once Soren and I leave home, and definitely not once everyone figures out that Soren and I are queer.

A wake of dust lifts from the long dirt road ahead that leads through the youngest apple trees to the main house and the barn. It's clouding up behind cars and trucks driving away from BATO. Two police cars take up the rear, their red and blue lights spinning, no sirens. Except for when one bleats twice to signal Dad to stop. When we are window to window, the cops' window goes down slowly. The officer in the passenger seat is a woman. She glances at me first and offers a smile.

"Ding, ding, ding." Soren whispers our gaydar signal as the officer takes off her sunglasses and looks at Dad.

"Something going on at the orchards?" he says.

"That is one impressive beard," she says. "What's that . . . more than a foot? Lots of beards on you 'menfolk' here." When Dad doesn't say anything, she continues. "We're checking on everyone up this way. Internet is out. Never any cell service here. Making sure you all know what's happening up north." She hands him a flyer. After glancing at it, he tosses it on the dash. Soren grabs it so we can both look at it. *Signs & Symptoms of Hypertoxoplasmosis,* it says on one side. I flip it over. *What to do if it happens to you.* At the bottom, in small print: *In the unlikely event that your loved one becomes aggressive.* Dad grabs it back before I can read any of the details. He balls it up and tosses it into the police car.

"Hey." The other cop leans toward the window. "No need for that."

"Exactly," Dad says.

"Where is it now?" our hypochondriac, Soren, asks.

"Yukon."

"That's pretty much still Alaska," Dad says. "Thank you for your concern, but we're going to go up and see our friends, have a good weekend, and then we'll go home. If we feel like it, because my freedoms as an American are well protected." Wait for it. Waaaaait for it. "God bless America, am I right?"

Shablam.

I think of the Ebola outbreak again, and how I never worried about it, what with so much water and sky in between me and it. This, though, is starting to feel like COVID. Never on my radar, until all of a sudden it was everywhere, and we all learned a new language fluently, whether we wanted to or not. If the world shuts down again, we'll be stuck at home again, just when Soren and I were finally ready to say goodbye.

Everyone at BATO wants to talk about the police and toxoplasmosis and how many guns people have in Canada's Yukon versus Alaska and if they'll "man up" and take out the threats. The trailers with the rolled-up canvases and frames for the market tents and the flatbed with the porta-potties wait for attention that doesn't seem to be coming.

"Let me at the zombies," a tall, scrawny man with zero Ren faire attire on says. "I'd shoot so many of them motherfuckers."

"Language," Lola's dad says. Bersi might be the only person I know who is more Christian than my dad. "No swearing. And no mention of zombies. There are no such things."

This kills the conversation enough that the talk shifts to the events of the weekend and the setting up of the market stalls and the competition arena and building the bonfire—which is the first one we've had in two years because of fire bans.

"That's cool," Soren says as we put together the frame of the tall peaked tent that will house our shop at the front and our cots behind the quilts hung across the middle as a divider. "We just have to worry about zombies instead of being burned alive. Actual *zombies.*" We'll keep the horses out the back, because we get to put our tent up against a little paddock, given that we're the Sigurdsons' closest friends. I am trying not to think about zombies. This will not be another COVID, with quarantines and years of trying to sort out what is bullshit and what is legit, which I didn't even have to do for myself when we were seven. All I cared about then was when the library would open up. But when you have a father who embraces all the right-wing conspiracies and white nationalism, it is hard to figure out what you think for yourself, no matter what the polarizing situation is. Confusing at first, and then deeply disappointing when you start to think for yourself and realize that you're living with a bigot who would rather see the government topple than have it pay one more cent to health care or any pursuit that could possibly benefit people who are different than you. The list of reasons that it's time for Soren and me to leave home isn't all that long, but with a reason like a paranoid, racist, homophobic, xenophobic father, who needs quantity over that kind of quality?

I can easily say that the pandemic is what made Soren and me wake up. Call us woke folk—a slur when Dad says it—or call us liberal sheep (one of his favorites), or simply call us Soren and Eira Helvig growing up and into our very own shiny and independent brains that look a lot different than our parents' do.

With the tent up and the shop mostly organized, Dad heads off to find the mead and the other men, and Soren takes off to wherever, maybe to find some of the Sigurdson kids before things start in earnest later. I change out of my shorts and T-shirt and become Eira the Viking Giantess: linen underwear and undershirt—Viking bras were more for show and, because of that, banned by the Christians, but I have to wear one to keep my big boobs in order—tunic, linen pants, and my belt and scabbard, with my dagger pointing down in its sheath, even though the Vikings carried their traditional seaxes point-up so they wouldn't puncture the leather. Mom makes us carry ours point-down. It's too hot to wear anything, but all that linen isn't as bad as it sounds.

Dad made my belt and scabbard, along with the buckles and fasteners. In fact, most people here own something made by the Helvigs. Now that my hair is short, I don't have to do anything with it except steer my longer bangs off to one side with a little oil. Cutting it was worth kneeling for twenty minutes on gravel. I claimed I had nits, but that made no difference. I never said that Soren was the one who chopped it off, but Dad punished him too, because if one of us does something behind his back, the other had something to do with it. So now we both have knees full of itchy scabs where the rocks dug in and stayed there. We spent that night picking them out, but there are always a few teeny, tiny ones that stay put and work their way out days or weeks later.

The most important part of the Viking Giantess costume is my long sword, Gertrude, which means *strong spear.* Not all that original, but it suits her. She is a full thirty-five inches of heavy iron; thirty of those are the blade. Dad made her for me in the forge this winter, when he was fulfilling the special orders he'd collected at faires all summer. Gertrude rides in the scabbard, angled across my back so I can grab her with my right hand, which is a skill that took well over a month to perfect. If I had to buy her, she'd cost thousands of dollars.

About halfway along the market path, I catch sight of Lola. She has a basket of garlic scapes balancing over the crook of her arm and is wearing one of my mom's dresses, tailored just for her figure. She's loosened the ribbon at the bust and crisscrossed leather cord across her chest to accentuate her breasts. Either she doesn't care if her parents or siblings see her, or she's ready for the consequences. Both of those super-brave notions make me want to do a heck of a lot more than kiss her. I stop in my tracks, not quite sure how to walk all of a sudden. Lola's talking to a boy I don't recognize, but as soon as she sees me, she squeals in delight and runs over. She catches me in a hug before I'm ready, pulling away just as I get myself organized to hug her back, and then reaches up to touch my hair while my arms are still poised for a hug.

"Your hair! It looks amazing!" She blushes so instantly that it looks like a ghost just dabbed her cheeks with pink powder right in front of me. I lower my arms, which now feel like lead at my sides. Lola gestures to the boy, who followed her. "This is Rob. He's from Seattle. He goes to an arts high school."

Considering he goes to an arts school, he sorely underdressed for the Renaissance faire—store-bought linen pants, tight white tank top, and new Birkenstocks. I feel my body relax just enough that I'm in charge of it again. I pull Gertrude out of my scabbard so fast that she whistles and, in one movement, catch a garlic scape with her tip and slide it to the base before grabbing it and taking a bite.

"Now your breath will stink," Lola says.

"I can smell it from here," Rob says. "You're the Giantess, right?"

"I doubt anyone else here could be."

"That makes you Soren's sister."

"You know Soren?"

"Enough to say that you two don't look much like twins," he says. "Except for the eyes. Maybe the jawline too." He traces mine in the air with a slender finger, nails painted black. So, by *arts high school,* what Lola means is *gay.* "Squarish, but not blocky. I wouldn't use a heavy line if I was drawing it."

Soren is five foot six, elfin compared to me. He wears his long blond hair in two braids and is waifish to my muscular. He looks like a Gelfling from *The Dark Crystal,* whereas I look more like a Landstrider. Eddie pointed out Soren's resemblance when he showed us the movie. Soren and I both have dark blue eyes that look like you'd end up in the deep ocean if you dove in. That's not my line. That's courtesy of Magda, when we made out at Ren Faire Northwest last year. The heat wave was in full force, and I spent the entire weekend drenched in sweat in my Viking Giantess outfit. Magda either didn't notice or didn't care. Buzz cut on one side, bouncy black curls on the other, light brown skin slick with sweat, she smelled like roses because she and her mother run a stall that sells all things roses. Perfume, petals, sachets, little iced cookies—

Wait. How does Rob know Soren at all? When would Soren ever have a chance to meet this guy?

"Speaking of Soren," Rob says, "I'm going to go find him."

Me too, because this has to be an internet hookup, which does not sound safe to me. Not at all. Even if Rob is on our territory. Before I worry about that, though, I have to get armored up and slaughter a couple of Saxons in the first bracket of the weekend's one-on-one tournament. I get to use my real long sword—blunted—in the historic martial-arts battles but foam replicas for the rest. I'm not competing in any mounted categories because my horse, Odger, doesn't love it, but I will clean up all the ones on foot.

Lola cheers me on as I defeat two Saxons easily—they are more growls and hairy eyeballs than skill—and one Norseman. None of them are as tall as me, but all of them are as heavy, easily.

That should level the playing field, but the three men wield their swords like they want to throw them at me, when the trick is to make your sword an extension of yourself. I will go into tomorrow as reigning champion, with a day full of fighting to defend it, even if there are hardly any spectators beyond us competitors and our families and friends and a handful of people not scared away by the cops and the news.

CHAPTER 2

Lola hands me her basket; I carry it for her as we walk through the village, which should be completely set up by this time on the Friday of a festival weekend.

"Where is everyone?" There are gaps between stalls, and only a fraction of the tents and trailers are set up in the camping area.

"Some COVID scare," Lola says. "Dad says we're going to lose money this year."

"It's not COVID," I say. "He didn't tell you about the zombies?"

"Uh, no." Lola laughs. *"Zombies?"*

I start to tell her, but it seems so far-fetched that I switch to talking about what I've learned about *Toxoplasma gondii* today. Like the fact that 11 percent of Americans over the age of six already carry it. So, something is different about it all of a sudden. When I stumble onto climate change, Lola stops me by putting one of her delicate hands on my thick, hairy forearm.

"Don't start with that." She pats my arm but then doesn't take her hand away. Instead, she glances around to make sure we're away from everyone else before sliding her hand down to hold mine. "Please."

Even with her hand warming mine, I have to bite my tongue to not say anything more about climate change. She's a denier, just like her brothers and sisters and parents, but I can always hope she'll open up to actual science eventually. When you grow up in a family like hers or mine, it can take a very long time to shake off the stuff you want to leave behind, or to even know what that stuff is. It's not as easy as just walking away—even if that's where Soren and I are at now—because we love so much about our families too, and where we come from.

"Let's talk about something else." I squeeze her hand, at the same time squeezing back what I want to say. Let's not talk about the fact that the same sort of people who deny basic facts are also the ones who would send us both to hell for liking each other the way we do. Let's not tell her that Soren and I are about to give up all the comforts and love that we *do* have at home in exchange for going out into the world to be who we really are, to live without secrets, and to fall in love with who we want to. And why? Because the people she's defending believe that we are sinners. Even if they might love us, they hate the sin. But we and the sin are symbiotic.

Another basic fact is that everyone has to arrive at their destination in their own time. Lola and I might want the same thing, but we're going to get it differently. Tonight, though? Tonight can be just about us; not our families, not our eternal damnation, and not zombies.

It's less than a minute before we have to drop each other's hands. There are a few people between us and my family's stall, which is the last one on the left this year. Lola's oldest brother, Calder, has his toddler on his shoulders.

"We just sent fighter jets up to British Columbia," Cal says, as if the planes belong to him personally.

His wife stands beside him, her arm hooked in his. She has their infant on her chest, asleep in a wrap.

"Without waiting for Canada's go-ahead." She sways as she talks.

"They're gonna carpet-bomb 'em," says the scrawny man from earlier. He's changed into a more suitable Ren faire outfit and actually looks pretty handsome now.

"That'll take care of it," Cal says. Lola's sister-in-law smiles at her as we pass, then she turns her gaze to me. No more smile. Cal glares at me too. When he turns his focus back to the group, he adds, "Canada can thank us later."

Our stall is the only one ready for sales. We have jars of Soren's first honey of the year, all the goods we crafted indoors over the winter, and the spring greens and radishes and carrots and peas. There's always a little pile of our younger sister's carved figures too, smoothed-out fistfuls of the basswood that our grandparents send her from California. Liv's carving got a lot better over the winter, maybe because she was inside more and had to sit still. She spends most of the year barefoot outside, scaling trees and wrangling her goats. Whatever the reason, her foxes and owls and bears and squirrels all look like what they're supposed to be. She always sells out anyway, but it used to be because it was cute to buy something that a little kid made. This year it's going to be because a kid made them but also because they're really good. And do not call her a little kid. She's never really been one. Truth be told, at ten Liv is far more serious than any of us have ever been in our entire lives.

Soren doesn't see Lola and me coming. Sitting nearly knee to knee with Rob behind the table, he barely looks up when he does notice us.

"Soren!" I shout in a whisper. "Dad will see you!"

"Or someone else will, and they'll tell him," Lola says.

"There's hardly anyone here yet," Soren says.

"Takes one person," I say. "And who even is this guy?"

"Hi, Lola," Soren says, finally putting just a little space between him and Rob. "You know better than to hang out with the Viking Giantess. She's nothing but trouble."

"I like her trouble," Lola says. This makes me blush so hard that I have to look away, but Soren notices. Before he can say anything, I give it back to him.

"And how about you? Does Rob-from-Seattle-who-goes-to-an-*arts*-high-school have any idea what he's getting into?"

"Little ol' me? Soren the Honey Maker?" Soren says. "I am entirely innocent." He puts a hand on Rob's knee and turns his blue eyes to Rob's big brown ones. "I promise."

"Soren, come with me." I grab his wrist so tight that he doesn't bother to protest. I lead him out the back, where the horses whinny happily to see us. "What is going on? Who is he?"

"I didn't want to say anything in case he didn't come."

"That's bullshit."

"Okay," Soren says. "I didn't want to tell you because I was embarrassed. *Am* embarrassed."

"We tell each other *everything*," I say.

"Not absolutely everything," he says.

"You arranged a hookup at the Ren faire?" I shake my head. "With Dad here?"

"How the hell else am I supposed to meet anyone?"

"In real life!" I say. "Not on some app."

"Well, he made his way here," Soren says. "All the way from Seattle. For me. To see me."

"And if you don't want Dad—or anyone else—to murder you both, then dial it DOWN."

"You dial it down," he says. "You look exactly like two teenage lesbians fawning over each other."

"We do not."

"Hey." Rob peers out from the canvas. "Everything okay?"

"It's fine." Soren takes his hand, thankfully in the shadows, and then steps toward him. Rob doesn't move. It's like they choreographed this before and are performing it now. This kiss, this sweet kiss that Soren leaves on Rob's lips. Rob blushes and then kisses Soren back.

Lola leads me deep into the orchard, along tree-lined rows of Galas and Ambrosias and Pink Ladies, and even though it's just now officially summer, the heat nearly cooks the new apples on the trees, still smallish and glinting in the sunlight, and positively stews the ones rotting under the trees and abandoned in crates at the ends of the rows. Even the dirt smells like apples here.

"This way," she says.

I would ask her where she's taking me, but I have no words

available, just a bounding heartbeat instead. She leads me to the center of the orchard, where she's laid out a blanket under one of the oldest trees, low and gnarly and full of lush branches to shade us from the sun. There is a basket too, she shows me as she invites me to sit. No more garlic scapes, but a thermos of iced tea and a bowl of wild blueberries and a little apple pie with a heart cut out of the crust.

"Did you know that it takes two pounds of apples to make a pie?" Hearing the quaver in Lola's voice makes my heart settle a little. Neither of us knows what we're doing right now. A light film of sweat breaks out along my arms and quickly cools in the breeze. "But this one is little, so it was only a pound or so."

"You planned all this?" My face heats up as I fold my impossibly long frame into a semi-reclining position. Make me nervous and I grow an inch by the minute. I am eight feet tall now, trying to arrange myself into a spot better suited for a gnome. "For me? For us?"

"It's just a picnic," Lola nearly whispers. "That's all."

I lean in—nearly crushing the pie—part my lips, and put one of my big hands at the back of her slender neck. I close my eyes as she lets me pull her to me until our lips meet. She scoots closer and takes my face in her hands and really kisses me. With her head tilted back to reach mine, she kisses my upper lip first, nibbling it softly before kissing my lower lip too.

This kiss is *different.* The apples above us turn to glitter. Sunlit sparkles rain down. Our kiss unfolds something, a dimension that did not exist with any other kiss until this one, which tastes of scapes and her and the fragrant orchard. My soul flips inside me, and my guts fall onto the blanket. The feeling is so overwhelming that when I pull away, I half expect to really see my guts pooled on the patchwork quilt, each square with a daisy in the middle and hearts along the edges, all of it covered in apple glitter.

From my height, Lola is a fairy beside me. She wears a crown of reeds woven with flowers atop her blond head, braids coiled up and behind her ears. I can see right down her top and the slope of her breasts, damp with sweat. Already tiny at five feet and a little bit, from this vantage point, she looks like I could put her in my pocket and take her home with me—instead of us having to go back to the faire, and then back to our homes, a day's drive apart, each firmly located in a world where we absolutely cannot be together. We can hardly even communicate between visits; I only get onto the computer at home for "educational purposes," with Mom standing by, or at the library, because my parents haven't figured out that Soren and I go on the computers there while they do errands around town.

After the Sigurdsons' fiddle performance at the bonfire, Lola's parents have Lola take the little kids back to the house, and with them goes my chance at seeing her again until tomorrow. I lie awake in bed trying to picture how it might happen. I'll cup her face in my hands, or maybe I'll put one hand at the small of her back and pull her to me. Just as I decide there's no point in trying to fall asleep, I do, maybe for an hour, minutes, maybe for just a few seconds, only to wake from a shallow sleep to the stench of thick smoke and a chorus of terrible screams surrounding me. At first, I think embers from the bonfire must've set the orchard on fire, but when I look out, I see that there are bodies *on* the fire. That cannot be right, but just as I'm trying to sort out whether this is a nightmare or real life, I lock eyes with Rob, frozen in place just beyond our stall. He lifts his arms as that scrawny guy—his tunic is soaked with blood now—runs at him and tackles him to the ground before mashing his face with Rob's in a grotesque kiss, coming up with flesh dangling between his teeth. The scrawny guy straightens and starts running again for the next closest person. I take a step, the first of however many it will take me to go help Rob, but then he rolls onto his knees and up to standing without using his hands, which hang limp at his sides now. He straightens, rolls his bloodied shoulders back, and runs down the path, heading for the crowd fleeing into the moonlit orchard.

Rob tackles a man to the ground and leans down as if to kiss him on the lips but instead opens his mouth wider than I've ever seen anyone do and sinks his teeth into the man's flesh. Rob jerks his head from side to side, tearing away the man's lips and cheek, dampening his screams into gurgles. Rob leaps away. He runs down the aisle between the stalls until he fixes on Cal's wife. She scoops the baby out of the wrap and throws her to a man who looks like he couldn't even run away from the neighbor's nasty dog and up his own front steps, but he holds that little baby in his arms and sprints into the darkness, leaving the woman behind to get her face ripped off by Rob too.

Not Rob. That is one of the zombies that were not supposed to exist, let alone make it here.

But I can still see Rob in it also—that is, what is left of him. In the same glance I see two other people locked in that same grotesque embrace. They land on a wheelbarrow and writhe there, a tangle of legs and arms and screams. When they both leap up, there is no way of telling who attacked who. They both have gaping wounds on their faces, and the whites of their eyes glint under the moon, their lids red-rimmed and wet, open bizarrely wide, like they are as unhinged as Rob's jaw seemed to be. They get up as if they have no need of bones and tendons and muscles. Then they run.

Dad runs toward me, waving his arms as the flames of the bonfire cast his shadow ahead of him. There's a woman behind him, so I step aside to let the two of them in, but at the last second he turns and shoves her hard. I catch a glimpse of her eyes then, milky and glistening. She stumbles and lands on her back; I see the hole in her cheek as she clacks her teeth and growls. It's not bleeding. In fact, the edges of the wound are almost clean, making a lacquer frame to shiny white teeth when she howls, high and screeching, like an eagle. She trains her eyes on us, focusing on me through her foggy film. She bites at the air in my direction. The veins on her neck are fat and nearly purple, bounding with each heartbeat, which come at an impossible rate. She stands as if being suddenly pulled up with a strong cable, using no hands, like Rob did. Like no one should be able to. She lunges for me, but Dad grabs my sword and plunges it into her easily, despite it not being sharp. Other than pinning her there and causing a pool of blood of that same red purple throbbing in her veins, it does nothing. She yowls and thrashes around it, alternately grinding her teeth and snapping, but can't organize herself to pull the sword out.

"Her head," Dad whispers. Then he hollers it. "Her head! Her head!"

Her head *what*? Part of me cannot put together what is happening before my eyes, here in this special place, with Lola's kiss still warming my lips. But another part of me—the one with the trapline back home, the one who wins every sword fight, the one who has been taught to kill intruders if they ever threaten our family or homestead—reaches for Dad's dagger on his belt and plunges it deep into her eye. Don't try to go through a human skull, Dad told us. It's harder than you think. Go for the tender spots.

The woman's knees buckle, and she falls backward, slipping off the knife. I can't stop staring at her milky eyes and the pool of blood.

"Inside! Get in!" Dad pulls the canvas slit closed behind him and grabs my shoulders. "Did you get any blood on you?" When he doesn't find any on me, he checks himself. "Do you see any on me? Where's your brother?"

"I don't see any," I hear myself say as my words slowly catch up to my thoughts. "I don't know where Soren is. These are the zombies, Dad! The ones you said would not get to us!"

"There are no such things as zombies!" he bellows. "We have to go! We have to go out there and find Soren and go."

"I killed her," I whisper. I reach for Dad, for him to hold me. Even though I've been taller than him for over a year, all I want right now is for him to fold me into his arms and hold my head against his chest like he did when I was little. I want to hear his heartbeat, right now, amid the unravelling around us, despite everything we have to do in these moments to find Soren and get out of here alive. I try to hug him, but he pushes me away.

"You did not kill that," he said. "You stopped Satan from possessing her. You killed a lame horse. A rabid coyote. The cat that got skinned trying to free itself from under that broken fence. Remember?"

"I just killed a person, Dad." I stand there with my arms out, still wanting him to embrace me. "She is someone. She has people who love her."

"Who loved her before."

The cat was called Boop, because she'd come up to you and bump her nose against you, as if she was the one booping us. She wasn't even a year old when we found her lying in the dirt beside a broken section of our post-and-rail fence. She'd gotten stuck somehow and then tried to free herself by scrambling under. She was almost dead when we discovered her. Dad picked her up and broke her neck in what looked like one single move.

"We have to find Soren." I grab my sword and my pack and then immediately freeze; if that was Rob ripping someone's face off, where was Soren?

"Make no mistake, Eira." Dad collects every weapon we have: the knives and seaxes and other daggers from the stall display. He unsnaps the holster on his belt, ready to draw his gun. "This is all part of God's plan. *'He will render His anger in fury. Rebuke with flames of fire!'*"

"God's plan better include Soren getting back here right now."

"This is all God's will." Dad shoves his things into his pack. He punctuates the air with his horn mead cup before shoving it into his pack too. Why are we bothering with any of these things? We need to find Soren. Get the horses. The truck. That's all that matters. *"And by His sword on all flesh, and those slain by the Lord will be many."*

"Dad—" I start, but there is nothing to say to compete with the screams outside, which have reached a fever pitch and are coming from all directions. Even as I want to deny it, I believe it too, this time. The end of the world has happened several times in my lifetime—or so he claimed it was going to each time, but then God's good grace shone salvation upon us.

There is no light now. Just hell, all around.

"We have to go," Dad says. "Where's Soren?"

"I don't know! He was with—" Rob. "I don't know! I don't know where he is!"

"I'll find him. You take the horses to the truck."

Dad disappears out the front. I stand at the back, my fingers grazing the canvas flap. On the other side of it is everything that doesn't make sense anymore. On the other side of this thin barrier is a kind of chaos I don't know how to think about. The pressure in my head is so massive that I wouldn't be surprised if my brains leaked out my ears and I died that way. I wait another moment, and when that doesn't happen, I pull aside the flap and step out into the night.

"Horses," I whisper. "Truck." The moon casts a silver light on the rows of apple trees, which stand like soldiers waiting for orders, while on the other side of the tent is the war they are waiting to join. Gunfire, screams, and the crackle of the spreading fire get quieter with each step I take toward the paddock and our three frantic horses. Thankfully, they settle when they see me, like they know that I'll take care of them, even though I don't know anything anymore. I mount my horse, and the other two follow.

They stay calm enough until they file into the trailer, and then they start stamping and tossing their heads. I secure them, then throw my scabbard and sword ahead of me into the cab and lock myself in the truck. I'll get the truck aimed for the back road out—I can already see the jam of trucks and cars that have blocked the main entrance—and then wait for Soren and Dad.

I stab the key into the ignition, start the engine, and grip the steering wheel. In the glow of the dashboard, I see a streak of that terrible red-purple blood on the inside of my arm, up by my elbow. I twist my arm and see another one just below the first. I grab one of Liv's rag dolls—the one she says lives in the truck with the fairy who lives in the headlights and keeps making them blink on and off—and scrub the woman's blood off my arm. When it's all gone, I roll down the window just enough to shove the doll out. Sorry, Liv. I will make you a new one. If this isn't actually the end of the world tonight.

I lock the doors and cut the engine. I open the glove box and take out the revolver Dad keeps there. There are four rounds in the chamber. I will need only one. I take off the safety and put the gun to my temple and close my eyes. The moment I feel my senses change, or if I feel an inexplicable heat, or coldness, or if my vision clouds, or numbness takes over—whatever sign I get that it's happening—I'll pull the trigger. I will do that to keep Dad and Soren safe. They have to get home to Mom and Liv.

A minute passes. Three minutes, at least. Would it have happened by now? I hear Soren shout my name. I open my eyes, even though most of me thinks I'm just hearing him in my head. But there he is, with Dad, stumbling out of the orchards ahead of me.

With the gun in my lap, I drive away from the view of the tents and the screaming and the fire that looks like it's about to consume the Sigurdsons' newly built log home, the one that looks more like a mountain resort hotel than a house. I shake my head. I can't think about them. I can't think about Lola. Tears blur my eyes. Just get to Soren and Dad. I wipe them away with the arm that used to have blood on it.

"I got some of the blood on me." I don't even stop the truck; I just slow down, so they fling themselves in. "I waited, with the gun, to see if anything would happen. It hasn't, but it might. And you'll have to kill me, Dad. You will. You'll do it, right? So you can get back to Mom and the others? So you and Soren get home safe?"

"Stop the truck."

"Not now. . . ." I ease the truck to a stop and put it into park. "I mean—"

"Of course not now," Dad cuts me off. "But you can't drive. We don't know how this works."

"The people I saw turned right away." Soren reaches for the gun, and then Dad takes it from him. "It's been twenty minutes at least, right?" Soren turns to me. "Maybe longer? Nothing's changed! You're fine. You are fine, Eira!"

"The one I saw . . ." I won't say Rob's name, even if I can barely bite it back. "He turned right away."

"Still," Dad says. "Soren, you drive. Eira and I will keep watch. I'll give you the gun if you need it, Eira."

"You'll do it, though, right, Dad?" I grip his wrist. He doesn't pull away, which says more than if he had. He's weighed all the information he has, and this is the conclusion he's come to, but he's not going to let his guard down. I love this about him so much in this moment, knowing that he and Soren will get home, no matter what.

As my heart rate slows, Soren navigates our way through the orchard and out the east gate, to a dirt track that leads to the highway. We're the only vehicle on this road, but when the highway comes into view, I'm not sure why I'm surprised to see that the traffic is truly jammed, to a complete stop. From here it looks like a long snaking light display, so many headlights and brake lights in the distance. Dad leans over and turns off our lights. He gets out and smashes our running lights too. Below, car horns and alarms and screams leak toward us. Five gunshots pierce the night, then the rapid fire of a semiautomatic, then more, a few seconds later, in response. There is a small explosion, and a car is engulfed by flames. Then another. We have to drive a bit closer to reach the ATV trail that will connect us with another forestry service road, which will take us northeast. We see some people, barely as big as dollhouse families to us at this distance, scurrying between the rows of cars. In other places we see knots of people, tackling others to the ground as violence consumes them. Seconds later, one by one, they stand erect again, drawn up in that unnerving way, like they have slap bracelets instead of backbones and have been set straight again. They take off running, each of them aiming for another one of those little dolls trudging along with suitcases and children and strollers and wagons. But when the dolls turn, the zombies don't climb onto the cars, and when the creatures get to a jam of vehicles, they just gather there in knots of chaos, clamoring and reaching.

CHAPTER 3

When we get onto the smoother forestry service road, we all relax a teeny, tiny bit. It's two a.m. The waxing slice of moon is fat and high and bright, and it makes me think of Lola and the apple glitter. I curl my fingers into tight fists until I can feel my fingernails dig into my flesh and the pain pushes away Lola, and the image of her home burning to the ground.

"Which way was the fire going?" Soren asks. We do this—tap into each other without knowing, or maybe we do know it at some level we don't have access to.

"Up the hill," Dad says.

Away from the house.

"Their workers will get it under control." Dad nods. "No different than an orchard fire. Same protocol. They've got plenty of water."

I take this. I relax my grip but keep my fists closed, holding in the pump trucks and the hoses and the giant water tower and the hope that everything will turn out all right, that this will be the romantically incendiary story of the night of our first kiss. This night will go down in history, but we'll keep going. Everything before, and then everything after.

We have all the windows down. The air is finally cooler. It smells of the lupines that line either side of the road and the muddy damp of the marshes just beyond. During the hot summer months, this is the only time of day that the air is cool.

None of us can get a full breath of that sweet air in, though. Our lungs and guts and brains are squeezed tight in the grips of bewildered fear and confusion as we try to make sense of what information we glean from the odd radio station we can tune in to and the chatter on the CB radio, which is mostly truckers.

This is so much bigger than whether or not the Sigurdsons' orchard is burning to the ground. Every continent except Australia and Antarctica has been affected by this rogue strain of *Toxoplasma gondii.*

CRN news on the hour: *"There is speculation that international governments have manipulated the common parasite in secret laboratories, with the most recent accusation being that the Russian government is—"*

Trucker Asteroid Larry on the CB: *"—weaponized it! Weaponized a Goddamned parasite that most of us have! They turned it into a mofo trigger! Gonna turn us all into killers! Turn us into Goddamn zombies, Goddamn undead monsters—"*

Some NPR scientist: *"While it is true the tests show considerable decrease in fear and increase in aggression, it remains highly unlikely that this perplexing iteration of* Toxoplasma gondii *cannot be contained."*

Along with the bewildering death counts, doubling with every mention until they don't bother with a number and just leave it at tens of millions—*tens of millions*—comes a name.

Hypertox.

When we get close enough to a cell tower that Dad can check the internet on his phone, we huddle around it, watching the tiny, devastating images of people being mowed down by the infected.

"Watch," Soren says. "Look at that." He replays the clip, pointing at the first zombie as it runs straight for an old lady, plows her to the ground, bites her face, leaps up, and keeps running. "Then these two." Two girls in sundresses and bare feet run in the same way to an old man tending to the woman. The girls pounce on him and beat him to death. It doesn't look like they bite him at all.

We search for information until Dad's phone dies, and then we keep driving, with it plugged into the charger and a plan to stop at the next spot where we think there will be coverage. In the spots where we get nothing but radio silence on all fronts, we don't talk.

The next trucker we hear on the CB has one message: *"Shelter in place. Protect your own. Hide. Wait this out. Let them take the weak. Save yourselves."*

We get three stations that say the same thing. *Shelter in place. Gather what food, water, medication, and supplies you can and find a safe place.*

Then, one by one, the stations stop live broadcasting, and the reporters are replaced with emergency broadcast messages.

"I really hope they got home to their families," Soren says.

"God willing," Dad says.

Not once do the radio news and emergency broadcasts use the term *zombie,* but that's all anyone talks about on the CB, which still has chatter. They compare the situation to every zombie movie and TV show Soren and I don't know much about. *Walkers, biters, zees, clickers, geeks, roamers, Romeros, Zekes, living dead, undead, rotters, runners, creepers.*

"Mom and Liv are fine," Soren whispers.

"Of course they are." Dad turns the radio off so I can't scan for signals anymore. "They're all tucked in at the safest place on earth."

I might've rolled my eyes at that declaration yesterday, but now I'm holding on to it for dear life.

What would've been a four-hour drive on the highway is turning into more than double that as the sun comes up. Dad lets me try to find a signal again, but the radio is just a scrolling series of static where some stations used to be and the same federal emergency broadcasts on loop.

"Attention. Attention. This is the Emergency Broadcast System. Take shelter immediately. Shelter in place. The United States is dealing with a highly transmissible, unknown neurological event that causes infected people to attack uninfected people. Watch for the following signs in the people around you: suddenly violent be-

havior, darkening of the blood, red-rimmed and/or cloudy eyes. These people are dangerous and will become violent. This is not a drill. Repeat: this is not a drill. Take shelter and tune in to this frequency for further instructions. Travel is not safe."

The last person we hear on the CB won't answer Dad. He just keeps talking. His words are rapid-fire. He barely pauses to breathe.

"—call them whatever you want. This is a zombie invasion. This is the zombie apocalypse. This is God. This is Pestilence. *This is His army of the undead, sent to cleanse our moral ruin."*

"Yes." Dad nods.

"Social decay is the scaffolding for this zombie apocalypse. A faithless worldview has brought us to this place. Homosexuality, feminism, immigrants. The woke. *We have become the outcome our Christian leaders feared. We are in the last gasp for a Godful world. If we stop breathing, He will tip the world and send us all tumbling into the depths of hell, where we belong."*

I take Soren's hand. He squeezes mine. We will not listen to some alt-right flat-earther bigot, even if Dad is clearly taking comfort in his words.

"And if you're listening out there? Are you listening out there? Is anyone out there listening to me say this? If you are, I'm giving you very clear instructions. Keep away, because the only thing I'll treat you to is a bullet to the brain, my friends. Mark my words. With God as my protector, I will kill you all."

"I bet he's got a good homestead somewhere in the middle of nowhere," Dad says as if the man is perfectly normal. "Prepared. Like us."

What I want to say is this: *You're excited, right, Dad? Part of you can't wait to put your preps to the test? You're thinking this is the second coming of Christ, right? How long before you end up at that conclusion and drag all of us with you?*

Soren is thinking the same thing, I bet, because when we lock side-eyes without Dad noticing, we just stare at each other. Neither of us will call him out on it, though. All bets are off. We're not leaving on our sixteenth birthday. We might not even make it that long.

CHAPTER 4

It's been three hundred and fifty-seven days since the Hypertox outbreak began, and we're all still alive. At first, all we thought about was what was happening out in the world, but now enough time has passed that Soren and I are back to thinking about running away and wondering if there is any world at all left out there for us to run to. Soren and I first ran away almost three years ago, on the night of our fourteenth birthday, which was just a few days after we got back from Midsommar at Lola's. We got as far as the library, when we were meant to be checking our traplines. We tied the horses up in the shade of the trees behind the building and went in to ask Eddie if we could camp on the lawn.

"Sure, the most flamboyant gay in the village takes in the little queer boy." He twisted the green silk carnation stuck in the lapel of his waistcoat. "That would rile up all the Bible-thumping Karens. Not to mention your father. *He* would murder me."

"He would not," Soren and I said in unison.

"He would! With his bare hands. Or with his Bible."

"Definitely not with his Bible," Soren said.

"Let me tell you," Eddie said. "I get it. I *actually* get it. I was homeless at sixteen, honey. I really, really get it. But there is no way you can stay here."

So, we went home.

We were going to leave on the night of our fifteenth birthday, but then Liv found us getting the horses ready in the middle of the night. She hardly makes a sound when she pads around with her perpetually bare feet. Neither of us noticed her until I glanced over and saw her standing there, scrawny, pale, her blond hair tousled and matted from sleep.

"You wouldn't go without me," she said.

We *were* going to go without her. And then we would come back for her, when she was old enough and made her own decision to leave, but in the meantime, we were better prepared for this second attempt. That was the first year the Bhosles said we could work there for the blueberry season and stay in the workers' bunks. We were pretty sure we could get Dad to calm down, if he found us there. Better to ask forgiveness than permission, we figured.

But with her standing in front of us in her nightgown and bare feet, I could feel the outside world falling away until it was just us three in the barn, with the animals rustling in their stalls and bats swooping in the light, hunting bugs.

"We're older," Soren said. "We'll have to go without you sometime."

"Not tonight," she said. "Okay?"

Maybe we didn't want to go that bad. Maybe he knew we

couldn't make it on our own. Maybe we knew for a fact that Dad would be apoplectic no matter where we went. But either way, all it took was a little kid with sleep in her eyes to get us to stay.

We made it home from BATO, and while the outside world was being torn apart, none of it touched us at our homestead. There were no zombies. Simple as that. We found Liv and Mom, safe and sound. Soren and I turned sixteen four days later, and we stayed put. We didn't even think about running away then, because where do you run away to in a zombie apocalypse when you live in the safest place on the planet? To honor what seemed like the now-dead dream of clueless newly fourteen-year-olds, we rode to the bluff where we used to be able to see the lights of Marion Gap before the power grid failed the day after we got back. We got off the horses and stared down at the neatly arranged streets in the far, twilit distance and realized that we had nowhere to go, and our lives to lose.

Dad says God excused us from the trials of Armageddon and that this is the promised reward. *This* is heaven, whether we are still on earth or not. He says we will never know if this is God's paradise, or just earth. Mom and Liv go along with that idea. I never really know what Liv thinks because she talks an idea up in one direction and then unravels it just as quickly. Soren and I say we've been "excused" because the zombies haven't found us, not by the will of God but rather the fact that we live in the middle of exactly *nowhere.* So, the zombies just haven't found us *yet.* And any of the few people who know we're here know better than to mess with Bjorn Helvig and his arsenal and fighting spirit. Or they're all zombies by now too. Or just plain regular dead.

We have one narrow dirt track that leads to our house from the south and another narrower one that leads away from a cattle gate to the north. Eight ATV paths snake through our 175 acres, and off of it too, where we hunt without permits—and with God's blessing, because how else would we bag a deer if not for His will?

Dad and I check the farthest-east edges of our land, where, yesterday, Dad claimed there was a tent-shaped flattening of the tall, thirsty grass in the meadow.

"It's probably just a deer and her fawn," I say as we near the spot. "Bedding down. Or a bear, maybe?"

Late spring means babies of all kinds, and mamas that need to lie down.

"There." He hops down and grabs a very old, sun-bleached, pre-zombie-apocalypse-era chip bag that probably blew this way on the wind. Salt and vinegar. What I would give for that bag to be brand-new, full of air and a bouquet of tangy, salty potato chip goodness. That is what God needs to do for me right now. Fill that bag anew, dear Father. Fill it so that I may fill my face. "What did I say?" Dad shakes the empty bag. "What did I tell you?"

Something else catches my eye. A smaller glint of another wrapper. A brand of beef jerky we boycott because the mega-corporation that owns it prints a tiny Progress Flag on all its packaging. That is not ours. Behind him, in the shadows of the trees, I spy an unused zip tie. Also not one of ours.

"You watch the pines." He gets back up on his horse. "I'll look north."

I stare at the pines and not at the zip tie. A million tiny worms of worry squirm in my gut. Goose pimples dot my arms. The sun feels impossibly hot, but I can't make myself move into the shade. Sweat runs from my forehead into my eyes, where a pressure of terrible anticipation and dread pushes from behind. Someone has been here.

Dad is back moments later. "There." He hands me the heavy binoculars he keeps in his saddlebag. "In the trees, your two o'clock." His voice is calm, which unnerves me more. He rests his hands on his revolver at his side while I scan the line where the grass meets the forest.

A small flash of silver pops against the dark forest, like a lure on sunlit waters.

"There's someone there," Dad says.

"It could be something stuck in a tree." There cannot be a person here. This is not an option. This is not happening.

"He doesn't see us," Dad says. "You stay here. I'll go around and drive him into the meadow."

"You don't—" My throat feels fat and pasty. I have to force the words out. This is the first person we've seen since we got home a year ago, and it is nothing but terrible. "You don't know that he's heading for our place."

"He's already on our land, Eira." Dad takes the binoculars back. "He might be infected."

We stare, searching for some sign that he's a zombie. But he moves like a normal person, maybe even slower. Not like the ones we saw at BATO. When Dad gives me another turn with the binoculars, I see the man clearly. Gray hair. Beer belly. Cargo shorts and a black shirt with a grinning bass fish on it and the words *Nice Bass!* in yellow. He's got a beard and a pair of thick, silver-framed glasses—that's probably the silver flash I saw—and neoprene braces on both knees.

"If a thief is caught breaking in at night and is struck a fatal blow, the defender is not guilty of bloodshed."

"It's not nighttime." With the binoculars still held to my eyes, I squeeze them shut, willing him to disappear by the time I open them up again. But when I do, he's still there. "And how would he even know he's on our property?"

"He's on our trapline. He wants *our* game. He knows. And it *is* nighttime. We are all sunk in the longest, blackest of nights, Eira." Dad clicks for his horse to turn. "Stay here. Wait for me." The forest swallows him up as he skirts north, and I don't see him again until almost half an hour later. Nice Bass stumbles ahead of him, arms up. He yells something, but I can't hear it from this far. I get Odger going in that direction, but we're only a few steps into the meadow when Dad lifts his gun and I hear the crack of one shot. All around the clearing, birds scatter up into the sky, startled, at the same time that the man falls forward, out of sight, into the grass.

I suck my breath in so deeply that I can't breathe out again, the opposite of having the wind knocked out of me. The sky unhooks itself and folds over and over until only black, starless night is left, even here and now, in the bright early morning. He was right.

We are in the blackest of nights.

My body feels too heavy. I'm going to fall out of my saddle. I lean over and hold on to Odger's warm neck. My breath doesn't come back, and that darkness just gets heavier and heavier, until I hear my father's voice.

"Get off the horse if you're going to faint."

"Exodus also says . . ." I shake my head. I cannot move. I can't find enough breath to tell him what he already knows. If the theft happens after sunrise, it's the defender who is guilty of bloodshed. "After sunrise—"

"This is eternal night," Dad says. "Despite the sun."

But we aren't one of those families that interprets the Bible. We take it word for word.

From atop his horse, Dad leans over and grabs my arm and yanks me off Odger. I might be half a foot taller than he is, but when he wants to, he can still wrangle me as if I am no bigger than Liv. He sets me on my feet, which I cannot feel.

I crumple to my knees and put my forehead to the hot dirt, where I can finally breathe out, in. Out, in.

"Is he dead?"

"He is."

"You can't just leave him there."

"Yet we will," Dad says. "Let the field mice and carrion birds and bears and wolves and cougars do their jobs, as we have done ours. The Lord giveth, and the Lord taketh away."

Dad tells the story of the "intruder" in the "nighttime" meadow at dinner, like it's any other story with a beginning, middle, and end. But the end in this case is a man's life. Dad didn't kill a zombie. The man wasn't a *draugr* from Dad's beloved Viking folklore. . . . Not even a trespasser, if he didn't know he was on our land, or if that even matters at the end of the world. All I can think about is the woman I killed that night when all of this started. Mom sits with her hands in her lap, her food forgotten. Liv is pale, fork in hand. She uses one of her chewed-up fingers to push the piece of rabbit off it. Soren watches my face the whole time. I stare at the meat on my plate, unable to swallow the bite in my mouth. When I finally do, I cannot imagine taking another. A rising nausea forces me from the table, but when I push back my chair, Dad shakes his head.

"Finish your meal," he says. "Nothing goes to waste in this house, Eira. Not before. Not now."

Throughout all of this, Mom keeps her eyes fixed on the wall beyond Dad, in the way that she does that makes it look like she's paying attention to him, and every word he says, but really she's got her eyes locked on the embroidery hanging behind him. *All Creatures Great and Small, the Lord God Made Them All.*

The next day there is a sign propped against the porch steps. It's a piece of old plywood, about the size of a poster. Dad obviously spent most of the night—actual, not metaphorical or biblical—working on it, drafting the text to be centered and even. He's carved each letter with his Dremel, with such care that it almost looks professional. My father is nothing if not naturally skilled, no matter what tool you place in his hands.

Soren and I see it first, when we come out just after breakfast to go on our rounds of the traps.

Trespasser:
This is God's land,
He blesses me with it.
He tasks me to protect it.
He trusts me to protect my family.
Stray onto it by accident,
Or aim for it on purpose,
Either way, you will be shot,
Or worse.
Trespassers killed to date:
IIII
Bjorn Helvig

Four? Both Soren and I know that Dad didn't just put those score marks there to scare people. He put them there because that is the true math, which means that he's killed three other "trespassers," technically on our land or not. This one is just the first the rest of us know about.

So, we aren't safe. Maybe from zombies still, but not from other people.

This isn't God's paradise.

And Dad has known for how long?

Dad has been a murderer for how long?

"Wh-when was the first one?" I force each word out with just enough air that I can summon from my lungs, which are flattened with panic.

Dad lifts the board; pulls two long, thick nails out from his pocket; and hammers it to the post.

—

The fifth line in Dad's tally is our closest neighbor, Jeremy Sosa. He lives four miles away. I never knew his last name, not until the middle of one night, when Dad's hollering wakes us up. I'm expecting a horde of zombies, but it's just one man and our bull, Cash, standing beside him, looking bored, a rope attached to the big ring in his snout.

"Drop the rope! On your knees!"

"I'm sorry!" Jeremy collapses to the ground. When he lifts his hands up to surrender, I see how thin he is, how his rib cage looks like it's the only thing giving him any shape.

"Jeremy Sosa," Dad says. "Intruder and thief."

"My family is so hungry." Jeremy weeps.

Mom ushers Liv inside and away from the windows, but Soren and I stay outside.

"The good Lord woke me up." Dad keeps his eyes and shotgun on Jeremy. "I dreamt of the Golden Calf. And here you are with my bull."

"The Golden Calf was made from melted-down earrings," Soren whispers. "When Moses left? That story, right? No bull?"

"No bull in that story," I whisper back. "No actual calf either."

Dad slides his focus to us for just long enough to make us shut up, then back to Jeremy.

"If a thief is caught breaking in at night and is struck a fatal blow, the defender is not guilty of bloodshed."

"He's going to kill him," I whisper.

"Dad, please don't," Soren says quietly. He bounces his hands out in front of him, palms down, as if he's trying to push all of this down, down, down into something he and I can manage. Mom comes out of the house. She has a gun too, her pistol. She holds it in both hands, like a prayer pointing to the floor.

"Bjorn," she says. "Let's bring him inside. Let him sit for a minute. Give him some water."

"The Old Norse word for *cow* and *money* is the same," Dad says, as if he's at the dinner table, intoning as usual. "*Fé.* Because cows equal wealth. As good as cash. Do you know our bull's name, Jeremy?"

Jeremy sits back on his haunches, arms behind his head. His white undershirt is soaked through with sweat, and his jeans hang low, even with a big black belt. He glances up at the sky, shaking his head a couple of times before training his gaze on our father.

"*My* name is Jeremy Henry Sosa," he says. "I'm fifty-two years old. My wife's name is Marietta. I have a thirty-year-old son from my first marriage. He has a new baby, but I don't know if they're okay. I have a ten-year-old we call Badger because he's really determined and can be really mean to his little sisters." Twins. I saw them a couple of times at the Co-op, always in matching overalls and T-shirts and pink cowboy boots. "They're going to turn four in three weeks."

Crack. Mom's pistol goes off. The bull bolts.

"What did you do?" Dad shouts at her, then at us, "Go get the bull!"

The commotion gives Jeremy just enough time to make the decision to leap up and take off into the forest. Dad lets loose an impressive Viking war cry as he runs after Jeremy, his equally impressive beard bouncing against his hairy bare chest. After a moment, all I can see is Dad's linen pajama bottoms disappearing into the woods, like he's a bisected ghost.

Mom puts the safety on the pistol. . . . "I don't know how it went off." Liv stands at the doorway. Mom takes her hand. "Better go get that bull. Liv, honey, let's get you back to bed." Just minutes into our search for the bull, we hear a gunshot. Jeremy Henry Sosa has just upped Dad's tally. We stop, but just for a moment, because having a task is a gift of distraction. Cash is as dumb as he is big, so he probably figured there would be no more earth under him once he reached the farthest edge of where he'd ever grazed. We find him about an hour later, munching grass at the far side of his favorite pasture, which is just a small patch between two strips of forest on either side of a little knoll. He lets Soren grab the rope, and then we make him climb up the bluff where Soren and I watch the space that used to be the lively little town of Marion Gap—the town where we exchanged our library books and talked to Eddie and Racer, the place with the drugstore on one corner and the hardware store on the other, the town where we were (very rarely) allowed junk food from the Sunoco, sold our wares at the farmers market in the ice rink parking lot, and always wished we could stay just a little longer before piling into the truck and heading back up here.

The sun is up and getting hot when we get back to the house with the bull in tow. Mom is in the outside kitchen, which she starts using when the house stops cooling off much at night. She dishes out eggs and buttered bread for Liv, who sits at the sewing machine that's set up on the porch. She's turned the heavy, antique thing so she can see her favorite tree, which she'd rather be climbing.

"Bugs are eating the buckwheat," Dad says as he sits down. Has he already talked to Mom about Jeremy Henry Sosa? Her stunt that didn't even work? "They finished the strawberries before they even got a good start. Likely got to his crops too."

So we're not talking about what happened in the middle of the night. We're a family of five, and four of us are being gaslit. Dad goes on about the lygus bug, which is also chewing through our alfalfa. No big deal that he's killed five people now. Let's talk about bugs instead. Would you like some eggs with that?

"Lord help us." I see Mom spinning through her mental inventory of stores. She's left the pistol behind and has blithely moved into the land of nothing-ever-happened. Jeremy? Jeremy who?

"He will," Dad says. Did God help Jeremy? Did He instruct Dad to let him go? Did Jeremy get to go home to his family? Are his wife and kids alone, wondering where he is?

"We're blessed with good stores," Mom says. "If we're careful, we can make it through a year with little yield. Even if the bugs keep taking over."

And what about zombies? What if they take over? Or intruders? What if it's one Jeremy after another, until someone manages to take over Gefjunland and kill us all?

"We'll do the math," Dad says. "Reorder the rationing. Get more meat. Do more drying and preserving. Focus on foraging. Our Lord helps and He provides." Mom puts a plate in front of him. "Smells amazing, Mother." He shovels in forkfuls of eggs. When he's done, he places both of his big hands flat on the smooth wood of the picnic table.

"Survivors are running out," Dad says as he wipes stray egg off his beard with a napkin. "They've lasted this long. But not anymore. They're running out of food. Water. Their morals. People want what we've got. Desperate people do desperate things to feed their families and keep them safe. Especially now. I understand this. Of course I do." He takes a long drink of his tea and keeps talking. "We are not desperate. We are protected by our heavenly Father. We are safe here, trust me. Gefjunland is holy land. We are chosen people. While we are all sinners, our sins are not so great that the Lord punishes us with death or worse. We're rewarded for our service to Him and for not straying from His word. We are holy enough. When held up to the sins of others. That is what it means to be *chosen.* And let me tell you, it is as much a burden as a blessing. The Lord can be grueling."

This is as close as he will get to bringing up the subject of Jeremy. Soren and I eat our breakfasts in small bites. Soren and I are not just simple sinners. Who we *are* is a sin. We are the ones he would blame if "death or worse" happened, if he knew what we are.

The bread is cardboard. The butter is concrete. All my spit has dried up. I don't know if I could form words and speak them, even if I was brave enough. I know what I'd ask, though. *Where is Jeremy's body? Did you just leave him for the scavengers too? What will his family think, when he doesn't come home? Will they come to look for him? Will you shoot a mother and her little girls too? Will you shoot me and Soren if you find out about the sin we bring to your Godly paradise?*

We have to go.

Gefjunland is not a sanctuary anymore. There are bodies in the woods, scattered and scavenged, ruined by bugs just like the wheat is being ravaged, just like all sensibility is being ravaged. When we were making plans to leave the first time, I remember thinking we were so mature and that our plan made sense. But it didn't. Each year after that, it still didn't make sense. We were kids in a fairy tale, thinking we could just ride off and find something better. It's almost funny to think that we thought home wasn't enough for us, when now it's far too much. We need to go. We need to find someplace Dad can't find us. Someplace we can bring Mom and Liv to. Someplace even safer than Gefjunland, because Dad won't be there.

CHAPTER 5

There is only one place safer than Gefjunland: Blessed Are These Orchards. The house may have burned to the ground, but there is a bunker there, buried beneath the orchard's giant compost piles. And Bersi's pride and joy, the bugout spot up that unnamed creek. The supplies for a huge family, all of whom probably died on that first night. Even Lola, who I've tried so hard not to think about for the past year. Now I have to as we plan our route to BATO to see if we can live there. Both Soren and I think most of the family is dead, based on what we saw that first night, and especially if they tried to defend their home and didn't flee right away. If there's no one else, or if it's just Lola and some of the younger siblings, we could live together. They'd let us join them and wouldn't try to send word to our parents.

"If someone is already there, we'll probably have to move on,"

Soren reasons. "One step at a time. This is the step that makes the most sense."

It's our birthday again. We stand on the bluff, watching the sun rise over the valley that used to be Marion Gap. We don't know what's left of it, or who is left in it. We are here, still, even if the end of the world already happened.

"We're doing this," I say. It's a statement, but I hear a question in my voice.

"We are doing this." There is no question in his voice. "Happy birthday." He gives me a small package. I peel away the waxed cloth to reveal five small squares of chocolate. I stare at him, mouth agape. "Save it," he says.

As if. I put all the chocolate into my mouth and let it melt. I close my eyes.

I reach into the pouch on my belt and pull out a nearly identical package.

"You have better self-control than me." I shrug as he reveals three squares of chocolate. "It was so hard for me to save even that."

This is the last of the chocolate. I let the taste of it linger in my mouth as we watch the shadows retreat from the valley, letting the sun shine on the unknown below.

We sit together at the outside table, where we're served pancakes with butter and honey and a treasured pinch of cinnamon. Dad and Mom and Liv sing "Happy Birthday." Bunting made from scraps of linen flutters between the trees behind us.

I grip Soren's hand under the table.

The time is right. Right now. I say the words in my head a few times before I dare speak them.

"We have an idea for a gift," I say. "That you could give us, Dad. Mom."

"Considering we're practically adults," Soren adds.

"We want to go up to the cabin tomorrow." I glance down at the honey and crumbs left on my plate. We call it a cabin, but it's not. Like the Sigurdsons' bugout location, ours is our off-site backup survival plan, a place to retreat to if home is compromised. By zombies, in this case. Or intruders. The "cabin" is a set of steel lockers and a lean-to hidden in a dense piece of forest above a year-round creek a long day's ride away. "There's nothing between here and there if we go the creek route. We can check on it. And stay over. Celebrate our birthday. Can we go?"

"Absolutely not." Mom reaches across the table and grabs my plate, as if it needs correction, not me. "Where did this insane idea even come from? We have no idea what's going on out there." Her eyes dart to Liv. "The good Lord would watch over you, but I want us to stick together. For all we know, this is the only place on earth that is truly safe."

Not for the founding members of Dad's kill tally, it isn't.

"God is our protector," Dad says. "Not this land." Those seven words say so much. He will let us go, I know it now. Not because he thinks it's safe, but because he needs to prove that his trust in the Lord is absolute. Either enough time has passed, and he thinks it's safe, or he is willing to send us out there to find out.

Or maybe, somewhere in the back rooms of his mind, he realizes that he can't keep us here, and so the best way to maintain his status of sage fatherly leader is to give us this.

I catch Soren's glance. He's still looking hopeful, if that's the right word. He eyes Dad, who is clearly thinking hard, even if I know the outcome on his behalf already. His fork hovers at the edge of his plate, his pancakes hardly touched. He looks down the length of the big table and beyond it, to the front door.

He has to trust in God's will. He *has* to take the side of faith, because that's the corner he's backed into.

"Dad," Soren says. "Do you think God wants us to stay here forever? For all the rest of the days of our lives?"

"Don't go," Liv murmurs.

"No one is going anywhere." Mom's voice rises. "We stay here. Together. For forever, if that's the Lord's plan."

"I'll be the one to decide that," Dad says. "I am the head of this family."

He pushes away from the table and strides down the porch steps and across the clearing to the barn. That's where he takes his deepest prayers, to the shaded company of his livestock and rusted tools and the cooing of the pigeons in the rafters.

The forest whispers and shivers in the early summer wind. After my chores, I head to Ivor's Bluff, above where we built the pyre for our little brother, who died when he was a baby. That was Ivor. He was born just three days after my and Soren's ninth birthday. I caught him; he came so fast. Soren went to get Dad from the trapline, but they didn't get back in time. He died when he was fifteen months old. He had a fever for three days, and then he just didn't wake up. He was in the big bed with Mom and Dad, lying in the crook of Mom's arm, when she woke to find him cold, his lips blue, arms and legs still pliable enough for her to run out into the snow with him clutched to her chest, where she keened for hours until her voice gave out. We never reported his birth—in that same bed—and we never reported his death.

I find Mom seated on the memorial bench Dad and I built. She's got something in her hands. Black plastic. Blocky. The satellite phone. She flips the antenna up and points it to the sky. She stands and turns to the west, then the east. She turns my way and sees me and immediately tucks the phone behind her apron.

"Eira!" Her cheeks redden. "You surprised me."

"Why do you have that, Mom?"

"I check every day," she says. "If I can. To see if it's working. To dial Grandma and Grandpa's number. Your aunts and uncles. The Sigurdsons. Just in case."

"You *do*?" I reorder my experience of her for the past year to include this daily defiant practice. That satellite phone belongs in Dad's domain. Not hers. "Does Dad know that you have it?"

"Of course not," she says. "Not that it matters. It hasn't worked since the beginning. I just keep trying. It feels good to try."

"I like this for you." As I say it, I realize that this is something I would say to Soren. That's part of our lexicon and doesn't include her. Sure enough, her brow furrows. "I mean, I like that you check every day, you know? It's hopeful. And sweet."

"Or just terribly, terribly sad," Mom says. "I miss all the people.

Grandma and Grandpa. Your aunts and uncles. Your cousins. Our friends. I miss town too. Just the cars going up and down Main Street, people bringing out their carts of groceries from the Emporium. Those old men leaning on their trucks at the Co-op, chatting to each other with their cheeks packed with chew. Remember?"

"I remember so much that it hurts," I say. Mom goes back to the laundry basket, which she left in the hot sun. I hand her one warm, steaming, wet item after another. "What if those old men are still there? Or even just one old man?"

"It's nice to think that," Mom says. "I *do* think that. Maybe not the old men at the Co-op, but something more hopeful than a useless sat phone."

"Marion Gap is still there." I want to say that five people survived long enough to make it to Gefjunland, so there must be more. The town is still there, and where there's a town, there might be people. Even now, after everything. The world is still going on out there. Away from here. It could be better now. Maybe it's over.

"It's not safe out there," Mom says. "Our home is safe."

"But for how long?" A new tally will start collecting lines. Until maybe someone manages to kill Dad first. And then what?

"Long enough that we'll be here when you come back." She takes my hands and looks up, straight into my eyes. "However long that takes."

At dinner, we wait for Dad's decree. He works silently at his rabbit sausage and salad. When he's finished that, he rips a piece of bread from the loaf and sops up the grease and dressing. He places his fork and knife across his plate and then sits back.

Here it comes. Soren stares at me.

We're already packed. We put new shoes on the horses, fitted them with their saddlebags and best saddles.

"Straight there," he says. "Then straight back."

Mom puts her hand to her face, the tears already wetting her cheeks.

"Your mother will pack you food," he says. "You'll stick to the ridge the whole way, both ways, in case I have to come after you. I don't want you using any of the supplies at the cabin, but I do want you to bring back one of the one-hundred-watt solar panels. The folding one." With that, he pushes away from the table. No mention of God. No mention of zombies.

For the rest of the evening, he shuts himself in his and Mom's bedroom. After we go to bed, I hear him go out of the house. I wait to hear the creak of the hammock's carabiners as he settles to sleep out there, which he does sometimes. But there is just silence. I creep into the kitchen and dare to look out the window.

He kneels at the foot of the steps. He's folded his pajamas up so his bony knees press into the gravel and dirt. This is his kind of flagellation now. He did use a whip, before Soren saw him doing it in the barn. We were five. Soren cried on and off for weeks. So, Dad does this now, looking for that grinding pain that will elevate his prayers and unknot some deep, deep relief inside him. He can always hide bloodied knees under clothes, and he never hobbles.

"The pain brings you closer to God," he says when he makes us kneel in the dirt as punishment. He's only ever made Soren and me do it. Never Liv. And never, ever Mom. Just us. Once when we snuck an anthology of queer science fiction home from the library, despite our protests that we didn't know what *queer* meant; another time when we stole candy from his personal stash in the drawer of his bedside table; and then again when I cut my hair the first time.

Everyone gets up to see us off, shortly before five a.m. Mom bustles around getting food together while Liv clings to me, then Soren, then both of us.

"You're not going." Liv rearranges herself so she's standing on my feet and hugging my waist. I walk her around the room like that.

"We are," I say. "We'll be back for—" I'm about to say *you,* which would then require explaining, but Soren saves me from myself.

"—sure. And we'll bring back some river rocks for you to paint." Soren kisses the top of her head. "And bird-of-prey feathers. If we find any."

Soren pulls Liv off my feet and to him in a tight hug. "Stay so brilliant," he says into her unkempt blond hair. He lifts a mat away from the nape of her neck. "Deal with this, small child."

"Deal with these, big child." Liv lifts Soren's braids, which are probably matted too, considering that I can't remember the last time he brushed them out. "And you deal with this, Eira." She jumps up to touch my hair, which I trimmed just the night before in anticipation of leaving. "You look like a boy. Soren looks like a girl, and you look like a boy."

"Can we move on from hair?" I see Dad outside. I don't want him to walk in on a conversation about gender expression.

"Shoot them right through the brain," Liv says, which confuses me at first, until I realize she's not talking about hair anymore. She's talking about zombies. "That's where it counts. Right here." She pokes her forehead, right between her eyes.

"There won't be any zombies between here and there." I bat her hand away. "The important thing is that you are good. You're going to stay good." I tuck our heads side by side and whisper, "You'll be okay here without us. And when the time is right, we'll take you with us. Away from here—"

"—to the cabin." Soren glares at me. *Don't blow this,* he mouths.

"You'll be back tomorrow," she says. "And besides, I don't want to go out there. Ever. You shouldn't either."

"Someday you might want to." Soren takes Liv's hand. "Until then, remember how much we love you."

Liv bounds ahead to help Dad get the horses ready, which leaves Mom and me on the porch. None of us want to say goodbye. She knows. She *knows.*

I bend down to hug her, and Soren joins too.

"Will you come back?"

We nod, tears streaming down our faces.

"He would always welcome you," she says. "No matter what."

We nod again, this time sobbing. I'm not sure if she's talking about God or Dad, but it's kind of the same thing, so it doesn't really matter.

"He loves us all." She pushes us away enough to wipe our tears with her handkerchief. "I know you've wanted to leave for years. I know this place is too small for you. I know that you're different, in a way that needs more than what's here. In a way that will always be hard for you."

"Mom—" Soren's face blanches.

"We never wanted to upset you," I say.

"This isn't what this goodbye is about." She holds up a hand to stop us. "Today, you're leaving. Another day, you'll come back. This is all my heart can take right now. It's as simple as that. Today, you go. Another day, you come back."

"Of course," we say.

"Don't let him keep you from me."

With that, she peppers us with kisses and *I love you*s and nearly pushes us down the stairs and all the way to where Liv and Dad have the horses at the rail by the stables.

Dad puts a hand on each of our heads. A thick, wordless moment builds, during which many others of his blessings replay in chopped bits and pieced-together parts. I don't mean to try to guess what he's going to say, but my brain goes ahead and does that every time. I wait for the intoning to begin, the near singsong voice he gets when he really starts to roll.

"The Lord will keep you from all harm. He will watch over your life; the Lord will watch over your coming and going both now and forevermore."

And that's it.

No verse after verse, no prayer on top of prayer. Just a simple psalm.

It's a good one. I don't mind putting that in my pocket as what could be the last prayer he gives me. I put my arms around Dad. Soren does too. This goodbye is different than the ones on the porch. The scrappy little paranoid part of my brain tells me that he knows exactly what we're doing, and he doesn't care enough to stop us. Two fewer mouths to feed. Two fewer rebel thinkers and weirdos in his midst. Two fewer bad influences on the only child who might turn out acceptable in his eyes.

His sour body odor stays on me when I pull away.

"Don't forget the solar panel," he says, instead of an actual goodbye.

I can still smell him as we ride away, east at first. When it's time to turn north to the ridge that leads to the not-really-a-cabin, we turn south instead.

"Maybe we'll always have his smell on us now," Soren says when we're far enough away from home. Pretty soon we'll be farther than we've been since coming home last year. I'm nauseous and light-headed, with a fat, prickly anxiety that makes me feel mentally bloated.

CHAPTER 6

We ride ten miles before it starts to get really hot. We stop at a creek and let the horses drink and rest. By now, Mom, Dad, and Liv will have finished the farm chores, even with the extra work. We have to start earlier and earlier these days as the heat gets unbearable so fast. Mom and Liv will have finished the breakfast dishes. Liv will be up a tree, while Mom and Dad will be drinking tea together on the porch, quietly writing out the Bible. Dad is copying out Revelation. Mom is writing out Exodus, when Jochebed gives birth to the child who will become Moses. Dad's scrawl and Mom's tidy printing have almost filled the leather-bound notebooks Dad bought at Midsommar last year, just hours before everything fell apart. Dad says that writing the texts out word for word is the best way to digest God's word, because it goes from his eyes to his hand to his brain and spirit, but Soren and I think it's because he's dyslexic, and this is the way that he can process it all, especially the Old Testament.

"Do you think he's at the part about how He created all things?" Soren glances over his shoulder, as if he can see our home behind us.

"Worthy are You, our Lord and God, to receive glory and honor and power, for you created all things . . ." Soren says the last part with me. *"And by Your will they existed and were created."*

"Science," I say. "Zombies."

"Queers," Soren says with a smile. "The Lord God made them all."

The first things we see when the forest thins into the grassy plateau that steps down into the valley are bright orange leaflets, everywhere, like wayward flowers, caught on shrubs and dotting the patchy, dry grass for as far as we can see. Soren hops down and grabs two. I unfold mine. The ink is sun-faded, and the page is rippled from rain and sun and damp and heat, repeated for who knows how long. It hasn't rained in seven weeks, but the dew would still dampen them most mornings.

On the front are the words *DANGER! HYPERTOX IS IN YOUR COMMUNITY!* and row after row of pictures with captions like you see on airplane safety cards: shelter in place; ration food and water; an icon-zombie running after a shocked-looking icon person; that same icon person with a bleeding head wound and X X eyes and then an arrow to it reanimated as icon-zombie, back straight and leaning backward just a bit, arms outstretched in that classic depiction of zombies—who decided they'd go with that?—legs akimbo to depict it running toward another unsuspecting icon person. At the bottom, there's a big check mark over an image of a person stabbing a zombie in the head, another over a person holding a severed zombie head, and a third check mark above a zombie being shot in the head. This last one has fine print: *gunshots and other loud noise (e.g., explosions, sirens, collisions) will summon any infected within a one-mile radius.* These kill instructions are followed by what not to do: an X over the image of someone punching a zombie and another X over someone knifing one in the gut. The final X is above an image of someone shooting one in the leg. The message here is make your noise count. Don't waste bullets on legs.

"See that?" I point out the warning. Soren has a handgun on his belt. I have a rifle along with my swords. With the butt up near the saddle, it angles down and under my stirrup. Odger and I hate the bulk, but it's what we would take if we were actually going to the cabin.

On the back is a notice in English, Spanish, Tagalog, French, Japanese, German, Russian, and about eight more languages. *Be advised, government services and disaster-relief assistance are no longer available and will not be for the foreseeable future.*

Odger shifts his shoulders, getting comfortable under my weight. He is big for a mustang, which is why Dad gave him to me. We used to buy our wild mustangs from the Bureau of Land Management, but for the last few years we've been trading for them with another prepper family who catches them illegally on the Virginia Range in Nevada.

“Do you still want to keep going?” Soren folds his leaflet and tucks it in his pocket, where it will likely wilt beyond recognition with sweat. I tuck mine in my saddlebag.

“No.” All the orange flyers look like so many land mines now. Every one of them screams, *Run! Run! Run!* “Yes.”

All of a sudden BATO seems impossibly far away.

“This is old news,” Soren says. “We’re going to keep going, right?”

“Right.” Two things are true; I badly want to go home, and I badly want to keep going.

Odger still faces Marion Gap, sniffing the air, eager to keep moving. He knows the farms and orchards along the way, and beyond that the neat grid of the town itself, the tidy streets lined with little boxy houses with front yards taken up with driveways and flower beds and kids’ bikes and barking dogs. He wants to go that way, where the guys at Valley Feed Supply keep sugar cubes in their pockets. I want to go that way too, even if my gut tells me to turn around, and even if I’m nearly positive that all the guys that had sugar cubes in their pockets are dead.

Instead of agreeing or disagreeing, or even coming to a decision out loud, Soren pats his horse’s neck. She’s called Rune—a mark of magic or myth. She’s not magical nor myth-worthy in any way, but the small, tilted gray Z shape on her forehead looks like the rune Eihwaz, which symbolizes stability and strength. Soren makes a quiet *click,* and Rune falls into step beside Odger and me. Rune couldn’t care less about sugar cubes, but she will follow Odger anywhere.

—

Even though I knew the interstate would be silent and clogged, it's another thing to behold it. At first glance it reminds me of that stretch of highway we saw when we fled from the orchard. If that looked like a writhing, dangerous snake of lights and chaos, this looks like a very lifeless version of that now. It's packed with cars, like a parking lot you'd never be able to get out of. The cars are like dulled scales, wedged up against each other, forming a dark serpent of mostly gray and black and blue cars and trucks, speckled with the odd yellow or orange or red or green. *Don't look,* I want to say, but that's weird. It's not coming for us. It's not even moving. Anyone inside those vehicles would be long dead or long gone. I half expect Odger to refuse to go any farther; he balks at even baby garter snakes. He keeps plodding forward, though, toward the hope of sugar cubes. This is the part in any scary story when the character steps closer and closer, unaware, toward the terrifying thing, and the people watching yell, *Don't go in the room! Don't open the door! Don't turn the corner! Don't open the box! Don't get into the car! Don't pick that up!*

We make another unspoken agreement to not go any closer to the cars than is necessary to make our way through the underpass, but even so, we can see that most of the cars are empty, their doors and trunks still open, windows down. There is dried blood everywhere: red-black pools of it on the hot pavement, rusty smears of it on windshields—inside and out—and covering the bodies slumped over steering wheels or folded over each other in back seats. Even Odger gets distracted from his singular pursuit of sugar cubes and starts stamping and balking. The smell is not as bad as I thought it would be. So much time has passed that the bodies are either bone and hair and sun-bleached clothes and shoes, or leathery, like a collection of roadside mummies slumped in their cars or splayed on the asphalt, as if they were prostrate in prayer when they died.

"How do we go on?" Soren sidles Rune up right beside me and reaches for my hand.

"We just do." I let his hand drop and take the reins tight in my fist. "Or we don't."

"All these people did people things," Soren says. "They fell in love, made mistakes. They had favorite movies and food and animals."

I half close my eyes, which softens the horror scene that spreads out in front of us. I can maybe go on like this, not seeing it all in grim detail. As we keep riding, I keep squinting. When Soren asks me what I'm doing, I tell him, and he does it too. That means that I have to open my eyes, though, because we can't both be blind at the same time. Amid the mass of cars choking the underpass are blackberry vines that have taken over without opposition. There is a narrow path still available where the cars are farthest apart. We pick our way between vehicles on the road, which slopes up on the other side and opens to a view of wheat fields gone to seed and a stand of willow trees we used to stop at when we rode into town before.

The biggest tree has a swing and sturdy low limbs perfect for climbing, but this time all any of the four of us wants is shade, and the horses need water. Usually we don't let the horses drink from the irrigation ditch, but it's so hot, we have no choice.

The shade instantly makes everything feel more possible, except for the water situation for the horses.

The irrigation ditch is empty, of course.

“No one to fill it,” Soren says.

I survey the dry concrete half-pipe that stretches out in both directions for as far as I can see. Its bottom is filled with dried leaves and the debris you’d expect from a winter. There is a stack of what looks like sandbags at the grate where a farm road crosses over a culvert.

“Those are not sandbags.” I put a hand on my brow and squint. “Those are bodies.”

After an hour detour to a spring we know of, where the horses and Soren and I drink as much as we can and we fill our bottles and two hydration packs, we redirect back to the road into Marion Gap. Marion is just a little town nestled in the knuckles between two mountains, although we call them hills. You can climb to the peak of either of them in under two hours from the town square. One is called Mount Sylvia, and the other is called Mount Robert. Robert, Sylvia, and Marion were the town’s founding father’s children and wife, all dead from scarlet fever before the family even reached the area. Ominous beginnings, I think now.

Main Street slices the town in half, with the ice rink at one end and a redbrick town hall, the library, and the elementary school at the other end. There is no high school; kids have to bus to Denman for that. Half the shops never reopened after COVID, and nothing even replaced them all these years later, so the town looks a little sad, like an old lady who wishes she was as pretty as she used to be. I can only imagine what the town looks like now. The corpse of that old lady who wished she was pretty?

"Let's go along the road," I say as we get close. "There's more shade if we stick to the east side." We've never ridden the horses into town any other way than by the multiuse trail, but there is no risk of traffic now, other than the gauntlet of abandoned vehicles. It looks like some toddler giant was playing with them and just left them there when they were called in for lunch and then forgot about them altogether.

I turn Odger's head toward the road, and he resists at first. I give him a nudge with my heels, hard enough that he rears just a little, shifting me in my saddle and making my sword slide down so that the tip hits the saddle with each step he takes. I cinch the buckle an extra notch and reach back to touch the hilt. I do this all the time. It's not just about making sure it's there at night. It's a habit. If I don't, I don't feel at ease. I thought about securing my other, older sword across my back the other way, but the weight of it and the hot leather and metal made me give up the idea of being some double-bladed badass bitch. So my old sword, shorter, nameless, and in need of a good sharpen, is tucked away in its own scabbard, securely strapped with my pack behind me, across Odger's haunches.

We're about a half mile out of town now, which is where the first houses closer to the road are. They're pretty far apart, and all of them are suffering from no one looking after them, even just after a year—or however long it's been since families breathed life into them before. Overgrown bushes, roofs dented by tree limbs, gutters sliding toward the unmowed lawns. A couple of them are burnt down.

There's a spray-painted message on the boards covering up

the window of one. *Jesus saves!* The same message is painted on the end of the driveway, where the gravel meets the asphalt. *JESUS SAVES!!!*

"Jesus did not," I say. "Actually."

The house is just a shack, no bigger than our woodshed. There's a swing set in the front yard and a sun-bleached toy baby buggy, overturned, with a naked plastic baby doll lying in the dirt beside it, limbs akimbo, hair matted with filth.

"Eira," Soren says with a tremor in his voice. He points to a livestock pen beyond the house, where a dozen or so dead sheep litter the ground, nothing left of them except skeletons and fleece. "They were trapped in there, with no one to let them out. All someone had to do was open the stupid gate." He hops off Rune and runs to the pen and opens the gate. When he gets back, we say nothing about it, but about a mile later, we both see a handful of sheep grazing in the distance. Someone thought to open the gate for them.

The ice rink—our next planned stop—is just ahead. When we see the big sign, we speed up, eager for a break. It's too far away to read, but it's a comfort to see it anyway. Racer used to change the sign every week, up on the ladder in his short-sleeved dress shirts, sweater vests, and bow ties. He's eight years older than we are and a good foot and a half shorter than me. He has Down syndrome, which he proudly tells everyone right before he shows them his Special Olympics ribbons and medals. He keeps his ten favorite ones—all gold—in his backpack. I don't suppose he does now, though.

He's probably dead.

My arms break out in goose bumps. I didn't know many people before the world changed, but I did know Eddie and Racer. They were good friends. Eddie was the only gay adult we knew. He helped us figure ourselves out—literally *out* to ourselves—and now I don't know how to even *think* about him and Racer. Are they dead? Or are they out there somewhere, surviving? Did they turn? Are they zombies now?

"You think Racer could outrun a zombie?" Soren asks.

"Absolutely," I say. "The ones I saw at BATO were fast but not as fast as Racer."

Racer's sign comes into focus.

PATTON FMLY
ALL LOST GO W
ME3T 09 WEDING

Something about this sign is worse than the spray-painted messages we've seen since we got to the edge of town. Someone had to go up there, take down what was very likely a very important message to the community, and then put up their own message. Without Racer or his approval.

This is how I know he's dead.

He never let anyone touch that sign. Eddie was his one designated alternate. Before I can think any more about who desecrated Racer's sign, there is a rustle at the edge of the forest to our left. Soren reaches for his gun, but I shake my head. I reach for Gertrude.

It's just a doe with a fawn, nibbling at the grass, not even noticing us here in the middle of the road.

"No guns, remember? Noise attracts."

"So this is essentially useless."

"Pretty much," I say. "Come on. Let's go check the concession." Odger is already turning in that direction, as if he read my mind.

"You don't think there's anything left, do you?"

"I do not," I say. "But we have to check, in case there are even ketchup packets or cartons of expired queso."

"Toilet paper," Soren says. "Remember that?"

The first thing to fly off the shelves with COVID. No big deal to us. Liv was in diapers, Mom and I used cloth, and all of us used a kind of bidet-in-a-bottle thing, one of which we have in our packs, as it happens. Shit happens. That is a proven fact.

We enter a huge patch of delicious shade, cut in half by a wall made up of big whiteboards on wheels. We get off the horses to take a closer look. Every square inch of space is covered with photos and messages, warped and weathered, with bleeding ink and curled edges and tape and tacks of every kind. *MISSING.* And *Nina! Go to Peri's!* And *HAVE YOU SEEN ME?* with a picture of a granny with a perfect, blue-tinged perm halo. And some missives: *GOD'S ZOMBIE SOLDIERS,* one pamphlet screams. I can't tell if that means soldiers *for* God or soldiers *from* God. School pictures of kids. Photos printed out on inkjet printers, ripped from photo books, and freed from frames in those hasty moments before people fled, now covered in scrawled directions and messages. And this, from Isaiah 14, in very neat printing with thick black marker on bright orange card stock, laminated, with the edges politely rounded:

> *The realm of the dead below is all astir*
> *to meet you at your coming;*
> *it rouses the spirits of the departed to greet you—*
> *all those who were leaders in the world;*
> *it makes them rise from their thrones—*
> *all those who were kings over the nations.*

For a moment I can't look away from that. But then my eyes slide over to a picture of the Girl Scouts group that met in the community room at the library. They're Liv's age, but she never wanted anything to do with their crafts and badges and pretend campfires on the lawn at the bottom of the steps.

MARION GAP GIRL SCOUT TROOP—ALL MISSING!!! SINCE JUNE 23rd!!! The first night. A note written on the back of another *MISSING* notice explains. They were camping at Umatilla National Forest and never came home.

They probably just wanted a real campfire. My legs wobble, so I slide to the ground, collapsing into a nest of fallen notices and tinder-dry pamphlets and warped photos. The fire ban had finally been lifted, and they went to have a real fire instead of their stupid fake fires with their yellow and orange cellophane flames and tidy sticks that looked like they came from the craft store.

Seven little girls.

"Remember when Dad went to the school board meeting to stop them from buying those whiteboards?" Soren puts an arm around me as I cry, harder for those seven girls than for anyone so far. I nod. "The man who homeschools his children barking about school."

"Those are my tax dollars! Waste of money," I growl in an impersonation of Dad. "Chalkboards do the job just fine. Just because Johnny has a 'sensitivity' to chalk dust? That's like peanut allergies—"

"Fake!" we say in unison. I wipe the tears away.

"Come on." Soren offers me a hand. "We can't stay here. We have to keep moving."

I grab the picture of the Girl Scouts and tuck it in the pouch on my belt.

There is an unholy stench that builds as we ride around the wall of whiteboards and head for the rink's loading bay, where we can go in without leaving the horses outside. I tell myself it's all the decay that comes with no electricity, especially of food, but it smells more like animal carcasses, so when the rear parking lot comes into view and we see the source of the smell, at first I think I'm looking at a big heap of dead animals, partially burnt.

Those seven girls? They broke my heart.

This?

I stare at it and feel nothing at all.

I feel nothing. But then, what feeling could possibly come along with the realization that my very own eyes are looking at a heap of mostly burnt human bodies, a pile as tall as me, layered like grotesque, knobby, charred pancakes?

Soren leans over and vomits, getting most of it on his leg and stirrup. He gags again and again while I just stare, thinking I'm seeing movement from the pile but also *knowing* that I'm not, unless it's maggots or rats.

The horses back up and turn around, whinnying and tossing their heads. We let them take us around to the far side of the building, where the Zamboni is usually parked just inside. It's gone.

"Can you imagine someone trying to escape on a Zamboni?" Soren does this: cuts the terrible thing with a funny thing, a distracting memory, an absurd what-if.

I do imagine it, and then I wait to laugh. We have to laugh, right? But that's when I start to cry, imagining someone driving away so slowly that the zombies are too perplexed to follow.

Soren and I get off the horses and just stand there with the reins tight in our fists. It's just midmorning, but it's hot enough that the air is thick with heat. We move into the shade of the inside. The rink is lined with army cots. Sleeping bags and stuffed animals and duffel bags and food wrappers are strewn everywhere, along with clothes and shoes and so many empty water bottles that they look like decorations, glowing just a little in the light from the leaf-and-scum-covered skylights above.

And no bodies.

We tie Odger and Rune up by the home team's penalty box and take our packs off their backs to give them a break. We park the packs by the horses and clear off two cots before pulling them closer and collapsing on them. It's deliciously cool in here, even with the midday heat pushing in through the big open doors.

"Where is everyone?" I stare at the dusty rafter as I say it. "I mean, I get that people left. And there are the bodies on the highway. And the pile here. But shouldn't there be more bodies? From the zombies? Like, in here too?"

"They all escaped." Soren turns on his side, his eyes rimmed with red. He's been crying, so silently that I didn't notice.

"You really think so?"

"I'm going to think so," he says. "I like that story."

"They're not all in that pile," I say. "Marion Gap might be a small town, but not that small."

My eyelids grow heavy. I'll rest them, just for a bit.

I fall into a dream about the Zamboni and the man who used to drive it. He had a terrific handlebar mustache, which he rocked with zero irony. In the dream, I watch him take his smooth, graceful turns on the rink, perfecting the ice as he goes. And then it's me driving it. I reach up and find that I have the fabulous mustache now. I twirl it with my fingertips, just as I hear someone screaming my name.

EIRA! Soren screams my name over and over as I take another sweeping turn, looking back at the unmarred ice I leave behind me. *Eira! Get up!* I glance at the stands. There's Lola! I wave. Eddie and Racer sit beside her. Dad and Mom and Liv are scattered in the bleachers. *Look!* I turn to tell Soren that everyone is okay. We're okay. But then I see Rob, and his mutilated face.

Get up. Soren yells. *Now!*

"Wake up!" Soren shakes me.

Footsteps, running toward us. Soren has his gun up, clasped in two hands. His arms shake as he points it at the sunshine, where the footsteps are getting closer.

"Don't shoot! There might be more!" I leap up and reach over my shoulder for Gertrude, but she's not there. I took off the scabbard when we tied up the horses. It is now a giant, flashing STUPID sign resting against my pack, about fifty feet away in the wrong direction. My old sword is nestled in the webbing of the pack, equally useless to me. Two swords and none at hand. *Idiot.* I set off for them at a sprint, but Soren has always been the faster runner. Not that either of us is an actual runner.

"I'll get her!" he shouts as he lowers the gun and runs for Gertrude.

I turn my attention to the big rectangle of sunlight, framed by the rink's open doors. A shadow appears in the parking lot. A man, I can tell by the bulk of him. He's big—maybe not as tall as I am, but close. He's running straight for me.

He's not a person.

He's a Hypertox monster. Revenant. Demon. A rabid fox. He runs at us with a strength that doesn't fit the decay, seemingly doubling his size as he closes the distance between us. I hear my father's voice: *Unholy beasts.*

"Hold on!" Soren shouts.

I can't, though. My only option is to run. I spin on one foot until I'm facing the opposite end of the rink, where the tunnel out looms dark but hopeful. If I can get out any one of the bank of doors before the zombie catches up, maybe I can ditch him.

I run.

The Vikings believed *draugrs* and revenants tormented those who wronged them in life, and even though I don't know this un-person, he runs after me with such focus that I half wonder if I do. He's still on my heels when I push through the exit and into the blinding sunlight. I keep running, but my stamina does not match my determination. My lungs burn. I'm slowing down. When I'm about halfway across the parking lot, I glance over my shoulder. The zombie is still coming for me, but so is Soren, lugging Gertrude with him.

"Here!" Soren tries to toss me the sword, but he fumbles it. This catches the zombie's attention, distracting him from me long enough that Soren has one more chance with Gertrude. He slides the sword across the hot pavement. I grab the hilt, pulling the blade out of the scabbard in the same movement that I use to lift the sword up and poise it above my shoulder for the short second it takes to widen my stance, and then I swing the sword down against the zombie's grimy neck.

His head is not quite severed. A pool of blood spreads away from the gash that exposes muscle and tissue and bone. I fall to my knees beside this not-man, who was a father, son, husband, employee, enemy, brother, uncle, or friend before but is now nothing but *beast.* His warm red-purple blood soaks my knees.

"Get away from it!" Soren shouts. The man looks about as old as Dad. He has a short, scruffy beard and mustache and also that familiar injury to his face, where he was bit.

And now I've killed him.

Correction: put that Hypertox motherfucker out of his misery.

This is how we have to think now. No exceptions. This is not Jeremy Henry Sosa. This is not another line in Dad's tally.

Our gas station is maybe half a mile from here. We call it "our" gas station not only because we filled up there and got treats sometimes—I like Cool Ranch Doritos, Soren lovesloveslove Heath bars, Liv likes Red Vines, Dad likes Cheetos, and Mom only ever got a cold iced tea—but also because that Sunoco has always been our family's emergency meeting place, if shit hits the fan and we're in the valley and get separated. It's the same wherever we go. If we ever split up while we're on the road, the plan is that we meet at the first—or last, depending on which way we came into town—gas station at the north end of whatever town we're in.

Dad tested Soren and me once. We were fourteen. We'd packed up the tent and horses at a Ren faire somewhere in Oregon, then Dad sent us to deliver a knife he'd traded for a doll for Liv. The doll maker was packing up at the other end of the market. When we got back to our spot, Dad was gone. After we looked around a bit, we asked the doll maker for a ride to the last gas station heading north, which would be the one we gassed up and went to the bathroom at on the way through town. Dad always filled the tank at these gas stations, and he always had us kids go to the bathroom. There he was, leaning against the truck, looking as proud as he had when I'd won two sword fights in a row the day before.

"Excellent," he said as he pulled us into a hug. "And if I wasn't here?"

"We'd wait," Soren said.

"And if you couldn't wait?"

"We'd leave you a message," I said. Neither of us was scared. We knew he'd be at the gas station. His praise felt unbalanced, like we didn't deserve so much of it, considering what wasn't at stake. If we'd arrived and he *hadn't* been there, that would've been different. We each had a Sharpie and a pad of rain-proof paper in the packs we took everywhere with us, to leave a message, but where would we have gone? We didn't know how to get home, even if we knew to follow our compasses north from there.

"Smart kids." He squeezed us both again. "I'm proud of you."

There are no messages for us now, although the windows are plastered with notes and photos.

"No one broke the glass," Soren says. "Because of all the messages." He's saying this as a way to say, *Look, Eira. There is still some good. Here, in the honoring of all these lost souls.* I don't see the good, though. I see through the jagged glass of the door, which *is* broken, into the shadows of what's left of the place where we kids walked slowly up and down the few aisles, admiring all the nutritionally destructive crap our parents wouldn't usually allow. The shelves are toppled, and whatever wasn't worth taking is spilled and smashed and tossed over everything, mixed on the floor with the leaves and trash that blew in over the winter.

"There's nothing left in there," I say. "Nothing left anywhere."

"There might be." Soren gets off his horse and approaches the door. He whistles our family's get-over-here notes: low note, then high note, repeated quickly, twice. When nothing comes out to attack—living or undead—he heads in. He comes out with a half-empty package of thumbtacks and a pine-scented air freshener. “From that weird shelf by the oil and bungee cords and coolant.”

I pick up the pine-tree-shaped air freshener, still in its package. I lift it to my nose and breathe in the familiar chemical smell. I don’t know if I’m making it up, if it has any scent left at all, in reality. But I remember it at least. It’s the smell of where we stood when we were waiting for the one disgusting bathroom to free up, beside the decks of cards, flyswatters, elastic bands, and weird assortment of stationery items.

CHAPTER 7

Even though Marion Gap is technically our town—we have our post box here and a dentist—Soren and I don't know much about the place. We know where everything is, which isn't saying much, but we don't have anyone to check in on, really, other than Eddie and Racer. And the dentist, I guess, although none of us kids like her. We didn't go to church here, because none of them would put up with Dad's ragingly controversial Big Opinions about everything from whiteboards that have nothing to do with him to the possible truth that the world is flat. Not many people know this, but he was born Kyle Becker. He changed his name to Bjorn Helvig when he was sixteen—and then legally when he was of age—and "claimed his birthright" as a descendant of Vikings and joined the very vile and very criminal Aryan Kin Associates, who recruited him from his foster home in Fresno. But then he met our mom when he was apprenticing as a blacksmith with her father at their homestead in Northern California. And he met my mom's two Black uncles, who grew up with my grandpa and were more family to him than his real family, who kicked him out to fend for himself when he was fifteen. When Dad sold his forge, Uncle Dan and Uncle KJ and Grandpa ran their own towing company, sharing two trucks among them.

The first Sunday Mom's family took him to church—a church with two thousand parking spaces and a rock band and a preacher who wore jeans—Dad got saved. According to him, the Lord took him by his hand and led him down to the stage and spoke to him in a voice clearer than his own: *I am the Father. The only Father.* Just what a kid without a dad wants to hear. Did that joyful congregation help him leave behind the Aryan Kin? Sure, because my mom wouldn't date him otherwise. But is he still a racist? Yes. Yes, he is. Maybe the worst kind: a racist who doesn't think he's racist.

We check the other gas station, the Kwik Pik, the grocery store, and Pinnacle Hardware, but almost everything of use has been taken. We add the remains of a roll of duct tape, a couple of tins of smoked oysters (they'd been kicked under the shelves), a sharpening stone for the dagger knives, and a few zip ties we find behind an emptied fish-bait fridge.

We see a couple of leathery, sun-dried bodies here and there, but most of them seem to be in that pile back at the ice rink. By the time we're nearing the library, I must be desensitized enough to make my first joke.

"What do people do when they realize it's the apocalypse?"

Soren says nothing.

"Take over the nearest toilet paper factory and *then* make sure their wives and children are okay."

"That's not funny," he says. "Not even a little."

"We're going to have to laugh." I twist to get my water bottle from the saddlebag, which is when I catch a glimpse of a figure dashing between two buildings. "Soren! Did you see that?"

"No." He looks around. "What was it?"

"Something. *Someone.* There." I point just as the same figure runs back into the street and stands there, frozen, for an instant before tucking his head down and running at us. "I can't kill another one. Let's go." We gallop around the corner onto Second Street, lined with what used to look like picture-perfect little houses. We called this Old Folks' Street, because everyone who tended those now-overgrown gardens and flower beds was a septuagenarian or older. Soren follows me as we cut up the middle of the narrow street. The trees that line either side give delicious shade, oblivious to all that's happened. Halfway down the block, we pause to glance back.

The zombie waves at us. One arm, then two. Then he's shouting our names.

"Eira Helvig! Soren Helvig!"

Lo and behold, it's Racer Menendez, in the genuine and unsullied flesh: sneakers, athletic socks pulled up as high as they'll go, the sateen short-shorts he took a liking to after going to Pride in Seattle a few years ago, and one of his ragged race or competition T-shirts, which is the only outfit he wears when he's not in his beloved short-sleeved-collared-shirt-and-khaki combo. The only zombie-apocalypse add-on is a fanny pack and a neon-green sheath holding a hatchet with a matching neon-green handle. When he gets close enough for me to read the four big black letters on the powder blue shirt, *ZARC,* I realize the shirt is not one from a race. The street-sign-simple graphic below is not quite as good as those on the orange leaflets, but it clearly depicts a little icon human running from a zombie, which lurches after them, arms out and leaning back, more Frankenstein than what we've seen so far. Racer is also sporting one of his hundreds of sweatbands and the aviator sunglasses he took from the library lost and found a very, very long time ago.

All I can do is stare at our friend, who looks so . . . *normal.* Like at any moment, there will be a clap of thunder, and God will set everything up right again. All those little old ladies and men will be puttering on their manicured lawns and waving us in for iced tea. I cannot reconcile Racer, here, just hours after I beheaded a zombie behind the same ice rink where I flirted with the girl who worked at the concession stand enough that she told Soren to tell me that she thought I was a creep and to leave her alone.

"Racer, *Racer.*" Soren breathes his name in, then out. "You're alive."

"Am I ever happy to see you!" I shout. I get off Odger and open my arms. Racer runs at me, nearly toppling me over as he grabs me in a hug. He's about as tall as Liv, which means he comes up to my mid-chest. I've never been so delighted to breathe in the cheap woodsy smell of his favorite body spray. He must have quite the stash of it, to still be using it. "Where's Eddie?"

"Gone."

Soren and I share a glance. If Eddie's dead, then how is Racer surviving on his own?

Soren hugs Racer too and then holds his hand and does not let go while Racer talks.

"He went to the next town," Racer says.

"So he's okay?"

"Yeah," Racer says. "He's okay. He rode his bike to Conlin. To find more members to be in our club."

Conlin is the next town to the west, about thirty miles or so.

"When did he go?" Soren asks.

"I don't remember what day he left." Racer shrugs. "You can count all the days. I'll show you. The calendar is at home."

"What club?" I squeeze his shoulders and go to kiss the top of his head, before the grease and dirt stop me.

Racer pulls his sweat-soaked shirt away from his chest and points to each letter. "*Zombie. Apocalypse. Running. Club.* I'm the coach. I teach people to run fast. Then zombies can't catch them."

The calendar Racer referred to is not at what used to be their home. Before, the brothers lived in the apartment above the nail salon down the street, but now Racer leads us straight to the side of the stately brick library building, to where the fire escape has toppled into a skeletal heap. Racer climbs over that, to a stairwell I've never noticed before. We tie the horses up and follow him. It leads down a few steps, to a metal door secured by a padlock and a dead bolt.

Racer unlocks both and lets us into the library's dim, fusty-smelling basement. It's cool. The only light is from the small soaped-over windows just below the ceiling, which is just above my head by a couple of inches where the floor slopes. My head grazes the cool surface in other spots. Anything that might've been stored in here before has been moved out, and most of the items from Eddie and Racer's place have been moved in, arranged exactly as they were in their apartment.

I take the lid off the big glass candy jar filled with Eddie's green carnations. He wore one each day: paper ones, felt ones, a beaded one so heavy that he had to use three pins, the big one Racer made him out of cardboard, and another Racer made him out of petals cut from a vegan ice cream container lid.

"Don't touch." Racer secures the lid back in place and pats it.

"How long have you lived down here?" I ask.

"When the zees came," Racer says, "we hid here."

I catch sight of a makeshift calendar tacked on the wall above the small, round kitchen table where Eddie sat with us and told us about the Stonewall uprising in 1969, which launched the modern LGBTQ movement. *If I don't fill you in,* Eddie said, *no one will. Especially not up there on your mountain. And the library internet is only good to a point.* Eddie is the reason why I know about Marsha P. Johnson and the Gay Liberation Front.

The calendar is made up of four pieces of light blue poster paper—Racer's choice, for sure—all carefully gridded in marker, with the days of the week printed in Eddie's neat block letters, all the *Y*s with their tails tucked under instead of pointing straight down. I do mine the same way, because of Eddie.

MAY

Starting on the thirteenth, Racer has crossed out each day with a green marker.

"Is that when he left?" A cold sweat soaks my pits and trickles down my back. Soren and I share a look, our expressions carefully blank.

"Yes." Racer picks up a jar that's half-filled with marbles. "This many days." Beside that jar is a pile of empty wet-wipe packages. There are two left and a note. ONE WIPE PER DAY. PITS THEN BITS. And another jar. This one with a single layer of marbles left in the bottom of it.

"You take a marble out every day?" Soren says. "And put it in the other jar?"

"Yes I do."

I count the marbles left. Twenty-one.

"What happens when you run out of marbles?" I put a hand on Racer's shoulders. I'm not sure I want to know the answer.

"I have to go." He lifts a compass on a string out of his shirt and studies it, moving until he suddenly stops. "That way. West."

"Can Eira and I go upstairs?" Soren's voice catches. "Wh-while you get changed? Is it safe up there?"

Racer nods. He takes another string from around his neck. It's a key that lets us up to the main floor of the library.

—

Either no one thought to come in here and ransack anything, or Eddie and Racer have kept everything shipshape. The shelves are still in order, the computers are in place, the children's area is tidy, with the play kitchen all set to cook supper, right down to the purple plastic pots and pans on the burners. I run a finger along the checkout desk. No dust.

I pick up the stuffed unicorn that Liv loved when we used to come here. She tried really hard to get the rest of us to believe that unicorns belonged in Norse legend, but Dad takes his passion for Norse mythology very seriously, so he told her over and over that there are no unicorns in Viking lore. This seems especially sad to me right now. Why couldn't he have just played along? Eddie did. He called this stuffy her *Einhorn.* That's just German for *unicorn,* but it sounded perfectly mythical to her.

"Eddie made everything better," I say.

"He's never going to know how much he meant to me." Sadness in Soren's voice weighs down each word. "I never thanked him for . . . for being the right person at the right time."

"Me neither," I say as we head back down to Racer. I wonder how we'll tell him, *when* we'll tell him, that Eddie is probably never coming back, that his brother is probably dead. But do we need to tell him? If we don't know for sure? If there is no proof? To find Racer here was a miracle in and of itself, right? Maybe there's room for another Menendez miracle.

We sit down at the table, where Racer sets out a can of kidney beans and another of condensed milk. He works on opening the beans with a manual can opener but fumbles. Soren and I know better than to offer to help. Racer asks for it when he wants it. Racer was the first person we ever met who has Down syndrome. Eddie explained to us that everyone with Down syndrome is different, and the only way to see each person's potential is to let them show you. Racer's speech, for example, is a lot easier to understand than his girlfriend Jessica's. Jessica's mom owned Kraftee Kathee's, but Jessica was the one that ran the place. I don't want to ask about either of them right now.

"I remember you had an electric one in your apartment," Soren says. Racer sets the opener down and uses the jagged lid to drain the liquid into what looks like a compost-and-gray-water bucket before he tips the beans into a bowl. Soren picks up the can opener. "Eddie was . . . *is* left-handed. This is for lefties."

Racer shrugs. He slides a scrawny onion and a knife my way. "Cut it into small pieces."

When I've cut about a quarter of the onion, he stops me and takes the onion and puts it into the bowl with the beans. He adds a bit of cilantro and a splash of balsamic vinegar and some chili flakes and ranch dressing mix. After dividing the beans into three smaller bowls, he opens the condensed milk and pours equal measures into jam jars. He adds a spoonful of Tang powder and some water and then puts lids on the jars and hands one to each of us. "Shake it."

"Where's the water from?" Soren shakes his jar, eyeing it suspiciously.

"The creek." He means the one that runs along the east edge of town. It never dries out completely, but it must be very low right now. "Don't worry, Soren. I filter it. Eddie showed me. You worry too much, Soren Helvig."

"Fair." Soren's face relaxes, and he starts shaking more enthusiastically.

"You're not worried?" I ask Racer.

"Sometimes." Racer chugs his drink—it tastes like a melted Creamsicle—and glances over at the jar of green carnations. "Maybe Eddie won't come back. Maybe a zombie got him." He stares into his empty jar and then lifts it, tipping it to send the very last drop into his mouth from above. "But he said he's coming back. He will. I know he will."

Is now the time to have the hard conversation? Did he just give us an opening? I glance at Soren, who shakes his head in reply. Not yet. I let out a breath that I didn't know I was holding. *Not yet.*

After supper, we survey Racer and Eddie's shelves of cans and boxes of food, all organized in alphabetical order. "So, it was you two who cleared out all the primo stuff." When Racer looks puzzled, Soren expands. "All the stores are empty."

"We didn't steal anything," Racer says. "We borrowed."

"Of course," Soren says. "That makes sense."

"Everyone borrowed. Not just me and Eddie."

"Where is everyone?"

"They all left." He claps his hands. "That fast." Another clap. "So fast."

"And the dead ones?" I say. "At the rink?"

Racer ignores me. He collects the jars and bowls and takes them to a stained utility sink and a beat-up counter. He sprays the jars with a bottle that says SOAP & WATER in Eddie's printing. He wipes them with paper towels and sets them back with the others.

"Did Eddie take a weapon?" I hope a different question will regain his attention. "A gun?"

"No guns," Racer says. "The noise makes the zombies come. He took his knife. Knives are better. And hatchets. Up close. Like this." He takes the hatchet out of its sheath and hits at an imaginary face. "We get zombies like that." Another stab. "Or like that."

"You've killed one?"

"No." Racer lowers his hatchet. "I run. I run faster than those zees."

I don't. The one I barely survived at the rink would've gotten me if I hadn't used Gertrude at the last minute.

"But Eddie?" I say. "He kills them?"

"We don't say *kill,*" Racer says. "We say *put down.*"

Put down. These are two words that feel immediately better than any others. They imply mercy. A gift. Terrible, but necessary. I would never let Odger suffer with a broken leg. I would never let a chicken gutted by a coyote bleed out in the dirt. I would shoot Odger. I would wring the chicken's neck.

Soren eyes me as he puts a hand on Racer's shoulder. "It's been a long time. Really too long."

"Yeah." Racer hugs Soren tight around the middle. "I have to go soon."

“This is my bag.” Racer pulls a backpack out from a closet. It has full water bottles in each side pocket and a sleeping mat folded under the lid. One thing is for sure: Eddie would not have prepared a go bag if it weren’t for meeting us. As much as he thought our dad was a paranoid nutjob, he did enjoy diving down the rabbit hole of “prepper lite,” as he called it.

Racer finds west on his compass again. “I go that way. Until I find more people for ZARC.”

“Why west?” Soren takes the compass and spins it in his palm. We face west right now, in this cool, dim basement. “What’s there?”

“Maybe less zombies,” Racer says. “And maybe me and my brother Eddie’s mom. In Portland. I have her address in my wallet. Eddie said good people will help me.”

Their mom kicked Eddie out when he was sixteen, and when he landed on his feet, she sent Racer to live with him. She never came to visit. She never sent money to help with Racer. She never even called her sons after that. So, if that’s the backup plan, to track down one shitty mother with the “help” of strangers running amok and taking advantage of each other, things are much, much worse than we thought.

Racer invites us to stay the night. One of us can have the couch—that would be Soren, because I won’t fit on it unless I fold myself into a pretzel—but we can’t have Eddie’s cot, because that is for when Eddie comes back. While Racer snores so loud I’m surprised it doesn’t summon the zombies like one gunshot after another, Soren and I try to figure out what to do.

"He's not coming back," I whisper. "Agreed?"

Soren nods. "Agreed."

"We can't take Racer with us," I say. "But what else are we supposed to do?"

"He can't come with us." Soren watches Racer sleep, chest rising and falling with each bellowing snore. "We can't keep him safe, right?"

"He's kept himself safe for over a month." I pick up the compass and point it west, toward BATO. "How do we know we could keep him safe at all? And if the Sigurdsons' doesn't work out, then what? Then where will we go? If we take him, that's another mouth to feed. We have supplies for the two of us to get to BATO."

"You're two mouths to start with," Soren says.

"So you want me to eat less? Faint every five miles? Blame the Helvig genes, not me. Maybe we could take him home," I continue. "Mom would take him in."

I say it, but I know that it's way more complicated than just taking him up the mountain and dropping him off, to take our share of the food and work. Soren agrees, because he doesn't say anything.

"Let's get some sleep." I eye Eddie's cot, but I don't want to upset Racer if he wakes in the night and sees me there. Soren curls up on the couch, which lets me double up our sleeping pads. I lie awake for a long time, wondering what Mom is thinking about. Does she think we're at the cabin? Or does she know we're not coming back? Dad doesn't know anything yet. When he does realize that we're not coming back, there won't be much he can do. He won't leave Mom and Liv alone to go look for us. Just when I think I won't fall asleep, I do, into a deep, dreamless sleep.

It's still blue-black dark when Racer wakes us up. It's just after four a.m. He shakes my shoulder and whispers—not quietly at all—in my ear, and then he does the same for Soren.

"Time for practice!"

"What?"

"Running practice. ZARC." He tugs my arm. "A shirt for you and a shirt for Soren." He throws one of the light blue shirts at Soren and one at me. *ZARC.* And in smaller letters below the zombie Frankenstein: *Zombie Apocalypse Running Club.* "Mine is special." Racer turns so we can read the back of his. *COACH.*

"We're not running." I roll away, using the shirt to cover my eyes. "I don't run. This large, fabulous body does not move like that. Wake me up when you need me to behead a zombie or skin a rabbit or work a garden or lift a car off a toddler or something. A small car. Maybe no engine."

"I don't know if the middle of a zombie apocalypse is the best time to sell us on a running club." Soren sits up. He rubs his eyes and then holds the shirt in front of him. "Oh. Hold on. It probably is exactly the time for a running club."

"This is a special, important club." Racer grabs Soren's shirt back. "Can you run away from zombies?"

I sit up too. The answer is no. Or barely. If Soren hadn't been there to toss me Gertrude yesterday, I'd be dead because I couldn't run away from a zombie.

"We can't run. We don't run." I hold the shirt against me. "And besides. This isn't going to fit."

"Follow me." Racer leads us to a small room where there are six stacks of shirts to choose from, at least ten in each size, all neatly folded on one of the old metal shelves from upstairs that were replaced in the upgrade, which Dad also opposed. All the shirts are the same pale blue, all silk-screened by Eddie and Racer in a very well-stocked craft corner that looks like it hosts at least half of Kraftee Kathee's shop inventory.

"You've got big hopes for this running club," Soren says as he selects a women's medium, with cap sleeves and a narrow torso to hug his. I find a men's extra-large, which fits, even if I have no intention of actually running in it.

We quietly hurry along the "safe route"—not sure what that means, but I'm guessing it means that Eddie said it was safe—until we get to the middle school. Racer leads us to the track and arranges us side by side, feet planted on the reddish rubber surface, which is still in good shape, even though the turf of the football field in the middle has long grown over and is now a carpet of the debris that has sailed over the chain-link fence in the span of one year's worth of stormy winds. A row of big plastic poster boards are fixed below the scoreboard, a giant letter painted on each in thick pale blue paint and outlined in blue: Z A R C ! ! ! And then below that: C O A C H R A C E R ! ! ! Zip-tied below that are a bunch of the plastic letters from the rink's sign, put together to make a sentence.

RUN LIKE YOUR LIFE DEPENDS ON IT!

"Eddie made that."

"It feels like a message. To us," Soren says. "Specifically."

"It is a message," Racer says. "Time to start *zee ay arrrr cee,* my friends." He leads us to a spray-painted line that crosses the width of the track.

"All right, this is going to *change! Your! Life!*" Racer holds his whistle but won't use it, he assures us, for fear that it will attract zees. He paces in front of us, clearly elated to have new members of ZARC after the one and only trainee has been absent for so long. "We are going to start with your five-minute warm-up walk." He lifts the whistle to his mouth, but just as Soren and I both hold up hands, gesturing for him to stop, he laughs and makes a whistle sound that's not actually a whistle but does get his message across.

I keep Gertrude across my back for the warm-up walk, but when that's done and Racer announces that it's time for our first ninety-second run, I'm not sure if I should put her with our water bottles and weapons by the gate that secures us in or learn to run with her. I have a flashback of not having her when that zombie chased me and decide to keep her.

Ninety seconds has never felt so long.

"It would feel longer if the sun was all the way up," Soren says when we get to stop and take a drink of water. He's not even out of breath.

"Good job!" Racer says. "Now walk for a minute."

"Then what?" Gertrude is hot and heavy on my back. My head feels padded with warm, moist batting, damping everything I see and hear. If ninety seconds of running is this hard, I might as well lie down in the weeds and let the zombies come.

CHAPTER 8

I'm not keeping track, because I don't want to know how slowly we're progressing, but each morning before dawn, Racer puts us through about half an hour of walk-run combos, the "run" part getting incrementally longer each time. After the first week, he makes us run from the library to the school.

This takes us along the safe route, marked by blockades of concrete barriers with *Marion Gap* spray-painted on with a stencil. Past Kraftee Kathee's and Fix-It Right Repair & Pawn. The barriers are topped with tangles of furniture and bike frames and lumber and metal and anything else to bulk them up with, most of which looks like it came from the big junkyard behind Fix-It Right Repair & Pawn.

Soren and I speculate that the original barriers were official, steering people toward a checkpoint early on. The burnt remnants of little wooden huts at the far end suggest that the idea was for calm order but that it didn't go that way.

"Zombies do not climb," Racer says when we ask him about the barricades.

"But they can go around?" Soren says, not breathless at all. He has a runner's body, with his long, slender limbs and wiry frame. And he's only carrying a dagger; I'm carrying a massive sword that adds thirty pounds to my already gigantic frame.

Racer doesn't answer. We can't get him to talk about much when it comes to the zombies and what happened in Marion Gap over the last year, other than what he told us that first day. When we asked him how all the bodies got to the ice rink, he said, "In the back of a truck." When we asked him who drove the truck, he said Eddie did. We asked him who put the bodies in the back of the truck. "Me and Eddie."

Racer is interested in two things: Eddie coming back and ZARC. In that order. He doesn't care that we're running out of food or that a zombie could catch him and beat him to death—or worse, turn him. He's confident that there will always be something to eat and that he can run from any zee that comes for him.

After another week of training and waiting with Racer, Soren and I decide that it's time to go. Eddie isn't coming back, and we need to leave or find a whole lot of food, really fast.

"There's food at BATO," Soren says. "We stick to the original plan, except we bring Racer with us."

"You're a lot more optimistic that BATO is going to work out," I say.

"Which means I'm pessimistic that any of the Sigurdsons survived," he says. "I saw more mayhem than you did that night."

I will not bring up Rob. I only ever did once, the day after we got home. Soren has never brought him up either.

"We're the only other people who know where their bunker is."

Across the basement, Racer marks another X on the calendar. It's been two months since Eddie left, but we still can't face the discussion that will result in one of two things happening: we either talk Racer into coming with us, with all the peril that might entail, or reconcile to leaving him here, and all the peril that will entail.

When Racer drops the last marble into the jar with the others, he takes out his compass and finds west.

"Time to go."

"Not yet," Soren and I say in unison.

"We have to make a plan," I say. "We at least have to find some food for the road."

We're down to one box of almond milk, half a small bag of farro riddled with weevils, three dented cans with no labels, plus the greens in Eddie and Racer's little garden. We have a lot of kale, some spinach, Eddie's prized asparagus, and garlic scapes aplenty. But that's not enough. We need protein. Chickens, eggs. Rabbits. Fish from the river. Squirrels, raccoons, deer, anything we can get without venturing too far.

The cans reveal (in order): cranberry sauce, some sort of stew that might be dog food and tastes how we all think dog food would taste, and sliced, rubbery mushrooms.

"I'm going out in the morning," I say as we chew through the tiny pile of mushrooms atop the steamed kale and garlic scapes.

"A human my size needs ten times this. Or I'm going to faint and never get up, and I'll die like that."

The chickens. Soren and I thought we'd be gone by now, but we're not. It's time to try to get the chickens again.

You'd think two farm kids could wrangle a few chickens, but we've tried together, twice, and left empty-handed. I'm going to go alone this time. The chickens hang around town hall, enjoying the lush grass on the west side, made green from whatever pipes are leaking under the stately brick building or whatever deep spring is keeping it hydrated.

"After ZARC." Racer picks off his mushrooms. He doesn't like kale either, but he'll eat it if he douses it in seasoning salt.

"*Instead* of ZARC." I transfer his little pile of mushrooms to my plate. "I want it to be cooler."

"After."

"We can skip a day."

"It's not a rest day," Racer says.

"Fine." I stab a stack of mushrooms. "But right after. Before it gets too hot. If I don't get us some meat soon, I won't have any energy left for running, Racer. At all. This is a large body to fuel."

I go by myself, along the safe route, with Gertrude reassuringly heavy across my back, my dagger and Soren's pistol on my belt. He has the rifle. The gun is the very last option, only to be used if I'm ready for an onslaught of zees that could follow. In that case, it might just be to put myself down before the zees do, so I don't turn. I also take a wagon, several burlap sacks, some rope, and a queen-sized bedsheet—white, with blue pinstripes. The boys stay behind to work on putting together a coop attached to the shed at the back of the library.

The rooster is nasty. He yells at me the minute I come into view, puffs his chest, and takes a run at me while his two cocks flank him on either side. Behind them are a dozen or so hens, although I'm not sure of my count because they're all running for cover.

The rooster puffs up even bigger, as if to say, *Look, look, giant lady human! Look how my girls run from you!*

When I toss some tender kale, he ruffles his feathers in recognition but then turns away and keeps watch from just out of any hope of reach. If I can sneak up behind him, I can throw the sheet over him. If I catch the rooster, the rest might follow without me doing anything. If he's wrapped up in the sheet, crowing and yowling, that might be all I need.

The stairs up to town hall are in shade now, so I sit on the bottom step and try to ignore the little beast that is going to be the biggest challenge of the day. The climbing sun casts shadows of the leaves in the wind, which make puddles of shade that shift and dapple everything below. It's enchanting, watching the shadows, with the warm wind keeping them from rest. The awnings of the ruined businesses shade in stricter shapes that creep into the street while I wait for the rooster to settle down. The mailbox casts a shadowy robot. The light posts streak the streets. And there, the tattered American flag that has been flying at half-mast over the office of the Ford dealership for a very long time shimmies, leaving a snake of shadow on the litter-strewn street far below. If Liv was here, she'd say something poetic about it. She's our writer, even if she doesn't know it yet.

My heart seizes at the thought of her, but then it knots up entirely when a different kind of shadow catches my eye, emerging from the narrow space between Kraftee Kathee's and the street-front church that never took off and has been empty for years. It's a zee. After weeks of not seeing one and even getting to the place where food seemed like the only really big deal, there she is, jogging up the safe route and then back down the middle of it. She's close enough that I can see her wet, red-rimmed, cloudy eyes dart back and forth, looking for someone to sink her teeth into, driven by the parasite that commands her every impulse and instructs her to do one thing and one thing only: pass it on.

A second zombie emerges between Kathee's and the church, and then a third. One is burly and bearded and still wears a flannel logger's shirt but likely walked right out of his jeans a long time ago. The one behind him is gaunt. His hair has mostly fallen out, and the hole in his cheek shows teeth crusted with dirt and debris. He's limping, from a broken ankle that doesn't faze him at all. He walks on it as if it's meant to be as folded over as it is, dragging a stump of a foot that has been ruined by gravel and concrete and rot. I'm not worried about him catching up.

I press my back against the wall of the stairs and force myself to take in more air. If I stay still, will they notice me? If I don't make a sound, will they just keep on going? How can they even see? I watch them as they whip their heads back and forth, seeking. The three of them have two settings: milling around or running. They never stand still.

The rooster turns his head. His comb wobbles, and then his beautiful tail feathers shake as he proudly marches toward me, crowing as loud as he can, which makes the first zombie sniff the air in my direction. She straightens, like she might be about to raise her hand in a church meeting if it were another time and place, long before the Hypertox apocalypse. But instead of raising her hand, she starts running. She aims straight for me as if she's being pulled along a rigid track. The two others fall in behind her, less coordinated. Is it a race to get to me first? Or are they working together? *Can* they work together?

That third one with the broken foot brings up a very distant rear, but the woman and the lumberjack are fast. I push myself up and reach for Gertrude. Her hilt is warm from the sun, and she's heavy as I start to pull her out of the scabbard. If I thought I could behead the rooster, I would. A few hens have gathered around him, pecking at the grass and *buck-buck*ing at him with affection.

I let Gertrude drop back into place.

I can't do it all. I can't deal with the rooster. I can't try to grab a chicken. I can't keep the zees at bay. I can't do all of it in the amount of time I have. I need three of me, or at least six hands. If only I could suddenly morph into a six-foot, six-inch insect, preferably with a very strong exoskeleton.

And what if there are more zees about to funnel out of the little alley? Maybe the safe route was "safe" back before Eddie left, but it is not safe anymore.

Out of the corner of my eye, I spot a plump, clueless hen that's wandered within reach. In one motion I squat and stretch just enough to scoop her off her feet. I carry her upside down as she protests and the rooster runs after me, pecking at my ankles and the backs of my legs.

I am going to eat my share of this chicken. *Today.* If that means outrunning zombies to do it, so be it.

There is a moving truck jackknifed across the road. If I can get to that, I'll be okay.

PART II

CHAPTER 9

I insist on rationing the dried bananas I found in the truck, but we eat the entire chicken in one greasy-fingered sitting, during which none of us speak. Awash with reverence and delight, we emit a few giggles, but mostly we each concentrate on our third of the roasted bird. No, I do not get more because I am the Viking Giantess with far more mass to feed. I don't want to deprive Soren and Racer of a single bite. We pick the meat off the bones and suck those bones until they look like they never had meat or sinew or gristle on them, as if they'd never been joined together by ligaments to be an actual living thing just a couple of hours before.

A couple of days later, my growling stomach wakes me up. I lie there listening to it and can easily admit that my parents knew what they were doing and that time is more important than water and soil quality and even the work involved in cultivating a harvest hefty enough to feed one person, let alone three or a family of five. What we're missing are the years required to build up the stores it would take to feed us.

"If we don't head for the Sigurdsons' soon, we're screwed," I say as Soren and I jog around the track. Racer runs ahead of us, listening to tapes on his grandma's Walkman. Soren and I both run with our weapons now, but Racer just likes to run. He's our carrot. It's easier trying to catch up to him than to just run with self-motivation as our fuel. He makes it look fun, which I never thought I'd say. "Unless we really spread out and try to find someone's root cellar that hasn't been picked clean yet. Someone's pantry. Kitchen cupboards. A garage, maybe."

"You don't think every house and garage and barn and store and empty building has been looted by now?"

"I don't know." I see Racer pull off his earphones. He stops in his tracks. "Racer? You okay?"

"No." He shakes his head. "The batteries are dead."

"Ah. I'm sorry, bud," I say. We catch up to him. I give him a hug. "We can go look for some? We have to look for food, so we can look for batteries at the same time."

"All the batteries are gone," he says. "Me and Eddie already looked. These are the last ones."

He furrows his brow and stares at his feet for a moment before opening the Walkman and plucking out the batteries. He throws those to the ground and then throws the Walkman and earphones to the ground too.

"You never know," Soren says. "Maybe we'll find some, somewhere—"

I put a hand on Soren's arm to get him to stop talking. I can see that Racer has something else to say, and I'm pretty sure I know what it is.

"Is my brother Eddie coming back?"

"We don't think so," Soren says.

"You think my brother Eddie is dead?"

Soren and I nod.

Racer nudges the Walkman with his running shoe, then he punts it, kicking up a little red cloud from the track. He takes off running. Not a sprint, because he's smart like that, but at a jog, along the track and out through the tunnel beside the scoreboard.

Racer beats us to the library, where we find him sitting on the steps in a patch of shade, his hands on his knees, head bowed. As we approach, Soren suggests we tell him it's time to go.

"Too soon," I say, and then, as we get closer, "Hey, Racer?"

"I'm going to get my horse," Racer says as he looks up. "Then we can go look for Eddie and batteries and food. I don't want to stay here with no more marbles."

"You have a *horse*?" I say. Soren and I share a glance. I offer Racer a hand, but he ignores it. He gets up and marches down the steps.

He leads us out through the south end of town, to a field of clover framed by cottonwoods all around and with a stream at the very far back, robust enough in the spring that it still has a trickle now.

There are two horses: Bolt and Grapes.

"This one is Eddie's." Racer pats the patch on the palomino's flank, which does look like a bunch of blond grapes. The other one nuzzles his shoulder. "Bolt is my horse. I named him after Usain Bolt. He ran the one-hundred-meter race in nine point five eight seconds."

"Why did Eddie take a bike?" Soren says. "If he had a horse?"

"He doesn't know how to ride a horse," Racer says. "But I do."

"This your Wednesday horse?" I ask. "From before?"

"Yeah." Racer gives Bolt a kiss on her nose. "Now I don't have to share her."

Star Therapy Riders worked out of a big stable not far from this meadow. I can't remember the name of the woman who ran the program, but I do remember that Racer walked over there once a week for lessons.

"Chelene." Soren answers my unspoken inquiry. "Short. Blond. She had longer hair than me." The past tense grates on me, so when Racer tells us all about her in the present tense while we walk Bolt back to the library, I am happy to listen.

After we get Bolt settled with the other horses, behind the empty chicken coop, we make notes. A dozen in total. Racer draws a compass and circles *west* on each one. Under each compass, he draws a green carnation. Under that, a heart, and under that, his name in capital letters: *RACER MENENDEZ.* Soren writes *BHOSLE'S* and draws a little basket of blueberries, taking such care with each one, shading in with Eddie's good colored pencils, working on them until it is nearly dark.

"Nice blueberries," Racer says.

To finish them off, I write our names and slip them upside

down into page protectors, to keep them safe from the rain that will never, ever come, it seems.

We leave the next morning. Or, closer to midday, after we help Racer tidy up for when Eddie comes back. We don't try to convince him that it's barely an *if* at this point. We just do what we're told, until the place is as spotless and organized as it can be.

We stick up notes at the library—front door, upstairs, downstairs—but also on telephone poles and storefronts. We save one for the Sunoco and one for the ice rink.

It's as simple a design as possible, but it's all we need.

Eddie will know what we mean.

We ride down Main Street like something out of a Western, only there are cars that have been bullied to the sides at some point, and we're a ragtag bunch who would've never been cast in a classic Western. The skinny, pretty boy with long blond braids; the giant girl with super-short hair; and the coach with three gleaming gold medals around his neck.

The only thing in our way is a carpet of leaves and the debris of a town that emptied out suddenly, like the flush of a toilet or a break in a dam: sodden, moldy clothes and shoes and stuffed animals, suitcases flung open and filled with a winter's worth of ruin.

It all smells musty, which is definitely the prevailing fragrance of a society that died over the course of a few weeks.

None of us say anything, so when the zombie with the neon-yellow safety vest comes tearing out of the alley, we're all surprised. Soren falls behind me, and Racer behind him. Racer starts yelling, which we agreed we wouldn't do but is totally understandable. Soren yells too.

"Get it!" He screams as I pull Gertrude out of her scabbard. Soren rests his hand on his gun but knows better than to even draw it. Ammunition is beyond priceless, and that loud a noise is the worst—best?—kind of zombie attractant.

This is up to me.

And you know what? I'm absolutely ready to slice that monster's head off. I don't give one flying fuck whose father or son or shitty boss he was before the apocalypse. I am so ready to enthusiastically "put him down" that I gallop toward him, thankful that Odger is cooperating, and come up on his right. I bring Gertrude up to where the sun makes a brief, blinding glint on her blade, and the blue, cloudless sky above is all I see for the split second before I bring her down at the steepest angle I can manage and slice his head clear off, and part of his shoulder too. His body collapses, but his teeth chatter and bite at the hot concrete. I get down and plant Gertrude in his brain.

"That's for the seven little girls, motherfucker." I unstick Gertrude and wipe her blade on his filthy safety vest.

"Eira Helvig!" Racer hollers as I'm just about to get back in the saddle. "Look!"

It's that stupid zombie with the broken foot, which is now completely missing. He runs—hobbles—toward us on his one good leg and the ground-down stump of his other one, which ends up with him landing on all fours every fifty feet or so.

"We'll leave him," I say. "But let's go before his girlfriend shows up."

“Maybe she was that one’s girlfriend.” Soren points to the headless safety-vest man and then to his bearded head a few feet away.

I laugh. Once, and then I catch myself.

“It’s funny,” Soren says. “Right?”

“It is.” I start to giggle. We ride past the one-foot wonder. I laugh even harder and then so does Soren and, finally, Racer too. This might be the only way to make it from one beheading to the other.

Laughing, wherever possible.

CHAPTER 10

The Sunoco comes into sight. It looks the same, with the busted-up sign and puddle of broken plastic under the rusting frame that's still up high enough to see from half a mile away. Don't get me wrong; it was rusty before. That's not an apocalypse thing that automatically happens the instant everything starts to fall apart.

The thing about gas stations is that they're *never* the same tableau. Vehicles come and go at the pump, the people in the convenience store are never the same. Not even the ones behind the counter, it seemed, whenever we stopped there for gas. A grumpy teenager, a rotating roster of grumpy adults, and the occasional way-more-cheerful elderly person who probably got bored being retired, or couldn't afford to retire, and knew better than to waste their time being grumpy.

We head for the shade of the roof above the pumps, which still stand at attention like four robot soldiers.

“I’ll just put it up really quick.” Soren fishes out the duct tape and tapes up a note he wrote for Mom, telling her we’re headed for the blueberry farm. “Want to put one of yours up here too?”

“No.” Racer pats the note with the blueberries and the compass pointing west that he has folded in his breast pocket, along with the first of the green carnations, both of which he’s going to leave at the community center. “This is not the message place.”

“Unless you’re in our family,” Soren says as he hops down. “We don’t like to do anything the same way everybody else does.”

Moments after Soren’s boots hit the ground, the door to the store opens a crack.

“Shit,” I say when Soren just stares at it. “Dagger!”

Soren reaches for his gun first but then pulls out his dagger instead. He lifts it with that same shaking arm as I jump down and pull Gertrude out so fast that she makes a *shhhing* sound I’ve never heard before.

Wait.

“Zees can’t open doors, Soren.” I lower my sword. Sure, they can push, but that door requires that you have the smarts to organize yourself to turn the handle first. “That’s a person. Get your gun.” We won’t have a choice but to shoot, if it comes down to a gun battle. There won’t be time for Gertrude. According to Dad, people are the biggest threat when society collapses and everyone is left to fend for themselves. Well, here we are. And while I disagree with Dad on most Big Opinions, I’m not ready to call his bluff on this one.

The door opens a little bit more, and then the person takes one step out onto the *It's a Sunoco Day!* welcome mat. Scrawny little leg, barefoot.

"Liv!" I rush to her and sweep her up into a hug, while Soren opens the door wider. Liv clutches something in one arm but holds on to me so tight with the other, her body racked with sobs coming from a depth I can't know. She's alone. I can tell. Something terrible happened.

"Mom!" Soren calls into the shadows. "Dad!"

When there's no answer, Soren hugs her too. And then Racer. We're a tight huddle with a quiet, trembling treasure in the middle.

"What happened?" Soren says.

"Are you okay, Liv Helvig?" Racer says.

"Where are Mom and Dad?" I look around as I say it.

"Are you okay?" Racer repeats.

"Liv? Are you?" Soren checks her over. She's filthy but unharmed. "Was it Dad? Did he hurt you and Mom?" He goes to check the arm that's holding something, but she won't let him. "What do you have there?" She doesn't give it at first, but when she does, we see that it's an unopened bag of Red Vines.

"Wow!" Racer says. "Look at *that*!"

"You found that here?" Soren glances behind us, into the dark, ransacked store. "We looked everywhere. We didn't find anything that good."

Liv shakes her head. "From home."

"Liv? What happened?" I have to force the words out of me,

from where they're lodged in a thick sludge of fear. "Why are you here?"

"The monsters came."

This is all she says about it. Soren and I share several desperate looks that try to say everything, but then we just silently come to the conclusion to give her a little time. Not Racer, though.

"Did the zees get them?" he says.

In reply, Liv takes her Red Vines and disappears into the garage. We follow her in to see Mom's horse, Ulf, and a little camp she's set up in the corner. She's stuffing her sleeping bag into her pack and tidying up the garbage from the rations.

"I've been here for days. But we can go home now," she says. "We can kill the monsters together."

"We can't go home," Soren and I say. I squeeze my eyes shut tight for a moment, to stanch the image of zombies milling around, between the house and the barn, in the stables, on the porch, wandering inside to bump into the walls and fall over the furniture, not focused on anything, really. Just waiting.

"We're going *home*." Liv is about to bolt. I can tell. She knows we'll follow her. I grab her wrist as she lunges toward Ulf. I carry her under my arm while she screams and thrashes. I set her on Soren's horse with him. He sits behind her and just holds her until something in her releases and she just starts sobbing again. I clutch Ulf's reins as we plod away from the gas station. None of us look back. Not at the Sunoco, not at what's left of Marion Gap, and not off in the direction of what used to be our home, which is not a safely tucked-away oasis in the middle of an untouchable wilderness anymore. Racer, Soren, and I all look forward, up the road that's ribboned with heat and littered with cars. Liv stops struggling and looks at the sky instead, at the fat popcorn clouds and songbirds flitting by. She clutches the Red Vines to her chest and rests her head on Soren's shoulder. She's asleep by the time we get to the on-ramp to the highway.

Even fast asleep—or pretending to be asleep—with her head lolling on Soren's chest, Liv looks upset. Her face never relaxes from the sad grimace she fell asleep with. I'm glad that she doesn't see the mess at the ice rink or any of the bodies we find along the way, including the four we ride past on the long gravel driveway that leads up to the Bhosles' house. Four men, splayed out as if they were running and got shot from behind, all face down, limbs akimbo. They've been decomposing in the sun for so long that they are leather over bone under their faded clothes. They don't look like Adnand or Lady, or any of their sons and daughters. They are four young men, maybe workers, if I judge by the jeans and T-shirts and boots. One still has really nice sunglasses atop his head.

"Do *not,*" Soren says when he realizes what I'm about to do.

"Do-*ing,*" I say as I jump down. I have always, *always* wanted this kind of sunglasses. Aviators. Cop glasses. Motorcycle badass glasses. Mirrored, with big lenses. It's because of what happened to Mom and Dad that I don't care one bit when I have to tug to get the glasses free from the dried-up hide. Not that they'd approve of me doing it, but the fact that they're dead, with no life left to live . . . that leaves us, to live all of it while we can.

CHAPTER 11

We head to Bhosle's Blueberry Farm because of a children's book. *Blueberries for Sal.* After seeing us every week during farmers market season for years, Mrs. Bhosle took me aside three years ago and gave me a copy.

"Thanks, Mrs. Bhosle." I didn't know how to tell her that I was way too old for a picture book without being rude, or if I even should. Mrs. Bhosle pressed my hands over the book. "Note inside," she said. "For you. Not here." She said something more, in Hindi, and then turned back to weighing the berries.

I could tell that she hadn't written the note. It looked like a teenaged girl had written it, with round, cheerful letters that landed somewhere in between cursive and printing. Probably her youngest daughter, who wasn't much older than us. I read it in the bathroom of the ice rink, not even two minutes later.

When you're old enough, if you ever need a safe place, or a job, we are happy to help. You can come any time, day or night. -Lady

I ripped out the page and burned it. Soren tucked the book away on his bookshelf. Forever after, the Bhosles were the first stop in our runaway plan.

We steer around the bodies to the berry-processing building, with its towering stacks of big plastic bins, which form a twenty-foot-high wall that extends the length of the metal barn. Everything smells of berries, pungent, like they've infused the molecules that make up the air itself.

Soren and I take turns sitting watch once it gets dark and Liv and Racer fall asleep. It's too hot for sleeping bags, but we've laid them out on the wood floor of the office in the corner to lie on, on top of the pads we have. Liv showed up with her bugout bag, so she has hers too.

There are two big, dirty windows, one on each side of the corner, giving us a good view of most of the rest of the yard. The office door is locked, and we've secured the big doors at each end of the building as best we can. After an hour or so, I get up to stretch my legs and peer out the office window, to the rows of blueberries beyond, though none of them are the happy, plump orbs of sugary goodness the Bhosles were famous for. They're halfway to being raisins, thanks to the lack of rain and no irrigation. Still, they're hopeful. And tasty.

A slice of movement catches my attention. Toward the west, where the moon is just a waning slit up high in the sky, casting almost no light at all. I nudge Soren's foot.

"What is that?"

"Blinds, blinds!" He grabs the cord and lets them drop with a clatter. After doing the same with the other blinds, we peer through the slats.

It's not zombies. Not people either. It's a pack of wolves, striding along the dirt track between two of the blueberry fields. I've only ever seen a wolf pack once before, even with being in the wilderness as often as we are. Soren and Liv have never seen a wolf in the wild. All of us have heard them, and now Racer will too, because one of the wolves stops, throws its head back, and aims for that sliver of moon, letting out such a long, plaintive howl that I start to cry right along with it. Soren too, as more of the wolves join in.

Racer and Liv come to the window beside us. We watch as the wolves fall silent and slink past, so casually that it's clear they know there is no human threat here, and that the zombies aren't interested in animals.

". . . Eight, nine, ten." Liv touches the glass, pointing to each one as they pass. She counts all the way up to thirty-two.

"That's not right," Soren says.

"How many did you count?"

"Same," Soren says. "Thirty-two. Have you ever heard of a pack so big?"

I put a hand on his shoulder. "Have you ever heard of a zombie apocalypse?"

When the wolves pass, Liv sits back and sighs. She puts her fingers to the necklace that I just notice around her neck now. Mom wore it every day: a thin gold chain with a hammered cross small enough that it disappeared entirely when she held it between her thumb and index finger. Dad gave it to her when Soren and I were born. She pinches the cross for a long moment and then opens her pack. She pulls out our smallest family Bible, and the leather zippered folio that I know holds the deed to the land and our parents' marriage certificate. I pick up three other documents I don't recognize. They're birth certificates for us, even though our births were never registered. I see the issue date is the same for all three: five years ago. Liv takes them from me, lays them out too, and then sets out the pack of Red Vines.

"Mom had them in secret," she says as she hands them around. "When the zombies kept coming and Dad fell, she put all this in my pack. And told me to go to the gas station and wait for you." She pulls out a bag of Cool Ranch Doritos—and a Heath bar. How long was Mom holding on to these? I can't even think back far enough to when she could've snuck them home, even before the apocalypse. Dad didn't mind letting us have a treat now and then, but only if he wanted one too. That was only ever on road trips. He did not allow junk food on the homestead. *Home is for your purest self.* I won't ever know why Mom had them, or for how long she had them. I won't ever know when she decided to get us birth certificates, or how she kept them from Dad. She's here, with us. In a way. In these gestures that went unrecognized until this moment. It feels oddly right to be sharing the chips and candy and chocolate among the four of us here, though, now, in the dark, cluttered office at Bhosle's Blueberry Farm, having just watched a parade of wolves. None of us wants to save even one tiny piece of our junk food treasure.

CHAPTER 12

It takes us a day and eight zee kills to ride to Timmons, the even smaller town we decide to stop at for the night. Liv squeezes her eyes shut for the first three kills, but after that, she pays close attention.

"For when I have to," she says after the last one I behead, within spitting distance of the IT'S TIMMONS TIME! sign at the edge of town. The smiling, sun-bleached people holding armfuls of smiling local produce all look down at us with their toothy grins as I send the granny's head rolling down the hill toward town.

"No killing for you," Soren says. "We don't want you getting that close to a zee. If it ever comes down to you, you and Racer just *run,* okay?" He points to her ZARC shirt, which Racer gave her when she first ran with us in the safety of the Bhosles' central compound. She is his most enthusiastic club member. It helps that she's already very fast, even barefoot.

The parts of the town that didn't burn down in the early days flooded, either in the fall or spring. Mud stains the walls halfway up most of the buildings still standing along the main street, and a terrible stench of mildew and rot persists, even with months of almost no rain. We let the horses loose in the baseball field behind the elementary school, a cinder block structure atop a knoll, which is still standing and is the least-water-ruined building we can find. The field is entirely fenced, which makes it easy to keep an eye on the horses. Racer is excited to put us through our paces out there for our next ZARC practice. I am not.

We set up in what used to be a third-grade classroom. The students' names are tacked above their cubbies, printed in teacherly handwriting on handprints cut out of colorful paper and laminated. While Racer and Soren take first watch just outside the door, with a good view of the horses, Liv and I rummage through the cubbies. She pulls out a wide-brimmed pink sun hat, a red-and-white dress made from crunchy polyester, jogging pants with puppies playing football on them, ribbed white knee socks that she finds balled in a pair of shiny plastic sandals, several sneakers, a bathing suit, and a pair of pajamas with tiny, smiley clouds on them. She sets them in little piles and then pulls off the name tags and sets them atop the stacks of post-apocalypse elementary school detritus.

She neatly folds the clothing and arranges it on the corresponding desks. Janiece's desk is reunited with the items from Janiece's cubby: a soft yellow cardigan with daisy buttons, three brand-new pencils, and a blank permission slip. Brendyn's striped gum boots sit where his eight-year-old self once did, with a construction-paper sunflower tucked into the left one.

"You can't run in those dumb shoes," Liv says as she places a pair of plastic white party shoes on Arlo's desk. She taps the rhinestone bows on each one. "These are the worst shoes." Says the kid who hasn't worn shoes since the last frost.

"What are you doing?" Racer asks Liv when he and Soren come in with an armful of greens.

"From the school garden." Soren piles the kale and spinach and chard on the teacher's desk and then roots in his pockets to pull out a couple handfuls of huckleberries. "There are lots more of these along the fence."

When the sun sets and it finally cools enough to open the door and windows, we eat a salad of berries and greens, with a box of expired Cheez-Its from the Bhosles.

"But do Cheez-Its expire?" I say. "Really?"

"Time to run, my friends." Racer pulls his Zombie Apocalypse Running Club T-shirt out of his pack and puts it on.

"No way," I say. "We can run in the morning."

"Practice starts in five minutes," Racer says.

"We just ate," Soren says.

"You call this eating?" I say. "This is grazing. I need meat, people. Meat."

"But I guess you have to run from zees with a full stomach too, right?" Soren says.

"Great news; I do not have a full stomach."

"Four minutes." Racer taps his watch.

"I'm ready," Liv says.

With as hearty a sigh as I can summon, I change into my ZARC shirt anyway, because we all know that Racer is smart to make us practice right now. Because zombies could appear right now. Any right now. Even if you've just eaten, or it's the end of the day and you just want to lie on your sleeping mat in the dark and try not to think about how hard it is to keep your people safe and fed and watered. Or what's going to come next.

Okay, I'll run the hell away from all of that for half an hour.

Racer's timer goes off. "Running time! Let's go!"

"Racer, my friend." I clap him on the back as we head for the field. "You are absolutely right. Again."

We do two laps before Racer stops us for warm-up exercises. Jumping jacks, stretches, push-ups.

"What do push-ups have to do with running from zombies?" I complain. I have 270 pounds of hungry, depleted body to push up, which is a hell of a lot more than any of the others. It's probably Racer and Liv combined.

Then we run. Or Liv, Racer, and Soren do. I take up the rear, huffing after five minutes.

"Zombies coming!" Racer says as he passes me. I lean forward, hands on my knees, heaving for a good, deep breath. If there really was a zee, I'd run. I need the zombies to make me run. Or for safer motivation, the promise of sausages, even just beef jerky. Hell, a jar of dried bananas. I might actually be able to run for my life for a stupid jar of dried bananas. But I cannot run just for the sake of running. I am the weakest ZARC member.

Racer, the gracious coach that he is, doesn't make fun of me at least.

Back in the classroom, as we guzzle the water we filtered from a trickle of a spring earlier, we hear a tiny voice that is not any of ours. We freeze for a second and then reach for our closest weapons. Soren's gun, Liv's bow, my sword, Racer's hatchet. It's barely a whisper, at the door. Or at least I think it's from the door.

"Hello?" It's a woman's voice, shaky and quiet. "Are you good people?"

What a dumb question. Soren makes a face and mouths, *What?*

The four of us spin, aiming our weapons at the door. Then the other door. I go to the window and carefully look out. I don't see anything but the scraggly field and the horses, happily munching.

"You're good people." She tries it on as a statement instead. "I've been watching. I know you're not bad people."

Good. Bad. How does any of that matter anymore? I eye the others and point up.

Up there.

Soren aims his gun at the ceiling.

"Don't shoot! Don't shoot! That will only bring the monsters!" A small rain of dust powders the floor as she moves the ceiling panel out of the way and sticks both hands out. Her hands are smooth; her long nails are manicured, each painted neon orange with an angled stripe of lime green. Liv stares at them. "Can I come out?"

"I wasn't going to shoot," Soren says.

"If you point it, you might shoot it." The woman scurries back into the ducts and lets herself down above the teacher's desk. The rest of her is in as good shape as her nails. Her hair is poufy and has a fifties-style flip around the bottom. She's short and stocky, but her clothes make her seem long-limbed and almost slender, they fit so well. Her face is drawn, with jowls pulling her mouth into a semipermanent frown. When she aims a red-lipsticked smile at us, her face becomes instantly beautiful.

"My, but you are tall," she says.

"Really?" I say. "It's the end of the world, and that's still the first thing people want to talk about when they meet me?"

"I'm sorry." She laughs, but it's choked with nerves and comes out more like a cackle. "My social skills are certainly rusty. You would be very good at basketball, wouldn't you? Did you play? In school?"

"We don't go to school," Liv says. "Schools are just factories for the unenlightened."

"Hello, Dad." I say it, then immediately regret it. Liv's face blanches. She visibly wilts.

"Eira, really?" Soren puts his gun back in the holster and pulls Liv into a hug.

"You three are all sisters," the woman says. "Am I right?"

"He's a boy," Liv mumbles.

"Well then, siblings." Her face puckers just the tiniest bit. "And homeschoolers. Well. Well, as a very proud public-school teacher, I do not agree with homeschooling, especially seeing as the student rosters helped us get the kids to the Villages safely."

"Are we actually having a debate about homeschooling?" I say.

"Silliness," she says. "You're right. We can talk about absolutely anything you want, once you put your weapons away."

"Do you like my bow?" Liv hands it to her to inspect.

"It's beautiful."

"I made it myself," Liv says. "When I wasn't going to school."

"Well. Good for you. What about math? If I were to ask you what—"

"Standardized testing ensures standardized workers. That's all." Now *I* sound like Dad. I grab Liv's bow back. "If you want us to go, just say so."

"No, no!" The woman grips my arm, and I lift Gertrude as a reflex. The woman's touch is gentle, though, and actually feels really nice—a kind of hug. That neon-orange nail polish nearly glows, even in the deepening dark. "Stay! I haven't ever had real visitors. And I have news. That's what I wanted to tell you. I couldn't let you go without telling you the good news."

"If you say *God* . . ." I peel her hands off me.

"No. Well, yes. Always *God.* He provides. He nurtures. He *cares.* And, in this case, He provides a train," she says. "Coming from the east. Heading west, to the coast. Soldiers came through last week, looking for survivors. There are refugee camps in California. South of the Children's Villages."

"What are those?" I ask.

"Places to keep the kids safe," she says. "Until everything goes back to normal."

“Which is going to be never,” I say.

“What about zombies?” Soren says.

“They’ve got fences, and guards. Even chain-link roofs in the yards, I think. Someone mentioned that. Barbed wire on the perimeters too. Very, very safe. Lots of food. Lots of things for the kids to get up to. That’s the scuttlebutt. I’m going to go be a teacher at one of them.”

“Sounds like jail,” I say.

“No way,” Liv says. “We’re not going there, right?”

“No,” I say. “We’re going to the Sigurdsons’. We stick to the plan.”

“The Sigurdsons’?” the woman repeats.

We three siblings say nothing. Racer takes one of her hands in his.

“Pretty.” He touches her thumbnail.

“Thank you, young man.” She pats his hand. “And you, I take it, are the coach?”

“Yes, I am.” He shows her his nails, long and ravaged by lack of attention. I feel a pang of guilt for not helping him with that, when I’ve managed to keep mine tidy. I add it to my nebulous to-do list. “Can you paint mine?”

“Not for boys, dear.” She holds his hands in hers and bows her head. “Lord, keep this angel boy safe,” she murmurs. “Amen.”

“I don’t believe in god.” Racer pulls his hands away. “Me and my brother, Eddie, are *atheists.*” He struggles with the word but emphasizes it nonetheless.

“The good news is that Jesus saved you anyway,” she says to him. And then to us, “If the train gets you closer to your mystery destination, you could get off it when it suits you. It's not prison, actually."

Blessed Are These Orchards is mostly west, but a chunk north too. I don't know where the tracks go, but if they go due west, they will get us closer. It might be an option, but only if we can take the horses.

CHAPTER 13

The woman's name is Mrs. Carolina. She doesn't give us her first name, but not like she's being weird on purpose. It's more like she's forgotten it, or set it aside. Or wants to hold on to the Teacher of the Year part of her most of all. She's taught in this classroom for twenty-six years. Same desk, same little bell to get her students' attention, same coat hook.

"Same *#1 Teacher* mug," she says as she packs it into her duffel bag the next day, which is when the train is due to stop at the far end of this tiny town sometime after dark. "This one is from my husband. He gave it to me on my very first day of teaching third grade. The kids know not to give me mugs as thank-you gifts. They all know that I like their homemade cards the best. And then flowers, and nail polish." She pulls open the desk drawer to show a cardboard box filled with rows of rainbow-bright nail polish. "Here, sweetheart." She waves Liv over. "Take as many as you want. You too," she says to me. "It's nice to look pretty when there is so much ugly around."

"I like the one you're wearing." Liv glances at Racer. "Which one is that?"

"Tangerine Tambourine." Mrs. Carolina hands her the bottle. Liv tucks it into her pack along with another three bottles: lime green, purple sparkle, and clear glitter. Maybe she's going to use them as paint for her carvings, because there is no way that anyone could get that kid to put on nail polish any more than they could get her to put on shoes, hats, purses, or socks, or to wear elastic bands in her hair. It's a fight to get her to wear underwear even. If it were up to her, she'd wander around in an undershirt, shorts, and nothing else, except for her archery tackle, which is kind of like another limb for her anyway.

Mrs. Carolina slides the drawer shut and sighs.

"Goodbye, Spring Brook Elementary." She pats the desk. "You've been very good to me. I'd like to think that I've been very good to you too. But now it's time to go." She kisses her fingers and pats the desk again.

Mrs. Carolina rides ahead of us on her bicycle, which has fared very well over the last year. The pink paint doesn't have a speck of dirt on it. The basket at the front is woven through with bright pink plastic flowers. The basket at the back is lined with red-and-white-checked gingham. She looks like she's headed for the farmers market, with her hair covered by a scarf and another one tied at her neck. She wears a skirt that is impossibly white, all things considered. She doesn't even seem to sweat, which surely must place her in the category of extraterrestrial being, what with the sun's endless assault these days.

"How does she not sweat?" Soren says as he uses a bandana to wipe his brow. His gaze shifts past me, to a berm in the distance.

"Zee," he says.

"I've got it." Just as I'm about to ride toward it, I hear one of Liv's arrows zing past. We all watch the arrow until it lands just to the left of him, kicking up a tiny scuff of dust.

"Liv! You don't have to—"

Liv squeezes one eye shut, draws her sinewy arm back, and pulls another arrow. Her fingernails are chewed ragged to the quick. Soren and I seriously need to get some self-care going on with all four of us.

"Now!" Soren yells.

Liv shakes her head.

"It's coming!" Racer yells.

"Let it come a little closer," I say. "I'll do it."

The zombie is close enough that I can see he has a bloodied head of black hair; an old cascade of blood is crimson against his light brown skin, which is just starting to gray. So many flies swarm his head that I hear them before I hear his footsteps. He wears a windbreaker and heavy work boots, the laces still done up. Most of one leg of his jeans is gone, and so is most of his thigh underneath.

I start toward him just as Liv's arrow zings by. This one plants deep into his left eye socket; you don't need much more force than you'd need to kill a rabbit to sink that. The flies scatter as he rolls his shoulders back, his arms slack at his sides, and then drops to his knees, where he stays for enough of a moment that he looks like he's praying, eyes to the heavens, except for Liv's arrow sticking out of his face. He doesn't make a sound when he face-plants, shoving the arrow deeper into his skull.

"Yes!" I shout. "Liv! You got him."

Liv slings her bow back in place, on her back, with the quiver Dad made her.

"You get that one." I point to the arrow that missed. I don't want her to have to wrestle the other one out of the mess that is this creature's pulpy head, but I am more excited than I should let on that there is one more person in our party who can kill a zombie without the crack-and-attract of Soren's gun or having to be close enough to use a hatchet. That is way too close. *Last resort* close. No eleven-year-old should know how to kill a zee, but I'm so glad that my little sister does.

Mrs. Carolina meets us about a mile down the road. None of us say anything about the zee. She waves us into a mechanic shop a little ways past the town's railyard, which is just a platform by the grain silos, likely the only reason the train ever stopped there in normal times. She tells us her instruction from the soldiers was to wait here, at Dan'n Ed's Truck's and Machine Repair. When it finally gets dark, Soren and I take the first watch while the others try to get some sleep in a cool corner of the big building. Racer joins us after just a few minutes, too excited about riding a train for the first time to try to sleep.

“Look what I found,” Soren says when he comes back from going to pee. He holds up two brand-new hatchets, still in their packaging, and turns to Racer. “We can match, if you want to. I know you like blue.” He offers the one with the blue handle to Racer, who rips off the packaging and takes off the blade guard before Soren even gets his black-handled one open. “And one for me.” He wrestles it open and then takes his belt off to slide it in place beside his gun. “Time to realize that the gun is going to be more trouble than it’s worth.”

“It’s still going to come in handy,” I say. “When shooting is a better choice than letting them get us.”

“Sure.” He rests his head on my shoulder. “But I wish we weren’t having this conversation at all. I wish there was no reason for it. I wish Dad was a different version of himself; then we wouldn’t even be here and he and Mom wouldn’t be dead. I wish I didn’t know about Dan’n Ed’s Truck’s and Machine Repair. I wish I wasn’t sitting here with you thinking about the grammar on that stupid sign.” Soren points to the enormous sign at the road. It’s been shot at a lot, either before or after, so much that the wood looks like it has an infection of pockmarks.

“Eddie would have some choice words to say about that,” Soren says.

“He would.” I feel a little swell of guilt when I realize that I haven’t thought of Eddie in days. When I think of Racer now, I just count him in our numbers, like he’s always been on the run with us in an apocalyptic world.

“Let me see if I can do him justice,” Soren says. He closes his eyes and squares his shoulders with a little shake, just like

Eddie does. *Did.* "I'd say that sign has some serious possessive issues. Someone"—he leans in a little to whisper conspiratorially—"*someone* should give Dan and Ed a really good talking-to."

It's after midnight, and the train hasn't come. We all sit in a circle in the enormous shop. Pigeons coo in the rafters. Mice scurry across the floor along the wall. Liv is on her knees with a margarine tub, hoping to catch one. She's lined the tub with a piece of clean rag and put in two noodles from her supper.

The rest of us are just waiting.

"Mrs. Carolina," I say. "Have you seen this train come through before?"

"No. This one is the only one planned. That's what the soldiers said." She smooths her skirt with her hands. It's a lot dirtier than it was this morning, but she wears it like she's just arrived at a dance. "If we miss it, then boo for us."

Boo for us. As if that really is the sum of it all.

"What if it doesn't come?" Liv says. "Then what?"

"What are we doing, just waiting here for a train that might not even come, and even if it does, it probably won't even be able to take the horses?" I direct this at Soren. We don't need this train. Sure, it will cut our time to the Sigurdsons' by a week. But what the hell is another week at this point? "Do we even want to be on a train? With *soldiers*? Maybe it's a trap."

"They were very nice young men." Mrs. Carolina picks an invisible something off her skirt. "I believe one of them was from Albuquerque."

"I like trains," Racer says. He's sitting beside Mrs. Carolina on the bench seat from a minivan. He's stuck very close to her ever since she appeared. "I want to go on the train."

A joyful cry sounds from the shadows. Liv runs toward us with the margarine tub. She cracks the lid to show us her treasure: a plump, fluffy mouse, its nose twitching, eyes darting with panic.

"His name is Piano. He was running across the keys." She points behind her, to where an upright lists to one side. It looks one blow from becoming kindling. "I don't want to go on the train. Let's just keep going. Like we have been. Riding horses and camping."

"You don't stand one single chance out there," Mrs. Carolina says in a way that makes it sound almost cheerful. "You truly don't."

"We stand all the chances," I say. "If anyone can survive out here, we can."

"Not with those monsters," Mrs. Carolina says. "Do you know, so many of us had toxoplasmosis already? That's why Hypertox spread so fast. So many hair triggers, lying in wait. Those Russians turned it into a biological weapon." She eyes Racer and Liv before lowering her voice. "They were going to start World War Three with it, but then it got away from them, and it started the end of the world instead."

"That's not a fact," I say.

"It might be."

"Or it might be from the melting ice caps," Soren says. "But you probably don't want to get into a conversation about climate change, I'm guessing?"

She takes a moment to consider and then shakes her head, thank goodness. "It really doesn't matter, does it? It's far more likely simply an act of God. Which is why we must all be saved. Our souls are truly what's at stake."

"All right, moving on. I vote for the train," Soren says. "If it ever comes."

"Smart boy." Mrs. Carolina smiles, as if she won something. She points at Liv. "You, my dear, are going to need something on your feet. The train will be absolutely disgusting."

"No way." Liv peeks at her mouse. "No shoes."

It's been dark for hours and hours when we finally hear the train in the distance, screeching as it brakes. As we get our things together, I have a deep pit in my gut, full of *don't get on the train.*

I don't want to go.

Liv doesn't.

Soren does.

Racer does.

I don't feel like I can say no, considering the ground we'll cover on the train. We'll be that much closer to safety and supplies, if our wishes come true and BATO is waiting for us untouched, unlikely as that sounds. We have to aim for it anyway, so we might as well be hopeful about it.

I lead Odger out into the hot night, behind Rune and Ulf. That leaves Bolt.

Racer isn't back from going out to pee.

"Racer!" I drop Odger's reins and start running. "Racer! The train is here."

I don't see him out the back, in the junkyard of car carcasses and rusting metal drums and sun-bleached traffic cones. "Racer! We have to go!"

The train stops. I hear Soren shouting for both of us. I run back to the tracks. There are half a dozen soldiers guarding the ladder leading up to the train and another six guarding the wide plank that leads into a cattle boxcar.

"I can't find him!" I shout.

Soren is arguing with the soldier in charge of the livestock cars.

"We can't leave any of the horses behind!" There is more fear in his voice than bravado, even though I know he's trying to take command of the situation. "We need them where we're going."

"There's four of you," the soldier says. "You can take two horses."

"Thirteen minutes!" another soldier shouts.

"I'm going to find him," I tell myself more than Soren. "I'm going to go get him and bring him to the train. You deal with the horses."

"If you're planning on taking that big boy"—the soldier points to Odger—"you're definitely not taking four. There's not enough room."

"We're getting off in Yakima," Soren pleads. "We're not going that far!"

I kick Odger's flanks. "Wait for us!"

"Nine minutes!" the soldier farther up the train shouts. "We don't wait for anyone."

Halfway down the dirt track that runs alongside the shop, I

slow. What if I *don't* find Racer? I glance back at the train. Then to the mess of engines and tarps and pallets. "Racer!" I scream. Then again, so loud that my throat feels raw immediately. "We have to *go*!"

I don't know what to do. I do not know what the correct decision is in this very moment, this instant, this *second*. Racer needs me, but I can't be separated from Soren and Liv.

"Two minutes!" The soldier is far enough away that I can barely hear him over the idling of the train, and the panic in my brain over the terrible subplot I've just backed myself into.

I head to the train at a gallop. Without Racer. Or Bolt. I jump down and lead Odger up the ramp to be with the other horses. I leave Odger with a kiss on his snout and run alongside the train to where Soren is leaning out, waving. The train starts moving as I put my foot on the first rung of the ladder up to the car.

As the train eases forward, I cannot take my eyes off the garage and junkyard. What if I see Racer *now*? I squeeze my eyes shut, afraid that if I open them, I'll see him running for the train. The only reason I could run along the train just now is because of him. We've been a team since the first day in Marion Gap, and here we are, broken apart forever because he had to take a leak at the worst time in the history of Racer Menendez.

"Racer is here!" I hear Soren's voice behind me. "He's on the train!" Soren helps me into the car, which is lined with rows of seats that face each other in groups of four. There, at the far end, is Racer, with a grin so bright and wide that it tells me he doesn't know that Bolt didn't get on the train.

"He left Ulf behind!" Liv bawls. "And you lost Bolt!"

“The plan was if they couldn’t take the horses, we wouldn’t get the train, Soren.” I look away from Racer, afraid that if I look at him I’ll cry. We came too close to losing him. “What happened?”

“By the time I realized he wasn’t going to let us take all four, Rune was already loaded, and then I saw Racer running for the train.” Soren covers his face with his hands. He draws them down, pulling his skin taut. “And then I saw Liv waving at him out the window. And you were *nowhere.* So, I made a call. I stayed with Racer and Liv. I figured you’d know where to meet us.”

PART III

CHAPTER 14

I expect everyone to be talking among themselves, but they aren't. Even Mrs. Carolina's charm can't get people talking.

"We're new here, so let's introduce ourselves." She stands at the front of the car and pats the seats on either side, which results in a serious frown from each of the seat occupants—one young man with a scowl chiseled on his jaw, and a woman about Mom's age but with bleached blond hair, right down to the roots. Who takes the time to bleach their hair in a zombie apocalypse? When no one takes her up on her suggestion, she makes her way to our seat, which is at the opposite end of the car. "That's too bad," she says, loud enough for people to hear. "We all have something very special in common. We could share our stories."

"Zombies came. The world as we knew it ended," a husky voice says as the lights turn off and the car falls into darkness for a second before the strip of tiny lights that mark the aisle starts to glow. "It's all the same story."

"Sit down and shut up." This is from the armed soldier who stands in the small circle of light thrown from the one dim fixture illuminating the passage between this car and the next. There's only one of him and at least fifty of us—not every seat is taken, much to my surprise—but I still feel uneasy when I see his uniform and his shiny black boots and his stony expression. I hear Dad's voice: *If it's government issue, you don't want anything to do with it.*

As the train slowly picks up speed and my eyes adjust to the dark, I look at Soren, Racer, and Liv, with tiny Piano cupped in her hands. Mrs. Carolina sits with two older men and a boy about my age, none of whom seem to know each other. Yet she keeps her mouth shut, no doubt resisting the urge to lead an icebreaker. Over and over, I look at my people, safe and sound. *We all made it onto the train, Eira. It's okay.* I didn't lose Racer. We're all accounted for: Soren, Liv, Racer. And me. Bolt and Ulf are the only casualties.

"Where were you, Racer?" My mix of anger and relief sharpens the words more than I intend.

"I saw the train," he says. "I ran for it. I ran so fast, Eira Helvig."

"I am very glad that you got on the train, Racer Menendez." I give him a hug and come away damp with the sweat he worked up running from the junkyard.

"Let's go see the engineer," he says.

"It's not that kind of train." Soren keeps his voice down. "Sorry, Racer."

"Let's go ask." Racer gets up. He takes Liv's hand. "Liv will come too."

Liv takes her hand back. "No, I won't. Soldiers are robots. Dangerous robots." Another Dad-ism. "I'm not asking them anything."

"These are good guys." I say it, even if I don't believe it. "They're making sure we all get there safely."

"We're not getting *there,*" Liv says. "We're not going where they're going." She tucks Piano back into the margarine tub and fishes in her pack for her carving knife and a knob of balsam no bigger than an egg. She wedges the knife into the wood and twists. "We're going to BATO."

We've only got a few hours on this train. It's going to save us a week.

"All our water is with the horses," Soren says. "I'm going to go ask if he has any."

"Don't bother," the soldier barks. "What'd you think? Nice, cold water bottles at every stop?"

A bottle of water, attached to a tanned, sinewy hand with blunt nails and three chunky silver rings—a skeleton with a cowboy hat, a crescent moon, and a tree with roots as deep as the branches—appears over my shoulder.

"Here," a voice says. "Take this."

I turn in my seat to see the person. Black jeans and a pair of beat-up turquoise-and-black cowboy boots with spurs; a pinstriped vest with a satin back; a stiff, dirty lasso neatly coiled and hanging off a belt beside a short, sheathed machete. The name *Cosmo* is perfectly tooled into the belt between two angled holsters, each cradling a sleek little Colt revolver, like you'd see in an old Western movie. They're not nearly as tall as me, but I bet they're at least five foot ten, not including the black cowboy hat.

"It's filtered," they say when I take the bottle.

When our eyes meet, something clicks. And I know I'm not making it up, because beside me Soren whispers, "Ding, ding, ding." My heart squeezes out a succession of quick, unsteady beats. This doesn't happen often, but when it does, it makes me light-headed. It happens sometimes when I meet someone queer, or when I get close to someone queer. It's not the same as a crush; it's more of a recognition. *My people.*

I stand up, which makes the soldier shift.

"We have water with our horses," I say over a pasty, thick tongue that seems to be contributing to my voice coming out higher and squeakier than it usually is. "We're getting off soon." I hand it back. "You're going to need it. But thank you."

"I'd be honored if you took it, Giantess." They return to their seat, which faces away from me, so I can't see them once they sit down.

"She called you Giantess!" Soren grabs my hand and squeezes it. "She knows you!"

"I doubt that *she* is the right pronoun."

"Sure, okay, but who carries *two* revolvers like that? Except Wild Bill Hickok." Soren leans forward, trying to get a look. "They totally know you. They're a *fan.* In all this bullshit, you manage to find a fan?"

The train stops at every town. The soldiers light it up and stay for exactly fifteen minutes, waiting for survivors to come. They take down zombies that come running at some stops, drawn by the screeching as the train slows. The shots crack the night, attracting even more of them, but the soldiers just keep shooting until it's time to pull away. The train noise draws them anyway, so what's some gunfire on top of that?

So far, someone has gotten on at each stop. At one town, a group of six people get on the car three ahead of ours, all wearing the same new-looking red tracksuits, with *ORCA SWIM CLUB* in white down each sleeve and on the backs, and *SWIM* across their butts. They don't look like a family, because they're mostly young adults, our age and older.

"Athletes." Racer grins. "Like us."

"I'm a way better swimmer than runner," Soren says. "Maybe I should go join their team."

"Zombie Apocalypse Running Club sticks together," Racer says. "Like they stick together." He points at the last of the swimmers climbing onto the train. It's a sweet thought, to think of them in a swim club from before, sticking together this whole time because they were at practice when it all started. But those suits are a very recent find. They're either all wearing the same thing because they think it's funny, or something happened that gave them no choice. For the sake of staying light, I decide that they think it's the funniest thing they've ever done.

It's dawn when I spot Cosmo again. From where I sit, I spot the top half of them when the train is about an hour past Kennewick. They take their hat off to run a hand through their black hair, shaggy on top, shaved on the sides, with a cowlick at the front, off to the left of center. They replace their hat, adjusting it back just a bit as they look out the window. There's a red-tailed hawk feather tucked into the band, and just as I'm looking at it, they reach up and touch it, as if for good luck, before dropping their hands to rest on the ivory handles of the revolvers.

"Enjoying the view?" Soren says. "You'll notice that absolutely everyone else is looking out the windows."

"What are they looking at?" People flock to the windows on the south side of the train.

When I half stand, I can easily see out the top third of one of the windows. All I see is a beautiful sunrise bathing the rolling fields of overgrown crops.

"Go ask your superfan," Soren says. "Maybe they know why the train is slowing down in the middle of nowhere."

"Absolutely I will go ask them, thank you very much for the excuse, Soren."

I take exactly two steps, and all hell breaks loose. Screams roll back from farther up the train, car by car by car. Gunfire echoes from *inside* the train and out. The wheels screech as the train slows down, suddenly enough that everyone in our car slides forward, dumping the window gawkers onto the floor, except for Cosmo, who manages to stay on their feet.

"Zees." They press a hand to the window. Then, much louder, "Zombies!"

"Go, go, go!" Soren shouts behind me. He shoves Racer and Liv ahead of him toward the door. Liv drops the margarine tub. She scrambles to get it, but Soren keeps pushing.

"Piano!" Liv screams as someone steps on the overturned tub, popping the lid off. The mouse scurries away, deftly dodging the stampede of feet.

"He's okay! He's okay! We have to get to the horses *now,*" I yell. "Stay together!"

Racer grips my hand so tight that my fingers go numb. When all our feet land on the ground, we grab hands and start running down the length of the train to the livestock cars. I glance over my shoulder, where screams and gunshots ruin the pretty, pastoral morning. The swim club members spill over each other to get out, all of them with bloodied faces and necks. Their red uniforms are darkened with blood at the collars and down the fronts. They flop up onto their feet and begin that terrible, lurching run, arms limp at their sides, as if they're steering with their shoulders.

"Run!" I scream. Soren takes off. Racer follows him.

"Good job!" he yells as he passes Soren. "Move those arms, Soren Helvig!"

"Liv." She stares at the members of the swim club, all of whom are running for her. "Liv!" When she still doesn't move, I grab her and tuck her under my arm like a football and sprint as fast as I can to catch up to the boys.

And by *sprint,* I mean clumsily close the distance even with a nearly catatonic eleven-year-old under my arm—thanks to the longest legs of anyone on this train, is my guess.

We are not fast enough.

A terrible idea takes over with a sudden and concrete confidence, blowing the *stay together* idea out of the water. I hate it. Hate it, hate it, hate—

"Liv, Racer, head for those trees." I point through the gap

between two train cars, to where a stand of enormous oaks borders the field.

"No!" Soren grabs their hands. "We stay together."

"They can make it," I say. "We get the horses. We meet there."

"Get up into them, okay? Liv, you help Racer up." I grip her shoulder. "You have to help him up into the trees."

Liv and Racer don't argue. They scramble under the hitch and take off into the field, where I can hardly see them for the expanse of ragweed that has smothered whatever used to be there. Soren and I make a run for the car with the horses. People have already opened it up and pulled the ramp down. Three horses bolt south, galloping away from the iron-heavy stink of blood as more and more people fall under the swim club members. Maybe they *were* a team before. They move faster than any of the zees that I've seen so far, like they were athletes to begin with.

Odger and Rune are still in the train car, their reins still looped loosely around the bar anchored to the wall. That we're not here for four horses makes my heart clench as I take Odger's reins and Soren takes Rune's.

"Good boy," I murmur to Odger in the low singsong voice he likes when he's skittish.

"Such a good girl," Soren says to Rune in the same way. "Sweet girl."

We're just about to leave when I see a very handsome quarter horse waiting in the shadows at the back of the car. I recognize the tooling on the saddle and the same turquoise leather highlights of Cosmo's boots. I grab that horse too.

"Come on, sweeties." I lead Cosmo's horse and Odger down the ramp ahead of Soren and Rune. As soon as we come out into the discordantly beautiful sunrise, the horses toss their heads and rear up. The screaming does not match the cloudless blue sky and the fox sparrows and finches singing in the field. The train-side massacre rolls ever closer toward us.

Once I'm in the saddle, I scan for Cosmo and don't see them. Instead, I see a fat, naked man running at me, a gold lamé fanny pack bouncing around his waist, which is streaked with blood from the zee bite on his cheek. What the hell was he doing five minutes ago?

We can't wait another second.

I gallop behind Soren, with Cosmo's horse's reins in one hand. We ride to the back of the train and then make a sharp cut across the tracks and run at a full-on canter back westward and north to the stand of oaks. I see Liv and Racer holding hands, running as fast as they can over the uneven ground. We push the horses harder, faster.

"Zees!" Soren hollers.

One of the swim club zombies heads for them, cutting diagonally across the field. She's short and stocky and running fast enough that the math says she'll get to Racer and Liv before we do. At the edge of the ragweed, Liv stops and fumbles for her bow. She doesn't even get the bow out of her quiver before the zee knocks her over.

"Liv!" I scream. Then, "Soren! Shoot it!" But we're too far, and it's right on top of Liv. Instead, Soren drives Rune even faster.

Ahead of us, Racer grabs his hatchet and raises it above his head with both hands gripping the handle. He brings it down, and even from this distance, I see the zee slump immediately.

"Liv!" I scream. "Liv!"

"I'm okay," Liv gasps. "I was trying to shoot it."

At first she looks fine, but then I see where the ground under her is dotted with fat splotches of blood. She has a small wound just below her ear. It looks like a vampire bite, though. Not a zee bite.

"No." I pull her onto my lap and press my handkerchief to her head. "No!"

"It didn't bite me!" She grabs a rock with a sharp, bloodied point. "This did."

When we get to the trees, Liv insists on climbing the tree herself. We only go high enough that the zees can't get us, and then a little higher than that. We're about fifteen feet up. I get Liv settled in front of me on a fat, stable limb. Soren and Racer sit just above and beside us. We're all very quiet, listening to the din of what's happening back at the train, and the very loud thoughts in our heads.

"Someone's coming," Liv says.

"Hey! HEY!" It's Cosmo. They hold on to their hat and run at full tilt, lasso and guns bouncing, glinting in the sun with each step. "That's my horse!"

Way behind Cosmo—but catching up—are three swim club members, faces smeared with blood, jaws snapping.

I scramble down and whistle for Odger. I gallop straight for Cosmo. I don't even slow down when I reach them. Cosmo lifts their arms, ready for me, like we planned it ahead of time and aren't making life-or-death decisions with each second. They grab the horn with one hand, my waist with the other, at the same time as I scoop them up and into place behind me. I turn Odger around and race the swim club members back to the trees.

"Get up!" I yell. "Climb!"

"My horse—"

"I saved her for you. Go! Up!"

"Did that kid get bit?" Cosmo scrambles up and joins the others in the tree. When they catch their breath, they add, "I saw the zee take her down."

"It's not a bite," I say.

"Better not be." Cosmo leans in for a look. They wipe blood away with their handkerchief to inspect the puncture.

"Back off." Liv swats their hand away and growls.

CHAPTER 15

It's late morning by the time all the zombies have gathered back at the train, like ants with a gummy worm. There are no more screams, just a lot of fresh zombies. We don't say a word as we climb down and get the horses. I point north, and we head that way in a tight group.

"We should have seen the highway by now," Cosmo says, hours later, as we head down a farm track along the edge of yet another overgrown field. We're aiming for I-82, which will take us to Yakima, which is just a couple hours' ride from BATO.

"How about we take a break?" I point to a snaking ribbon of green in the distance. "There's a creek, for sure. There will be water and shade."

The creek is only about ten feet across, but it's cold and flowing fast, so we drink straight from it. We settle in the shade there to rest.

"I don't know about you all," Soren says, "but my body is vibrating and my brain won't stop going over my apocalypse inventory of truly terrible things. There is no way I can rest."

"We'll all crash," Cosmo says, "if we're tired enough."

Liv finds a pool that is deep enough to swim in. I can see trout fry flitting back and forth in the water. Liv ducks under. After about twenty seconds, Cosmo starts squirming.

"Tell me she can hold her breath for a long time."

"She can go for more than a minute," I say. "Strongest swimmer in the family."

Liv kicks herself even deeper, until she touches the bottom. She flips, pushes herself up with her feet, and then breaks the surface, rolls onto her back, and sculls her hands against the current. Cosmo sighs with relief.

"Hey," they say.

"Yeah?"

"Where are you guys going?"

I am so thankful for this basic question that I actually have the answer to.

"Our friends' apple orchard," I say. "Kind of near Yakima. Northwest. A couple hours' ride. What about you?"

"Astoria," Cosmo says. "On the coast. Do you think anyone would mind if I travel with you until you go north?"

"Join us. Please. Safety in numbers." I know Liv will mind, but too bad. "What's in Astoria?"

"One of the Children's Villages."

"That's got to be a euphemism for something bad," I say. "Right?"

"Better not be." Cosmo digs in their pack and pulls out a pamphlet. "My little brother is there." The logo is a clover of hearts within a wreath of hands.

> UNICEF Children's Villages—safekeeping for children 12 and under. Let us take care of our future, while you take care of rebuilding your lives. The Villages provide adult supervision, safe housing, education, exercise, fun activities, three meals a day, and snacks. You will be reunited with your children and assigned family housing when you get to the Children's Village. Until then, we'll be their guardians, in accordance with the United Nations Global Emergency Children's Plan, ratified on July 7, 2029.

I remember Mrs. Carolina's mention of children and villages. "They took him?"

"I *let* him go," Cosmo says. "I handed him over. I signed on the dotted line, like I was shipping a parcel. We should've stuck together. But it was early days, and I was so scared that he'd be hurt, or worse. So, when the UNICEF reps came, I bought what they were selling. Here we are, floundering at the end of the world, let's band together to save the children. Our parents were gone. He was all I had, and I gave him away. And now I'm going to find him." Before I can gently question the likelihood of the Village still being there, Cosmo puts a hand up. "I'm not thinking about that, so don't ask."

I guess plenty of other people have, but I don't say that either. "What's your brother's name?"

"Bailey." Cosmo glances over at Liv. "About her age, I'm guessing. He turned twelve in March."

"She turned eleven in April," I say.

"You're lucky you didn't run into any Village convoys."

I want to say that there is no way in hell that I would have ever let her go, but of course, I don't.

"What happens after you find Bailey?"

"Well, if the Villages are as good as they say, then I'll stay there with him." Cosmo shrugs, but not in a way that says they don't care. It is a big, big shrug, with a big, big breath to go with it. "And if I need to get him out of there, I will."

Cosmo takes their boots and socks off and then shimmies out of their jeans to reveal black boxer briefs. In the same second that I wonder if they'll take their top off, Cosmo does. Red scars about the size of pencils underline each nipple, about three inches below. None of us Helvig kids have ever seen top surgery scars before, but all three of us know better than to stare. As for Racer, he doesn't stare either. So even while this creek scene looks nothing but idyllic and sweet, it's made up of actors who are pretending not to be traumatized by what happened when the train stopped, pretending that seeing someone with top surgery scars is no big deal, and pretending like we have a handle on all of it.

We travel until sunset and then set up camp. When Soren and Racer take over watch, Cosmo puts away the deck of cards that was keeping us awake while I roll out my sleeping bag. Cosmo unrolls theirs beside mine. I listen to their breath slow into sleep. My exhaustion and worry fold over themselves, driving me into the deepest sleep, so thick that when Soren shakes me awake just before dawn, it takes me ages to orient myself again. At first, I think I'm home, in bed. I smell sausages. I hear Liv and Mom talking, and birdsong. It all falls into place as I sit up, though, especially my rumbling stomach. There is birdsong, but Mom is dead, and there is definitely no sausage.

Racer stands on a boulder between the rest of us and the creek.

"Zombie Apocalypse Running Club!" He pretends to blow his whistle. "Practice time!"

"What's happening?" Cosmo stirs beside me.

"Here." Liv drops one of the ZARC shirts directly onto Cosmo's head. "Oops."

Cosmo does not put on the shirt, and they do not do the laps along the skinny trail we came in on, between the bridge and our creek-side camp. They offer to keep watch, like it's a sacrifice. Cosmo waves the rest of us off as we head up the trail. The only reason we all got away from the train yesterday is because our cardio was better than most of the peoples' on the train. And the reason my cardio even exists is because of ZARC.

"You laugh," I pant when I pass them for a fourth time. I'll admit, the wedge of shade and the bottle of water freshly filtered from the creek both look far more enjoyable than this run. "But it works."

"Weapons work." Cosmo offers me the water. I shake my head. I'd get a stitch. "Strategic avoidance works even better."

"Until it doesn't." I head up the trail for my fifth and final lap. "And then you run!"

As the others pack up, Cosmo and I head off to collect a couple of saddled-up horses that are curious enough about our horses that we might be able to catch them for Racer and Liv.

"Are you going to use your lasso?" I say as we ease our way closer and closer. Cosmo slows to a stop.

"Won't need to." Cosmo clicks their tongue, which makes the horses swing their heads our way. "Hup, hup! Let's go!" Cosmo makes a few kissy noises, and the horses come right over, swinging their heads, happy to see us.

"I'm very disappointed," I say.

"Why?"

"I wanted to see you use your lasso." The horses plod along behind us, no doubt hopeful that we'll lead them to something better to eat than this dried-up grass. "That would've been kinda hot."

"Hot?" Cosmo laughs. "Interesting choice of words."

My cheeks are on fire, but the smile they beam at me is worth it.

Racer names his horse Chris Nikic, after the first person with Down syndrome to finish an Ironman triathlon. Niki for short, for the rest of us. Full "Chris Nikic" for Racer, every single time. He wanted to name Liv's Ben Heitmeyer, after the first athlete with Down syndrome to compete in the first triathlon in Special Olympics World Games history, but Liv named her Buttercup, after her pony at home, her favorite chicken, two pet rabbits she had, and a goat with three legs.

Cosmo's horse is called Leus, short for Equuleus, which is a mouthful and a constellation meaning *little horse,* named by the astronomer Ptolemy. When I ask Cosmo if they know a lot about astronomy, they shake their head.

"I can name a few constellations. Not much more than that. My dad named him," they say as we head west, which leads to both Astoria and BATO at the moment. "Leus was tiny when he was born. We didn't think he'd make it. So my dad named him for a tiny horse that is over a billion years old."

This mention of their dad is an opening to ask them more about their family, but Cosmo seems to realize that too, and they pull Leus's head to the right and separate from the group to ride about fifty feet away, which seems like a pretty clear message to me that they don't want to talk about their family. All I've gleaned so far is that Cosmo was by themselves at a junior sharpshooter competition in Wyoming when everything fell apart, and then they headed home. They mentioned getting to their grandparents' house, then a cousin's house, their principal's house, and their girlfriend's house. And, according to them, they "just kept heading for home."

With the horses, we cover just over forty miles and don't see a single zombie. No people either. Just mountains, rivers, lakes, blue sky, and puffy clouds that take the shapes of all the light and fluffy things we can come up with. Bunnies, ice cream cones, turtles.

CHAPTER 16

Cosmo and I take first watch on the third night. While Racer and Soren toss and turn, Liv falls asleep almost immediately.

"She's always fallen asleep like that. And she can sleep through anything," I say. "Maybe not the best quality to have in a zombie apocalypse, but I've always been jealous. She used to fall asleep with her head on her plate at supper sometimes, even up until just a couple of years ago." This gets us whispering about before. We don't mention zombies or anything to do with them for at least an hour. This is how I find out that while Cosmo is a three-time junior sharpshooter champion of the western division, they try not to shoot zees, because it just brings more.

"So yeah, ace shot, but also not necessarily the best zombie-apocalypse skill to have." They draw their machete. It's a cheap one you'd find in any hardware store, with a plastic handle and a blade that is nicked and scarred but also very, very sharp. "This is my best friend. The guns are for scaring off people." We sit side by side with our backs against a log. "Another problem with guns? I'm down to half a box of ammunition. I know my machete is a piece of crap, but it's the one we had in the garage, so I took it. It's nothing like your sword. Your dad made your sword, right? I saw your stall at the faire."

"He did." The idea of Cosmo knowing me before sends a wash of uneasy goose bumps up and down my arms. It's weird to imagine them watching me in tournaments or holding one of Dad's knives in their hand. I show them my dagger. "It's a seax. Viking dagger, basically."

"You use your sword mostly?"

"Yeah," I say. "Her name is Gertrude."

"Is there a real Gertrude?" Cosmo says like they're asking about a girlfriend. I blush and am grateful for the dark.

"It's just a name. Basically means *strong spear.* So original."

"You had a different sword in Pinedale. At the Ren faire. Twice. The two years before Hypertox. I would remember this one."

"That was my old sword. My dad made that too."

"You know, I've been keeping my eye out for a sword. Ever since I saw you with yours, actually. Would you believe me if I told you I've thought of you a few times since then? Not in a creepy way. Just wondering if you were out here beheading zees left and right in the Hypertoxalypse."

"Is that what people call it?" I ask.

"Some, I guess." Cosmo shrugs. "Doesn't really matter what you call it. So? You've been out here the whole time, lopping off heads and conducting a widescale campaign of badassery?"

"Not at all." I glance at Racer and Soren, both asleep now. What if we had left before Hypertox? Last year, the year before, or even the first time Soren and I meant to, when we were far too young. We would've lost Liv too, and not just our parents. This last year at home was worth it to have Liv. She and Soren and Racer are all that matter now. "We've been at home this whole time." I tell them about Gefjunland and what happened to our parents.

"I'm really sorry, Eira." When I don't say anything—because I don't know what to say—Cosmo breaks the silence. "Did your dad make those daggers too? The ones you and your brother have?"

"He did." My cheeks are suddenly hot. I squeeze my eyes shut and I'm back home, standing too close to his forge, watching the steel glow orange in the mold. He glances at me. Down at me, when I was still shorter than he is. *Was.* Was. I blink away the image, but not before he smiles at me, that big beard-shrouded grin that was mostly up in his eyes. I open my eyes and look out into the velvet-black forest in front of us. "He was a blacksmith," I croak. "By trade. But mostly he just loved having a homestead."

When I fall silent, Cosmo puts their hand on my arm. "I get it. I miss my dad too."

But I don't miss *him.* I miss Mom, and home. And he was a part of that, so I suppose I miss those parts too. I loved him, absolutely. But I do not *miss* him.

"You'll only have one dad," Cosmo continues.

"Can we talk about something else?" Because if we talk about him, and why we left, then I'm going to find myself standing in front of the thing I do not want to acknowledge as real. If we had not left, my parents would still be alive, and home would still be there to go back to. They died—and home died too—because we weren't there to help defend them.

"Sure," Cosmo says. "Boyfriend? Girlfriend? I had a girlfriend, but I haven't seen her since before."

"I guess I had one too," I say. "Sort of." I tell Cosmo about Lola, about the night of the outbreak. When I'm done, my limbs feel so heavy that I can't lift my hand to wipe away my tears.

"All right. New topic: stupid and effective zombie weapons," Cosmo says. "I'll go first. Cans of food. Canned peaches. Alphabet soup."

"That won't kill a zee." I feel my breath coming easier. "How about a mop?"

"That's any better?"

"The stick end," I say. "Obviously."

"Okay, on the theme of 'stick ends,' let's add toilet plunger, cheerleader batons, chair legs, serving spoons—"

"Rulers, toothbrushes, safety scissors," I say. "Toilet scrubbers. Trowels."

"Who even says *trowel*? TROW-el." Cosmo laughs. "Yeah. All stupid. Our blades are the best. *Yours* is, I think. Or maybe it's just because you kick ass at using it. That thing's meant for *two* hands, you know." Cosmo says it knowing full well that I know that.

"Two hands for you, sure." I have an idea. "Back in a sec."

I free my old sword from its scabbard on the outside of my pack and bring it back to Cosmo. I lay it across their knees, where it looks like it's suspended in the moonlight, their black jeans disappearing in the dark.

"Try it," I say.

Cosmo stands up and then tightens their hands around the hilt. They point it at the dirt. "I don't know how."

"Like I do." I stand behind them and reach to close my hands over theirs. I guide the sword up, up, and into a fighting position, angled, pulled back, ready to load tension and power and intent. "It's not like a gun. There's not just one point." I run a finger along the blade. "There is all of this. So much more to work with."

"Yeah." I hear a catch in Cosmo's voice. "Okay." They widen their stance and bounce the sword a little.

"It gets heavy fast." I hold their forearms up. "I'll help. Concentrate on your posture instead."

We are inches apart. I look down at them while they focus on the sword. I slide my hands along their forearms, the friction heating the palms of my hands. Cosmo sucks in a breath.

"What are you doing?" Liv appears out of the dark. She's a pale ghost in a white tank top and shorts, fists on her hips. "Why does she have your old sword?"

"I'm giving it to them," I say.

"You are?" Cosmo gasps. "Really?"

"No, you are not." I know Liv wants to shout at me, but she controls herself. Barely. "Dad made that for you!"

"I don't need it. It's too small for me. Do you want it?"

"I hate swords." This is only because she wants to be good at something that isn't the thing *I'm* good at. Hence the bow. "Give it to Soren."

"He doesn't want it for the same reason you don't."

"Dad wouldn't want you to give it away."

"It's *my* sword," I say. "It's a way to say thank you."

"For what?"

For the offer of water on the train. For them just *being* on the train. For the way they let me lift them up onto Odger without hesitation. *For seeing me before.* Soren sits up.

"Doesn't matter what for." He's over there grinning in the dark, I am sure. "It's Eira's sword. Not yours. You don't want to give Cosmo your bow? Cool. That's as far as your say goes."

"I'll take good care of it." Cosmo wrestles the machete off their belt and tosses it into the darkness. They fix the sheath onto their belt, ahead of the Colt on their left side. "Thank you."

"Dad would be so, so mad." Liv flops back onto her mat and yanks her sleeping bag over her face, even though it's far too hot for that, even in this, the coolest part of the night.

Add another thank-you for the fact that Cosmo didn't try to argue with me about giving it to them. This is someone who knows the peril and appreciates the sword in exactly the right way. I open my arms to hug them, but then I hesitate when it suddenly seems awkward. They don't, though. Cosmo moves right into the hug. It occurs to me that I haven't hugged anyone outside of my family and Racer since that night with Lola in the orchard.

"I bet she doesn't even know how to use a sword," Liv says from inside her sleeping bag. "You'd have to teach her. Like, from scratch. Like, from zero. From completely nothing."

"I can do that."

"She can't come with us. And you can't give that to her!" Liv sits up again. She grabs her bow and readies an arrow. "Dad made that! And you're just giving it to a stray dog?"

"Put that down, Liv." When she doesn't, I close the distance in two strides and grab it out of her hand.

"Give that back!"

"Apologize," I say.

Liv crosses her arms and tries to stare me down.

"That's okay," Cosmo says. "I'll take your silence as an apology."

"Well, that's stupid," Liv says. "Because it isn't one."

"And my pronouns are *they* and *them,*" Cosmo says.

"What?"

"Don't call me *she* or *her,*" Cosmo says. "Don't call me *he* or *him.* Call me *they* or *them,* like everyone else here is already managing to do without any drama."

"That makes no sense," Liv says.

"You've seen me with my shirt off. Aren't you curious? Don't you want to ask me about my scars?"

"I thought you had cancer."

I was not expecting her to say that.

"I did not have cancer," Cosmo says.

"Then what did you do to your—"

"Eira. Soren. Come on," Cosmo says. "Am *I* really going to be the one to have this talk with your kid sister?"

"No!" Soren leaps up. "No, you're not."

"And yet you two ended up very—" Cosmo nods slowly but stops talking when I make the widest eyes possible and shake my head.

"We did," I say to shut them down. When does one come out to an eleven-year-old sister who still idolizes her father enough to threaten someone with a bow and arrow in his honor?

"But you're a girl—"

"Liv! Enough." I grab Liv's arm.

"But she *is*! She's a girl!"

"Does this sword have a name?" Cosmo keeps their eyes locked on me. I see that we are collectively changing the subject now. "Like Gertrude?"

"I never gave it one."

"I'll come up with something." Cosmo looks a bit wrung out from the exchange with Liv. "So, you'll teach me?"

"Sure," I say. "I'll teach you."

"So stupid," Liv mutters as she buries herself in her sleeping bag again. "She is a *girl*."

Back at our places against the log, I let out the longest exhale. "I'm sorry about your pronouns," I say. "She's just a kid."

"Kids are usually the ones who catch on pretty quick."

"She's never met anyone like you before."

"And you have?"

"Yeah. Actually . . ." I'm just about to tell them about the Norwegian folk dancer who I made out with in a shadowy corner of a baseball dugout in the little stadium where the Puyallup Ren faire was being held, the summer before everything fell apart. When I stop talking, Cosmo doesn't fill the silence. It occurs to me that they're waiting for me to come out as nonbinary too. "Oh, I don't mean me. Someone I made out with once. Just the one time. We didn't date or anything. I don't date. I mean, I would. But my parents don't really let us have friends. I mean, not outside of family friends. . . ."

Lola. I feel her pressed against me, her head tilted up. My lips on hers. A rush of warmth floods my body.

"I bet you're a good teacher," Cosmo says.

"What?" I realize I've missed something. "Making out?"

"No! No." Cosmo laughs. "I've got that covered. It seemed like you wanted to change the subject, so I did. Back to swords."

"Ah. Yes. I am a good teacher," I say, even though I don't actually know if that's true or if I wanted to change the subject.

"Guess I'm going to find out for myself just how good you are." It's dark. I'm not even looking at Cosmo, yet I fully hear a little grin shaping their words. I've heard that same grin from every single person I've ever made out with. It takes me a few seconds to clock it, to realize what's actually happening here in this little pocket of forest in the middle of nowhere, with the apocalypse raging all around us.

Cosmo is flirting with me.

Cosmo's flirt lands on my cheeks like two hot mementos of who I was before. Who I *still* am. I would like nothing more than to forget about Mom and Dad and the zombies and lose myself in Cosmo's embrace for even just five minutes. If you offered me a plate of sausages and mashed potatoes and a glorious, garden-fresh salad, with Mom's berry crumble and whipped cream on the side, I would still choose five minutes with Cosmo. I'm starving, in both definitions of the word.

When I wake up, Cosmo is coming back from a dip in the creek after having just reshaved the sides of their head with a plastic pink razor.

"Are you going to run with us today?" Racer asks. "You are

the only one who is not a member of the Zombie Apocalypse Running Club."

"I'm good, Racer." They secure their cowboy hat for the day, even though it is barely sunrise. "I wouldn't want to get all sweaty again right away. But thanks."

"Running is very important." Racer holds out a shirt.

"But think about it, Racer. If Cosmo is the worst runner out of all of us," Liv says, "she'll be the one to go down and get bit. While the rest of us get away."

"*They.* And I can run faster than some barefoot kid," Cosmo says.

"No, you can't," Racer says. "Liv is my best runner."

"Can so."

"Prove it." Racer drapes the shirt over Cosmo's hat.

"Seriously, not today." But Cosmo doesn't give the shirt back this time.

CHAPTER 17

So, their competitive spirit is what gets Cosmo running on day five of us traveling through the nearly zee-less mountains. Racer picks the cracked-mud, slightly sloping embankment of a river that's dangerously low, instead of the pebbly bed of a creek that's dried up altogether.

"I could've done the rocks," Liv grumbles as she and Cosmo line up to race.

"In bare feet? Sure," Cosmo says. "As if. And if you think I'm going to fake a loss just because you're a kid, think again."

"Trust me." Liv sets her sights down the river. "You won't need to."

"Three, two . . ." As Racer counts, Cosmo bounces and shakes out their hands. "One and a half." He laughs. "One and a quarter . . . one, and go!"

Liv takes off at a sprint, her scrawny legs driving her forward, but Cosmo keeps an impressive pace, even with one hand keeping their hat from blowing off and with their guns bouncing. Cosmo might even win, because steady always does. Liv is looking to impress, so she's set off too fast.

"We didn't make a finish line," Soren mutters when Liv gets so tiny in the distance that we can hardly see her. They eventually stop. They look no bigger than bugs from here. As we get a bit closer, we can see they're splashing water onto their faces and laughing.

"Tie," Cosmo says.

"Definitely tie," Liv says. "They're a good runner. I can admit that."

None of us say anything about Liv using the correct pronouns all of a sudden, as if doing so will jinx it.

Just as we turn to go back to camp, Soren spots a pair of zees cresting a little hill. They fall over themselves and straighten up in that uncanny, immediate, graceful way that they do. They head straight for Liv and Cosmo.

"Run!" Racer yells.

They don't have time to run, though. With one hand, Cosmo grabs Liv and pushes her behind them. With the other, they draw their pistol and fire two shots in immediate succession. The zees drop as if one bullet felled them both, even though they're at least fifteen feet apart. The first one's nightgown catches the air and poofs out like she's curtsying at a Victorian ball. The other one only wears tattered boxer shorts, but he has a scarf of freshly torn ivy around his neck and trailing behind him. A third one appears out of the trees. Soren draws his gun. He shoots once and misses but gets him with the second shot. . . .

We wait to see if any other zees come running, and when they don't, we head back to camp. Cosmo and I walk side by side behind the others. Our arms are so close that I can feel an energy lifting off of Cosmo, either from the zombie scare or from the exertion. Or both. They're soaked with sweat and smell of sage and body odor. Whenever they find a sage bush, they rub a bunch in their hands and then all over themselves. A heat rises from my crotch to the top of my head, making me feel suddenly faint and also compelled to kiss them.

Is it because two queers at the end of the world *have* to hook up, in the same way that the last cisgendered heterosexual couple is contractually obliged to make babies for the new world? But we're not making babies.

I could take their hand. Just their hand. I could take some of the vibrating, nervous energy off of them. I could hold it tight. Steady them. I move my hand toward theirs and then lift it suddenly, to shield the sun as I try to make sense of what I see happening beyond the far side of our camp.

More zombies. We all stop. Between us and camp are the horses, nibbling at the green grass above the river. Beyond the horses are the logs we dragged to sit on by the fire ring Racer and Liv made from rocks, and our packs, propped up side by side against a fallen tree. And beyond that, the zombies. I can't tell how many, but there are enough that when their heads come up over the knoll, at first they look like a low row of big rocks—only these ones weren't there before, and they're moving. *Fast.*

"Zombies!" I head for Odger. "Hurry!"

The others follow. Liv and Racer aim for the camp and the packs that are waiting for us and the gear all around.

"No! Leave it!" This is the first time I've heard Cosmo yell. They've got a holler louder than any of the rest of us.

"That way!" I point north. "Straight toward that peak. The one with the cell tower. Right there. See it?" I make sure she and Racer know the one. "Head for the tower. We'll catch up with you."

"Our stuff!" Liv cries as she rides off.

"We'll get everything!" I shout. "Just go!"

All this time we've been so careful not to use the guns, and this *one* time—the farthest we've ever been from civilization—they show up. "Like Black Friday when they open the door," Cosmo growls as they tug Leus's reins. "And *we* are the hot-ticket items."

"We don't have time," I say as Cosmo starts for the camp, even as the zombies crest the hill. From this far, I can tell that they all turned a long time ago; there is not a fresh zee among them, just gray, human-shaped sacks of decay, all still equipped with the lurching, unfair speed that is the Hypertox driving them at us. "We can come back for everything once we lose them."

"I'm not leaving my—" Cosmo straightens as they watch the zees close the distance. *"Shit."* They pull out a revolver and take a shot, dropping what should be a frail old lady to her knees. She falls back, her head hitting a rock. The zee behind her steps on her chest as he keeps coming. The crack of the old lady's breaking ribs makes my skin crawl. "Let's go! Let's go!"

I steer Odger north, leading the way. Our three horses know what's good for them; they canter across the meadow and into the forest, eager to get away from those monsters. When I look back, I can't believe how many there are—at least twenty, which is the most I've seen together.

We catch up to Liv and Racer about ten minutes later, but when we emerge from the forest and look up to orient ourselves with the cell tower, we don't see it anymore.

"We'll wait, right?" I say. "Then we'll just retrace our steps."

"They'll move on eventually," Cosmo says. "Then we can go back."

Problem is, after hours pass and we all agree that now is the time, we can't find the meadow that leads to the river. We cannot find an entire river. We three mountain kids who've worked traplines and found our way in thousands of acres of wilderness cannot get us back to our packs. A pair of ravens follows us, laughing at our misfortune. Everyone was riding so hard that no one took note of landmarks—boulders, fallen trees, cliff faces—other than the cell tower, which seems to have vanished off the face of the earth. And here in the wilderness, there aren't many human-made markers, like fences or burnt-out cars or buildings of any kind.

We find a river just as the sky softens into the pastels of a beautiful sunset, but it's not the river we left behind earlier.

"We're not going to find our stuff?" Liv starts to cry. Racer too. The ravens cackle, thoroughly amused. "You lost me and Racer's horses, and now you've lost everything else? What about all my new nail polish? And our Bible?"

Food, more importantly. And the stove. Sleeping bags and pads.

And the birth certificates we only had for the briefest time.

"Eddie's notes!" Racer sobs. "Eddie's green carnations! What about the picture of my family?"

"We can make more notes for Eddie," Soren says. "We can make more carnations too. But I'm really sorry about the picture. We can find nail polish anywhere, Liv. That's easy." He doesn't mention the Bible, or the food, or anything else. The rest of us don't say anything about the treasures we've lost either, as if doing so would make the loss that much more painful.

We have the things on us—clothes, weapons, hats—and everything in our saddlebags, including twelve rather unhelpful ZARC shirts in various sizes in Racer's, but that's it. I still have a tarp, which is pretty much useless after weeks of no rain and which I would trade for pretty much anything in my pack, including my menstrual cup. We can't survive with just our weapons and the gear in the saddlebags.

When we stop for the night, we take the saddles off the horses to use the filthy, stiff blankets under them as very pathetic bedrolls. Gone are our ultralight sleeping bags and mats. Gone are our two stoves and pots and fuel and lightweight shade tarp and our food, except for whatever we had on us, which was a bag of peanuts and exactly four smashed-up granola bars. We tip the crumbs into our hands and eat them by licking our fingers and sticking them into the oats and sugar. We do this slowly.

Here we are in the middle of nowhere with very few supplies and just a few expired energy bars among us.

A zephyr rustles the trees, and there are a lot of birds, singing. The ravens haven't abandoned the drama; they laugh at us some more as they hop from branch to branch.

"Huginn and Muninn." Liv names them after Odin's ravens; the names mean *thought* and *memory.* "That's a good sign." Liv offers up a peanut in the shell. Thought and memory didn't help us find our camp. Thought and memory aren't going to make a meal either. None of us tell her to save the peanuts, though, because we can't bring ourselves to talk about our lack of food, or because it's more important that a kid in the throes of unending crisis should get to offer a majestic raven one lousy peanut.

The bigger raven scoffs at her, but in the morning, the peanut is gone, and the ravens are still there.

We have to find food and supplies to replace the ones we have to stop looking for. This means taking the first dirt road we find and heading west, no matter where it ends up. We ride silently, watching Liv squander her last few peanuts as she tries to befriend Huginn and Muninn. They travel with us, eyeing the peanuts she patiently offers up until her arm gets tired and she has to switch.

"Look at those peaks," Soren says when we're halfway down a sun-baking-hot stretch of dusty, exposed road. "Do those look familiar?"

"They do not," I say.

"Boob Mountain." He points them out. "That's what the Sigurdson boys call it. In between. In the cleavage."

"That's BATO!" Liv cries. "I know Boob Mountain!" The ravens swoop up high and fly in a messy figure eight, as if they know what her excitement means.

"How did the boys get away with saying *boob*? And how have I never heard of this?" I say. "Out of all of us, I should've been aware of a cleavage reference."

"Well, dear Eira." Soren makes sure he has my full attention before he continues, with his best deadpan face. "Maybe you've never been this far south of the boobs."

"Ha!" Cosmo guffaws. "How far away is it from here?"

"More than a day's ride," Soren says. "But we don't know what we'll find."

Maybe we'll find Lola.

The moment I have that thought, I chastise it with another. It's not just as likely that she's dead; it's *more* likely that she's dead.

Yet, the smell of sun-hot, ripe apples is suddenly as real as if I'm just about to bite into one. Soft and rotting, cloyingly sweet. Her lips against mine. I don't mean a memory; I mean I *feel* her lips against mine. I put my fingers to my lips, both holding the sensation there and also willing the ghost of it away.

She's dead. BATO burned on that very first night. The zees were already there. BATO and the Sigurdsons are gone. Dead. Burnt. Turned. We don't talk about it much, but Soren and I have an investment in them not being there. Even if we want them to be there, even if we want them to have survived, we can't stay with them. It would be the same as being at home, in good ways and bad.

If this doesn't work out, we do not have a plan.

"Guess we'll part ways soon." Cosmo eyes the rounded peaks and the valley in between. "We'll hit Highway 12 before your friends' place."

My stomach flips at the thought of Cosmo leaving us. I'm so hungry that this terrible thought punches down, and I'm suddenly nauseous.

"You've lost all your gear," I say. "How will you survive?"

"I've survived this long," they say.

"But with nothing?"

"No." They look away from the mountain and at the four of us: Soren, Liv, Racer, and, lastly, me. "I've never had this little. But everything I need is out there. I just have to find it. Same as you."

"Come to BATO with us," I say. "Even if it's ruined, it's not likely any strangers would know where to look for their supplies. They're a prepper family. Like us."

"And if they're alive? Rural prepper-survivalist types are not my people. Bet they're not yours either, when it comes down to it."

"There won't be anyone," I say.

"We saw what happened that night," Soren adds.

"I'll think about it," Cosmo says. "But it's already taken me three times as long as I thought it would just to get here."

We head as due north as we can, with the ravens leading the way. After a couple of hours, we find a grimy hunting cabin no one else has come across yet, but it doesn't have much to offer.

There is a crate on the greasy, scarred table. In it are two cans of diced tomatoes, a box of mashed potatoes that has been ruined by mice, two cans of chicken, and a small can of clams. Soren and Liv go off to gather some dandelion leaves, and then I put it all together in a gross sort of clam chowder. Thank goodness there is a salt shaker with a small cake of salt at the bottom. I stab the salt loose and dump it all in.

We eat without comment and do not mention any of the food that is back at the creek.

"Rock, paper, scissors for the bed?" Soren suggests.

So, Liv gets the bed, while Racer and Soren take first watch. I lie with my hands folded on my stomach, head resting on what is left of the hunter's down vest, most of which has been emptied by rodents. I try not to think about Lola and her family, but when I close my eyes, I see their new front door and Lola's mom opening it with a smile. *I'll give you a tour!*

Cosmo comes in from the crumbling-but-functional outhouse. I hear their belt and holsters creaking as they step quietly to our little triangle of space between the table, the bed, and the door. They undo their belt and kneel, so close that I get a waft of sage and sweat. They set their sword, belt, and guns to one side and then stretch out on the floor beside me with a folded-up dish towel to cushion their head.

"You're thinking so loud that I could hear you from the john," they say.

My mental tour of the Sigurdsons' house ends with Lola's mom giving me a disapproving look as I see Cosmo jumping down from Leus and walking toward me, their swagger backlit by the sun. But there is the stench of rotting apples again. And Lola. And the new house, engulfed in flames.

"Do you remember that last Ren faire in Pinedale?" Cosmo keeps their voice low, even though I can tell by Liv's breath that she is deeply asleep. "You won four battles in a row." Two of those Saxon opponents were the same two I defeated at Lola's during those last hours of *before. Lola,* again. I shake my head, but the apple fragrance lingers, like some kind of spell. I fold my arms under my head, even if only to smell the reek of me instead of the ghost of the Sigurdsons' orchards.

"I remember." I squeeze my eyes shut tight.

"Sorry," Cosmo says. "Don't want to talk about it?"

"I'd love to talk about it," I say. "Especially if it clears my head."

"You're thinking about Lola." Cosmo reaches over and gently taps my head. "Right? It's always some*one* who gets stuck in there. Especially someone we love. She's in there, taking up all that handsome real estate."

Handsome. No one has ever used that word in reference to me. I like it so much, so instantly, that I have to catch my breath before I speak.

"I don't want to think about her," I say. "She's dead. There's no point."

"I still think of everyone. And I mean *everyone.* Not just my family or my girlfriend, but I think of our mechanic, and the woman with the flower shop by the movie theater. The kids in my classes. The old man and his wife who sat on the same park bench I passed every day after school."

It's strange to think of Cosmo before. Cosmo who walked

their little brother to and from school each day. Cosmo who went to high school and got good grades and had friends and a girlfriend and who belonged to a sharpshooter club and the Junior Rodeo. Cosmo, with a mom who worked at the grocery store and a dad who drove a tow truck, I now know after collecting the shiny bits from our conversations. I want to reach for their hand. But if I do, things will change. Right now, we're so many well-oiled gears doing a pretty good job of keeping ourselves and each other alive, with the exception of what happened at the river. This isn't the time. This isn't the place.

But there might not ever be the right time or place anymore. Not in zee-land.

I want to feel the warmth of Cosmo's skin against mine, our fingers entwined. I don't want to think about Lola. I want to stop thinking about . . . *everything.* I want to be still in this exact moment and stop thinking about how to *be* in the greater midst of this apocalypse. I want to remember that I am *Eira the Viking Giantess.*

Cosmo is not dead. And now the urge to hold their hand grows into an entire scene playing out in my head. To hell with it, I'm going to shift that into real life. I sit up. Lean over. Put my hand on their chest and leave it there for just a second. My fingers trace the shallow bowl of their collarbone and into the crease of their neck and then up to the fresh stubble on either side of their mop of hair. I feel the dull pinprick of every single hair they shaved off as I run my hand up higher.

Cosmo takes my other hand and lifts my wrist to their lips. They kiss it once, which is more erotic than any kiss on the lips I have ever had. But then they kiss me on the lips: a brief, blazingly hot moment that is even better. They don't linger. Instead, they keep holding my hand to their chest as they lie back and fall asleep, which seems nearly instant, while I awkwardly settle without moving my arm and don't sleep at all until it's our turn to keep watch just after midnight.

CHAPTER 18

I wake up the next morning to Liv kicking my shoulder. It takes me a moment to put together where we are and what she's seeing: Cosmo and me, entwined on the floor. Cosmo has their arm draped over my hip, one leg over mine, and their head tucked between my shoulder blades, sleeping soundly.

"Usually, the smaller one is the little spoon," Soren says from where he sits at the table. "Cosmo looks like they're trying to stop a giant from running away." He pauses. "Guess that makes sense. Sort of." He looks at me. "Except for the running-away part."

Liv kicks Cosmo's boot, which has to hurt her bare foot. "Get up!" Cosmo wakes and leaps up in the same second, hands going to where their guns would be.

"What the hell!"

"Yeah." Soren folds his arms and grins. "What the hell indeed, dear people?"

Cosmo blushes as they grab their belt and cinch it across their hips. "Who doesn't miss cuddling, you know?"

"Good news," Racer says. "Today there is no ZARC practice. Today we head for Boob Mountain. To see your friends."

The ravens aren't there as we saddle up, but they show up as soon as we start riding. They yell at Liv now and then. She whistles back, the same trill she used to use with the goats. The day gets so hot that even before the sun is all the way up, we have to snake from one shaded grove to the next until we finally make it to the edge of the heavily forested swath that is like a green moat separating us from the four hundred acres that make up Blessed Are These Orchards.

And here comes a zee, running straight for us. He shoulders a big backpack. His long hair is tangled up in the straps. He wears a leather vest and the tattered scraps of what is left of blue linen pants.

"Mom made those! He's from Midsommar." Soren's cheeks drain of color. He covers his face.

The zee runs at us, his backpack bouncing. He must've been a lot beefier before, because the only reason the very loose pack doesn't fall off is because of the waist belt and chest strap, and the fact that his hair is gnarled up in the buckles and webbing.

"I'll do it." I gallop toward him and veer to his right, drawing him away from the others. I ride longer than I need to, because it's different, killing this one. I might not know him, but he was *here,* with us. He runs at me so fast that the rest of his pants come away, weakened by a year of weather and wear, revealing a pair of linen underwear that I would recognize anywhere by the red stitching. Mom made those too.

"Do it!" Cosmo yells.

"Eira!" Liv screams. "Eira! Kill him!"

He's close enough that I can see that zigzagging thread. I try to lift Gertrude, but I can't. Cosmo draws up beside me, my old sword in their hand. They run it through the zee's eyeball, where it catches on the skull from inside, so he hangs there for a moment before Cosmo lowers the sword and he slides off it. He falls onto his pack, back arched, arms splayed, head tilted back. He looks almost Christlike.

The first of the apple trees appear over a shallow hill in cheerful, squat rows of big green pom-poms. We ride in between a section of Pink Ladies and another of Fujis, on the overgrown track the farmhands used to drive the big machines down. The big, orange plastic drinking-water containers are still perched on the break tables at the ends of each row, their spigots like little white thumbs. The shade umbrellas have been ripped to shreds in the weather and are now just white metal skeletal remains.

"I have a name for the sword," Cosmo says out of nowhere. "Want to hear it?"

"Yeah," I say. "Any distraction from what we're riding into is welcome."

"Alice."

“I like it.”

Liv pulls up on the other side of me. “Watch this.” She whistles. The bigger raven swoops down and lands on a branch ahead of us. By the time we catch up, the smaller one is perched there too.

“That’s really cool.”

“Yeah.” Her brow is furrowed. She stares at the building that’s just come into view.

“Is that the house?” Cosmo points.

“That’s their old house. Now it’s the workers’ quarters,” I say. “Or, it was. The new house is about a quarter mile past that.” Liv still stares. “You okay, Liv?”

She nods, but I don’t know how an eleven-year-old *can* be, amid all of this. Making friends with ravens, mourning her dead friends, all in the same day. There were ten Sigurdson kids. Liv was closest with the nine- and eleven-year-old girls, Astrid and Darby.

Whatever hope I reluctantly harbored disappears when the ransacked workers’ quarters come into sharper view, along with a pile of long-beyond-rotting bodies. Wider than high, it’s just a jumble of sun-leathered skin and gnawed-on bones and fabric ruined with viscera and weather. There’s no way to tell how many bodies there are, or who they are, or how old they are. I can’t tell if they’re the workers, whoever might’ve trashed the place, or the family. I hold Odger still as I scan the jumble of decay. I know exactly what I’m looking for: that reed-and-flower crown, even though that’s impossible.

Lola’s dad, Bersi, and his brother and their ten boys between them built their sprawling two-story log home. It was done and furnished and decorated just before we visited them that New Year's. The girls were not allowed to help, other than to make lunches.

Lola dared to shave not even two inches of an undercut of her butt-long wheat-colored hair, and she got paddled for it. She painted her nails with acrylic craft paint and got spanked. That was when she was thirteen, put over her father's knee, bare-assed and screaming for him to stop.

I don't know what I expected when their home—or what used to be their home—comes into view. We behold the terrible vista in a line of five horses across, like a cover for a Wild West zombie-apocalypse movie. It's no movie set, though. Judging by the rubble, the fire we drove away from must've flattened their home that first night. Even so, the stench of old burnt debris is a tang in the air, an acrid perfume of plastics and chemicals and cloth that has been clinging to the trees and the ground and the ruined house.

"There's nothing left," Soren says.

"Not of the house," I say. "But we have to look for the family. We need to check on the bunker."

Soren gives me a look. I know what it means. There is no good news here, even if the bunker is intact and we can move in. There is only bad news, all around.

"I'm really sorry," Cosmo says.

"Me too," Racer says. "I'm sorry about your friends."

Liv bends over and rests her cheek on Buttercup's neck. She stays like that, crying, and lets the horse follow us as we head for a closer look. But then Racer starts crying too, and then Soren, so the three of them hang back in the shade while Cosmo and I go ahead to check it out. It's bizarre, riding through the orchard, past all the cheerful young apples crowding the trees. It only takes a quick, still-far-away assessment to tell that there is nothing and no one left at the house.

"I'm really sorry for your loss," Cosmo says.

"I'm not sure what I'm supposed to feel sorry about," I say. "If they'd survived, we couldn't stay here. If they're all dead, we have a new home."

"You want to stay here?" Cosmo gestures at the mess around us. "This is where you want to set up house?"

"If the bunker is good."

"You're going to live in a bunker?"

"Maybe," I say. "If no one has touched the bunker, it'd be a good place to stay for a while."

"This isn't your isolated mountain homestead that nobody knows about," Cosmo says. "This is a working farm! You can probably see the processing plant from the highway. People know about it. There are probably still signs for it on the road in."

"Just doing our best. For our family. Like you." I feel the prickle of agitation cool my skin as I say the words, and the instant heat of regret as Cosmo scoffs and shakes their head. "Like you going to get Bailey, I mean."

"Yeah. Got it. I'm just being honest." Cosmo splays out a hand and starts making points, one for each finger. "One, lots of people in the family, so any number of them *could* still be alive and lay claim to this place. Two, this place is exposed. Hills on all sides.

Perfect vantage points for bad guys. Three, no matter what state the bunker is in, those supplies won't last forever. Four, where are you going to get more food? This brings me to the last point: Where is the water source?"

It's hard to imagine that I woke up with Cosmo's leg over mine and their face nuzzled against my back, because looking at them right now, I just see hard angles and sharp tacks.

"There's a solar water pump," I say. "A few, for irrigation. And we can hunt. And trap. Bersi planned for this."

"He wasn't just going to leave it up to his pretend Big Daddy up in heaven?" Cosmo laughs. "That doesn't show a lot of faith."

"Nice." I steer Odger ahead and hope that Cosmo doesn't follow and see my red face.

"Wait, wait." Cosmo catches up. "I'm sorry. That was a shitty thing to say. You believe in God. I can respect that. But I don't, and I hope you respect that too."

"You *just* disrespected it."

"And I'm sorry."

"You don't believe in anything? No God?"

"No. I believe we die, and there is nothing after."

The three huge piles of farm compost lie about half a mile to the east of the house. The piles used to be giant, steamy, loamy mounds, easily twice as tall as the pump house that stands nearby. The bunker is a shipping container buried under the first pile, accessed through the pump house. Once formidable, the compost piles are just mounds of dirt now, after having nothing added to them and a year of the elements and neglect.

The pump house looks exactly the same, though. The gravel around it has even kept any encroaching weeds and blackberry vines at bay. I know it isn't locked. The Sigurdsons kept it full of crap. That way no one would bother breaking in, and there wouldn't have to be a key to the bunker to keep track of. It had to be easily accessible, because Tonna Sigurdson's worst nightmare was her children not being able to get in if they needed to. Even the solar panels are hidden. Unless you're looking down from above; the false edge to the pump house roof hides the panels from view.

I remember Dad and Bersi discussing the best way to hide an entrance.

"Keep it simple," Dad argued. "In the floor."

"Go up to go down," Bersi insisted. "Everyone looks at the floor."

Above a pair of dirty coveralls hanging on a hook is a section of the drop-ceiling panel with fingerprints in the grime. Not such a great hide after all. The sunlight shifts to shadow behind me.

"Someone's been in there," Cosmo says.

That odd twist of equal parts dread and excitement turns my stomach. I bend over, hands on my knees, and retch. Cosmo pats my back, and when nothing comes of it, I straighten and shift the panel to reveal the rectangular opening into the attic.

"Boost me?" I say, and to their credit, Cosmo bends over so I can step on their back, all 270 pounds of me. Or, a bit less, after weeks of missing my mother's cooking three times a day. Once up, I crawl along to the ladder at the back. It's a tight fit, but Bersi was a big man, just like his oldest sons, so I can shimmy down to the small, airtight door with a big, heavy handle that I have to shove up to get to release. There is a *ffft* of air when it does.

It looks just like it did when Lola showed it to me a few years ago. We weren't allowed to be in there, but she showed me anyway.

"Only thing is," she said as we each claimed one of the top bunks, "it's just for four people. That's why we're getting a few more bunkers."

Upon closer inspection, we can see that it has been used. The stores are about a quarter gone, and the bedding is wrinkled.

"They were just bare mattresses before." The sheets and pillows were under the bed, in a big clear plastic bag that zipped open. The bag is still there, except now it has clothing in it. Jeans and a pair of coveralls almost big enough for me. There is some dirt on the floor and a little black comb sitting on the bathroom sink. Considering the Sigurdsons number more than a dozen, if you factor in Calder's wife and kids, it could've been anyone, but not many, or even more than one or two of them. Or maybe it wasn't the Sigurdsons at all. Maybe someone else knew how to get in here.

Cosmo and I, and then the others too, decide that it's been long enough since anyone has been there and we'll chance staying the night in exchange for clean, comfortable bunks.

"I'll leave in the morning," Cosmo tells me before Soren and

I head outside for first watch. He and I have to decide what to do next. That person who fits those big coveralls might be back.

Cosmo takes my hand. "I'm sorry about earlier. I think I'm getting a little messed up at the thought of leaving you guys."

Soren and I hardly speak while we sit watch, even though we need to come up with a plan. We just gaze up at the night sky for shooting stars, as if wishing on them would help us figure out what to do next.

In the morning, after we have cleared out of the bunker—we made that decision at least—Racer pulls on his ZARC coach shirt and puts his ornamental whistle around his neck.

"Yesterday you had a break," he says. "Practice time. Everybody put your shirts on. Let's go! Before it gets too hot."

"No way," Liv protests at first, which surprises me so much that I want to go along with Racer just to get her a little bit back to herself. "I'm not running at BATO. Not when my friends are dead." Somewhere in a nearby apple tree, Huginn and Muninn caw in solidarity.

"Maybe a short run?" I hold up my thumb and index finger, just a whisper apart. "Up and down one or two of the rows?"

"Full practice," Racer insists. He fishes in our saddlebags and finds our musty shirts.

Racer looks at us one at a time. When none of us say anything, he grabs the shirts back and throws them into the dirt. "You're stupid!" He gets onto Niki and takes off, slowly, but still.

"Racer is right. You are stupid." Liv collects the shirts and shoves them into her saddlebag before taking off after him, as if she wasn't the one who just refused to run.

"He's right," I say. "We are stupid."

Liv brings Racer back, and we all put on the foul shirts and set off to run laps of three rows of Ambrosias. I wish I had a watch, because this feels like the longest practice ever, even though Racer insists that it is half an hour exactly. When we're back at the pump house, Cosmo excuses themselves with a roll of toilet paper. When they're not back after a few minutes, I go to check on them.

"Zee!" they holler as they run toward me. "Kill it!"

Close on their heels is what is left of one of the Sigurdson boys. Gunnar. A year younger than Lola.

I can't kill him because I don't have a weapon.

"Stupid," I growl as I turn and run too. "Stupid!" Complacency kills, Dad says. Cosmo and I fall into step, even though my legs are so much longer than theirs. They're holding their pants up with one hand; their belt with their guns is slung over one shoulder. "Why didn't you shoot him?" We turn the corner and see the others standing ready with their weapons.

"I was taking a shit!" Cosmo shouts as they collapse to the ground. Soren whacks Gunnar in the temple. He drops immediately. Before Liv can figure out who he is, I drag his body away.

I expect praise for how fast we ran, but when I get back to the group, I see Liv vomiting in the dirt.

"Are you too hot?" I ask.

I take her into the coolness of the bunker and wipe her face. "Do you need water?" She takes a sip, then vomits some more, her body convulsing like a zee about to rise up for the first time. Maybe she did see that it was Gunnar. But that idea fades when Soren comes down with Racer. He's crying and clutching Soren's hand.

"Him too." Soren sits Racer on the bed opposite Liv. He's brought a five-gallon bucket with him, cracked and brittle from being out in the sun.

"We'll have to stay put until this passes," Soren says. "We're not going anywhere."

"Where's Cosmo?"

When Soren isn't back minutes later, I go up to check on him, only to find him crouched beside Cosmo's body, which is curled up in the shade of an apple tree at the edge of the orchard.

"Cosmo! No! NO!"

"I'm not dead." Cosmo lifts a hand and then rolls onto their knees and barfs into the tall grass. "I'm just sick too. Maybe the rabbit?"

I think back to the rabbit we roasted over the fire last night. It seemed fine to me. "Soren and I are fine. Something in the water, maybe?"

"We filter everything," Soren says.

"Not when we found that waterfall earlier," I say.

"Look," Cosmo groans. "Just help me inside?"

We put one of the mattresses from the upper bunks onto the floor so no one has to climb, find another two decent buckets from up top, and get everyone as comfortable as possible, considering what is exploding from both ends of all three of them.

I head to the first aid kits, which I saw when we first got here, on their assigned shelf—two big red duffel bags with white crosses on them. The Imodium and antibiotics aren't there, and neither are the trauma packs, IV kits, or bags of saline. There's everything you could need for a minor wound and a full obstetric kit for delivering babies, but no medication. No anti-diarrhea pills, no analgesics, no narcotics, not even a stupid anti-inflammatory.

I can't stop to think of who went so carefully over this place, because the barfing sounds and the accompanying stench have taken over the entire space, no matter how efficient the ventilation is. Soren and I go outside, into the fresh air, to make a plan.

"I can find the bugout place by myself." Soren traces his finger over the back-roads map book that was stored on the communications shelf, along with the useless radios and sat phone. "Here we are." He notes an X at the edge of a patch of green. "It's somewhere northwest of here. Only a day's ride. I remember it took about five hours, but we weren't moving very fast and there were a lot of us, and supplies. How about I go, and you stay here?"

"What about an ATV?" As I say it, I realize that the four ATVs that were always parked in a shed were not, because that's where I got the other barf buckets.

"Gone." Soren pencils a line along a back road and up along a tiny blue thread of water. "ATVs can't go up the creek bed. Bersi got most of the supplies helicoptered in. It's that far in. Bet you the first aid kits there won't be touched. I'll go, get what me and Rune can carry, and be back tomorrow. Tomorrow night at the latest."

"You're not going alone." I shake my head. "No way."

"You're okay leaving three sacks of vomiting misery alone?"

"They're safe," I say. "It's more dangerous out there."

"Okay. Let's go, then." He rips out the page, folds it, and tucks it into his pocket. "Fresh air would be amazing."

There are four bugout packs on the bottom shelf in the little storeroom. The laminated inventory card lists fifty items, all of them top quality and brand name and perfectly suited to a zombie apocalypse. Leave it to Bersi to outdo Dad even in the backup bug-out bag category. I wish I could tell him about it.

CHAPTER 19

We should be back tomorrow. The others are going to stay inside, lock the entrance, and try not to worry about us for at least that long. We told them not to worry until three days has passed, though, because we don't want them coming after us if we're only delayed.

"I would kiss you goodbye," Cosmo says out of earshot of Liv. "Only . . ."

"We can save it for when I get back," I say. "When everyone feels better." Especially if we're flattened by whatever is turning their insides to explosive sludge.

At every junction, Soren takes a long pause, scanning the horizon, the trees, the roll of the hills, and the ground right at our feet, like he's tracking a deer and not a creek bed.

"Once we get past Naches," he says when the town is in sight, "we'll see a feed place with two big silos. That's what we're looking for next." He lifts the binoculars we took from the bunker and looks in that direction. "Zombie alert. One o'clock."

There it is, careening toward us so fast that it's like watching a fast-forwarded movie. This one looks different; its stature is all wrong for the distance.

And that is because it's a little kid. As if Gunnar wasn't bad enough.

"What's that pink thing?" Soren squints.

"Hell, no," I say.

"Fuck, no." Soren actually backs his horse away, as if that will end the situation.

"That's not a kid," I say. "That's just a zee, right? A smaller zee. Just a zombie. Just a transmitter of a very nasty parasite. A machine. A monster. Nothing left of what she used to be. Nobody's kid."

It doesn't matter how many words come out of my face in an attempt to convince us that she is anything other than a child, a daughter, a sister, a friend. She runs at us with the same speed of the grown ones. Chubby and gray, she wears a filthy blue-and-white-striped swimsuit and just one pink arm floaty. Her face is contorted in a snarl waiting to turn into a bite.

Soren doesn't reach for his gun. I don't reach for Gertrude. Neither of us reaches for our daggers. We just sit atop the horses and stare until the horses start to protest.

"Should I shoot?" Soren says.

When she is close enough that I can see that her dirty-blond hair is matted with big burs, but I still cannot move, Soren grabs his hatchet and coaxes Rune ahead until he can reach for her. He loses his grip on the hatchet. He leans farther out, trying to catch the handle as it falls, but he falls instead.

"Get up!" I whistle to get the girl's attention onto me, and me alone. "Run that way. I'll draw her off and come back." Rune swings her head back and forth, looking at Odger, then Soren, before deciding to stick with Odger.

The girl runs after Odger and me, which is exactly what I wanted. I crest a shallow hill, planning to gallop ahead and get some distance before turning back to get Soren. I am not killing that zee. No way.

I find Soren up a tree. Once I tell him that I couldn't kill the little girl, we decide to canter out of there as fast as we can so we have no chance of running into her again.

We steer clear of Naches, which is about four times the size of Marion Gap. Soren finds the creek bed as if he were looking at a map. It's dry as a bone, and the rocks and pebbles clatter under the horses' hooves. We make good time and get there in the late afternoon, not only because of Soren's ace navigation but also because we don't see any zees after the little girl with the pink floaty.

"There." Soren points up the steep bank to the BATO cow brand burned into a cedar tree that looms above us, still in the stale air. We cut into the forest at a forty-five-degree angle, heading almost exactly northwest. "That's the only sign," Soren says. "Back there at the bank. It's a straight shot from here. About a half hour ride, if I remember correctly."

About half an hour later, we see the massive slab of granite that reaches up to the sky and then the metal door fitted into a wall of concrete and granite. When I see the dead bolt and combination lock, the heat of the day sloughs off and the cool of the shaded forest leaves me so cold that I shiver. Either the stomach bug is hitting me in this exact moment, or—

"We don't have a key." The sadness in my voice makes it thick. "Oh, Soren. We need a *key.*"

"The door was wood when I was here," Soren says.

"Not anymore." I get down and put both hands on the door. "Because that would be too easy. Who needs just one little break in a freaking zombie apocalypse. Hell, not us, right? Nah. Not us. We're fine, right? Absolutely excellent."

There is no way in hell we can get into the Sigurdsons' bunker. There's a camouflage trail cam secured to a tree to my right and another one just behind me, both doing absolutely nothing at all now.

"What are the chances we'll find a bolt cutter nearby, Soren?" I'm not joking. It could be that there is one hidden, in the case of not bringing the keys and combo. If Bersi and Tonna didn't want their family to not be able to get into the bunker at home, surely the same logic applies here.

"If there is, we'll never find it."

But we look anyway. We spend an hour searching the forest around the door, spreading giant ferns only to set off clouds of spores and not finding anything. We look all along the granite rock, looking for nooks and crannies, anything that might look like a geocache.

Then we find it. A fake rock, wedged in a small pile of rocks that look just like it. It splits in two, and there it is: a note in a waterproof capsule.

1. Our family number
2. The "key" to Mama's heart

There are more clues, to what we guess is the code. But there's no point in trying to figure them out. Without a word, we replace the capsule and the rock, get on the horses, and ride back the way we came. We ride until it gets dark, and then we bunk in a small stable with open windows and just a gate. The horses happily bed down in the bigger stall, and we unhappily bed down in the smaller one. Zees can't figure out a gate, or what it takes to climb in a window, but we still take turns staying awake to keep watch.

We move in slow motion the next morning, and don't say much to each other. We sit in silence for long stretches of time, long enough that the sun is all the way up and the heat of the day is in full swing, and we still haven't put our sleeping mats away or had anything to eat. Neither of us is in a hurry to tell the others that we couldn't get in.

"Who even has a family number?" Soren says when we finally get going around midday. "Is that even a thing?"

Four zombies later—they looked like they could've been a family: a grandpa, a woman, and two teenagers, even though I know it's impossible that they belonged to each other before—Naches comes into sight. Shortly after that, we see three horses heading our way, but only two people. It's Racer and Cosmo, each with one of the new packs on their back. Liv's horse is loaded like a pack horse, with three pillowcases from the bunker stuffed like sacks from the gold rush.

"Where is she?" I holler as I gallop their way.

"She's safe—" Cosmo puts up their hands, like I'm the one who might shoot.

"*Where* is she?"

The four of us sit there, atop our horses in the middle of the road, exposed in all directions and in the blazing sun while Cosmo and Racer tell us what happened.

"Racer and I woke up, and she was gone," Cosmo says. "She left a note to say she was going outside, that she felt better. She said she'd see if she could find some eggs. We were still feeling really rough—still are—so we went back to sleep. She still wasn't back when we woke up again, so we got the horses and went looking for her. We found this stuck at the top of the driveway. There are fresh vehicle tracks all the way out." Cosmo holds out a flyer. Even before I grab it, I recognize the logo. That circle of hands around a clover of hearts.

UNICEF Children's Village ambassador Parvin Hakimi CVA #079 was here August 3, 2030. We've taken LIV INGRID HELVIG, DOB: 04/13/19, into our care and will act as her guardians until you can be reunited at CHILDREN'S VILLAGE PNW 4 ASTORIA. The kinship agreement is on the reverse, as is the Covenant of Care outlining the rights of children in our care and the responsibilities of the Children's Village.

Stay safe, and may you and your loved ones be together again soon.

In trust,
Sen. Dr. Rhea Haddad

PS. Liv has registered Eira Helvig and Soren Helvig as her next of kin and reunion adults.

"Why would she go?" I can barely find enough breath for the words. I have to squeeze out each one. "Why didn't she just climb a tree and refuse to go? Or hide? Why didn't she go back to the bunker? I don't understand."

"They said something," Soren says. "They had to have said something that made sense to her."

"That's what they do," Cosmo says. "They make it make sense. They make it so there's only one good choice."

For the first time since running from those zombies with the chicken in hand, I think I might actually die. Right here, right *now.* Everything else, every other time my life was at risk, it was just that. At *risk.* But I am going to fall off Odger and lie in the dirt and convulse a few times and then just expire. "Why did she *go*? I can't—" I gasp. "I can't breathe. I'm dying. I can't—I'm not an adult. What if they won't let us get her? What if they make us wait? What if something happens and we can't—"

"You can!" Cosmo urges Leus close enough that they can haul

off and slap me across the face. "Guardians can be sixteen and over. I'm going to get Bailey, and you and Soren are going to get Liv."

"Ow!" I put a hand to my burning cheek. "But, but, but . . . ," I splutter. "I don't understand. This is *Liv.* She wouldn't go! They had to have forced her! What if she's scared? What if they hurt her?"

"Get a fucking grip!" Cosmo points to me, then Soren. "They make it so there's only one choice because they *can.* We're out here barely surviving, but like it or not, the Village can keep her safe. Until you get there. They're keeping Bailey safe until I get there."

"You're only saying that because you have to believe it," Soren says, backing away from Cosmo, who still has their hand raised.

Are there any half-full cups in a zombie apocalypse? Because here comes our first obstacle: five zombies who clock us as we make our way alongside the highway around sunset, when it's finally starting to cool. They lock on us at the exact same moment, all straightening and swinging their heads in our direction like a herd of deer startled by a threat. The fastest of them forms the point of a tidy V. From a distance, he looks like any young man sprinting. But as he gains on us and I look back, I see his gray skin and where it's sloughing off his shoulders.

"Why are they together like that?" Soren yells as we head for a break in a fence that will let us out of this field. "Cosmo! Shoot them!"

"There might be more nearby!" Cosmo shouts. But even as they say it, we all know there is no other choice. Cosmo twists backward while Leus canters toward the fence. Their hands alight on their holsters for just a second, and then *pop-pop!* Two of the five drop, including the fastest one. Another *pop-pop!* and one more drops.

We make it through the fence. Racer lags behind for a moment, but when he gets too far behind for Niki's liking, the horse tucks his head down just a bit and drives forward, closing the distance.

This works until the next field crumbles away to a slope with dirt and boulders and a tangle of blackberry vines. The horses slow.

"Hup." I dig my ankles into Odger's sides, but he hates blackberry vines, and the other horses are used to taking his lead, so if he's mincing his way, so are the others. The two zees are closing in.

I cut left, out of the vines and up a steep slope that will get us onto the highway.

"What are you *doing*?" Soren shouts.

"Taking our chances!" I pray there will be space to ride through the gridlock up there. Please, God. Please, please, *please.*

It's a tangle, but I see a path to the next exit. When I'm sure everyone is behind me, I ride as fast as Odger will go. I aim for the exit and follow it into Naches, according to the signage. I barely have time to take in that every single building leading into the downtown is a pile of deliberately arranged rubble. I see a wrecking ball, parked in the distance to the north, and count three diggers. A line of shipping containers stacked two high forms a wall. Loose tangles of barbed wire block our way.

"Watch out!" Soren hollers beside me. "Stop! Stop!"

"This way!" Cosmo yells as they veer sharply to the left, down a wide path defined by more broken concrete and busted-up wood and old drywall, all carefully piled to form a channel. We have no choice but to follow it as it narrows.

The first shot zings quietly past my left ear, so close that I feel it slice the air. *Zip.* One zee hits the ground, letting out a surprisingly loud *oof,* like it was just some football player who went down hard and got the wind knocked out of him. Then another shot, and the second zee crumples. The shooter has a silencer. *Zip. Zip. Zip.* The shooter drives more bullets into the bodies.

When the shooting stops, quiet reverberates, except for the horses' loud, hot breath. They are exhausted, and so are we. Soren and Racer slump over their saddle horns. Cosmo sits very still, covered in a slick of sweat that makes them glisten in the sun.

"Where the hell are we?" Cosmo looks all around.

"Eira, look." Soren points to the end of the channel, to a barricade of more rubble, where a man stands tall atop it, gun pointed at us.

Two men and a woman join him before the sniper lowers his gun, which he only does because the other people's guns are bigger, and they're bigger too. The shooter has dark brown skin and long dreads bundled into a wide ponytail. The two other men are stocky white boys with dull brown crew cuts. The woman has nothing on my height, but she is built like a pit bull—broad chest; big, blocky head; and scrawny haunches—and taller than the sniper by half a foot, so either he's tiny, or she is tall. All of them look like they were either in the military or are in some kind of paramilitary force or militia now. Their uniforms match, but they're not government issue. Racer is impressed, though.

"Soldiers," he says. "They can help us."

"They're not real soldiers," I whisper. "Those uniforms come from a surplus store. And this place isn't anything official. Just the opposite, okay? We do not trust these people, got it?"

"Okay." Racer's disappointment is obvious. "But Eddie always says to look for the helpers. Mister Rogers said it first. But Eddie says it too."

"These are not helpers," Soren says. "Trust me."

"Greetings!" the woman shouts. "We don't take your weapons here. But you will unload any guns and put them away. Now, please." We unload our guns, and then we all put our hands up, even though they didn't order us to. "Come closer."

We ride two by two, as close together as the horses agree to. When the woman holds a hand up, gesturing for us to stop, Soren and I gasp at the same time, our eyes locked on the biggest of the men.

"Holy shit," Soren says when he catches his breath. The largest of the buff white dudes is Calder Sigurdson, in the flesh.

"No way," I say. "That's Cal!" I say his name louder. "Cal! Hey!"

Eldest of the children, Cal is six years older than Lola, with two little kids and a wife. The last time I saw him was that night, with his toddler perched on his shoulders and his baby tucked in a wrap on his wife's chest, until she yanked the baby out and tossed her to that man, who ran off into the dark.

"Cal!" Soren waves. "It's me! And Eira! The Helvig twins!"

Cal's facial expression is now as it has been his entire life—like he's just watched you do something very stupid and is not amused. I want to ask him everything: What happened after we left? Where is everyone? Where is *Lola*? And why is BATO abandoned?

Oh, shit.

We *stole* all the supplies we took from the bunker. When there is at least one Sigurdson still alive to use them.

Another man appears, barely as tall as Racer. He's *old* old. Eighty at least, if not even older. With trimmed gray hair and a beard to match, he's wearing a white short-sleeved dress shirt and two parts of a dapper three-piece suit—pants and vest. A fat ring on his right hand glints in the sun, even at this distance.

"Whether you know Calder or not, you are not welcome here," the old man says. "Not yet. Let me explain. You've found yourselves among the Tars. This is short for *tardigrades.* Do you know what tardigrades are? No shame if you don't."

"We fucking know what water bears are," Cosmo growls in a whisper. I don't, actually. I think I did at some point, when Liv was in her deep-ocean phase.

"Tardigrades would survive a nuclear winter. They survive in outer space. At the bottom of the ocean. *Anywhere,* under any conditions, no matter how punishing. As do we. As will you, if you join us. Otherwise, you'll perish."

"Guess they didn't want to be cockroaches," Cosmo mutters.

"Cocks for short," Soren says.

"We're getting the kids." I do a quick and quiet poll. "Hands up for yes."

We all raise a hand.

"We're not joiners," I say louder, on behalf of all of us. "We're just passing—"

"—through, yes." He drones on. "You have two options. One,

we admit you, you submit to our screening process and subsequent assignments—"

"Assignments?" Soren says under his breath. "Hell, no." He raises his voice. "Cal! Calder! Where is everybody?"

He keeps his stony gaze looking everywhere but at us.

"Or *two,*" the old man shouts. His expression does not give away anything. It matches the others', as if they all rehearsed in a mirror together. Don't let it crack, no matter what. "Leave now. Never return. Take your chances out there. Your chances don't work out in your favor? You decide you want to come back to the civilized community we have here? Join the Tars? Enjoy our shelter? Food? Water? Community? Too bad. No second chances. Submit to me and to our process now, or go. And do not dare to come back."

"Cal! Is Lola okay?" I yell. "What about the rest of your family?" Cal just stands there, not even looking in my direction.

"Calder? Calder Sigurdson!" When Cosmo hollers his name, he glances at them. "Okay, so that's you. I just wanted to be sure I had the right asshole who ignores his friends asking about his family after rage-fueled human hosts of a weaponized parasite have destroyed life on earth as we know it."

The glance turns into a glare.

"You've always been a fucking dick!" Soren yells, surprising me so much that I start to laugh, and then can't stop. I try. I hold my breath, pinch my arm, but I keep laughing.

"A dick!" I howl. "You have, though, right? You've always been a dick!"

"A total dick!" Soren echoes.

Cal finally cracks. "Better than what you do with dicks!" he yells. "Faggot!"

The old man nods slowly. "The decision has been made for you."

"We didn't want to join your pretend army anyway," Cosmo says. "Right, everybody?" The rest of us nod our agreement, although I can tell that Racer is still pining a little over the uniforms.

Without another word, we turn and let Racer and Niki pick a careful path over the zombies' bodies, hoping no one is coming the other way, human or not.

Back at the highway, we pause in a rectangle of shade behind a Children's Village billboard with a spray-painted water bear and *Join the Tars!,* which I didn't notice on the way in as we galloped by the flattened Exxon station.

"Keep moving," a voice says from above us. Two soldiers sit on the platform, between the floodlights. They look no older than us.

"You saw us come in!" Cosmo laughs. "You could've shot those zees right here!"

"Move on," the other one says. "Now."

"Eira." I hear someone say my name, and then again, closer. "Eira, hey."

I turn.

It's Lola. She stands there like a video game skin of the Lola I kissed that night. This one has hair in a short ponytail and wears a uniform like those of the two dummies on the billboard platform. She has a gun slung across her back and shiny black boots. She's wearing makeup. Not a lot, but enough that I know one thing for sure.

"Your parents are dead, right?" I pull her into a hug. Her smallness still feels big in my arms, like it did that day in the orchard. "Even an apocalypse wouldn't make your mom and dad let you wear makeup and pants."

"Yours are dead too," she says through tears. "Otherwise, you'd still be at home."

Well. Not exactly. There's so much to say but only so much oxygen available for this interaction. I feel it thinning as we hold each other, crying.

One of the boys climbs down and strides over. He takes Lola's arm and pulls her away from me. He drapes his arm across her shoulder.

"You know this WrestleManiac?" He looks me up and down.

"She's a friend." Lola's cheeks flush as she says it. "Eira, this is Preston—"

"Of course that's his name," Cosmo says.

"Ah." I nod. "Nice. . . ." But it's not nice to meet him. Or to see Lola like this. I'm not going to judge her for how she's surviving out here, or for who she fell in love with, or for wanting more than just stumbling from one near-death experience to another. But it's not nice to meet him and see the way he owns her in one gesture; and worse, she lets him. I hug her again, holding her longer than I should. When I pull away, I take the heat of her reddening cheeks with me on mine.

"Better get on your way." Preston glares at me.

"You take care, Lola." I reach to tuck her hair behind her ear, but then I think how gross it was to watch *Preston* own her in a similar way, so I tip my hat to her instead. She does the same.

"I'll make you another apple pie," she says. "Someday."

"Probably not." I don't even want the pie if she makes it here, in a place that welcomes everybody, but not if you're queer. "This kind of place isn't meant for people like us."

When she doesn't try to convince me otherwise, Preston nails down the point.

"We live by the word of God here," he says. "So, yeah."

"And on that note . . ." Cosmo tips their hat too and gives Leus a nudge to get moving. "We're out of here."

Racer follows them, but Soren and I linger, both trying to think of something to say. No words make their way through the anger and disappointment of coming across this shithole of supposed Godliness mixed with the relief and happiness of finding two people we know alive. *Knew,* I realize as we finally leave. We don't know them anymore.

CHAPTER 20

Cosmo doesn't know how to use a compass properly, not beyond heading in a specific direction. They can't plot a course on a topographical map, so their plan since leaving Wyoming has been to stick to the roads they highlighted on a AAA map they brought from home, which was lost along with everything else when we lost our camp. Soren and I know this route, though: go over the mountains on Highway 12, then follow I-5 south, and then look for the signs for Astoria. We can't remember what that road is called, but it will be obvious so long as even a couple of signs are still standing. And then there are the billboards, which will lead the way too.

"Seems too easy," I say.

"They want it that way," Cosmo says.

We see another one about an hour outside Naches. This Children's Village billboard has been spray-painted with the Tar symbol too. This one is a stencil, much tidier, and depicts what looks like a lumpy piece of colon, a butthole for a face, and seven legs.

As we get farther away from the valley and start to climb, the highway is less of an obstacle course of abandoned vehicles and weather-ruined corpses and the confetti of personal belongings that always look like they've been tossed up like party decorations by some pixie who ran through after. There is no stretch of road without at least one piece of decaying evidence of the time when people thought they could flee by car, having not considered every apocalypse story ever produced, in which the roads clog up within hours of the desperate exodus, just like we saw that very first night. But there are fewer abandoned cars and trucks up here, at least. Most people didn't even get this far.

It's an eerily quiet ride to Bear Canyon trailhead, where we decide to spend the night. We could go farther, but Cosmo and Racer are still wrung out from being sick. Once we've set up in a small clearing by a little creek, Cosmo and Racer show us what they took from the bunker and stuffed in those pillowcases, which, thankfully, neither Lola nor Calder recognized or thought to ask about.

"It's mostly stuff from the bugout bags." Cosmo hands out new inflatable sleeping pads, still tightly coiled in plastic. "Tell me, why do you need bugout bags in a bunker?"

"In case you have to leave said bunker," Soren says.

"The sleeping bags are all the same color," Racer says. "I don't like that."

"We'll write our names on them," I say. "Or you can even draw on yours if you want."

The moon is almost a new one, so the night is very dark when Cosmo and I take our turn to keep watch. We sit on our new sleeping mats and lean against a log, near a circle of rocks someone arranged for a fire before. There is no discussion of starting one, though. It's still uncomfortably hot, and we don't know who else is up here. Not of the zombie variety—they aren't attracted by light or flames or even smoke—but of the human variety. Tars, specifically. I watch the sky, looking for shooting stars. When I glance over at Cosmo to see what they're doing, they're stargazing too. They glance at me and take my hand. My hand is so much bigger, I feel like I should be holding *their* hand instead. But it's nice that someone wants to hold mine. That Cosmo wants to hold mine.

"You know a lot about the night sky." They direct the statement to the stars.

"I do." I look up again too.

We fall silent for several long minutes, and then Cosmo lets out one little laugh. "Guess I can't impress you that way, huh?"

"Sure you could," I say.

They fold down all my fingers except for the pointer one. They lift it in theirs and point it to three bright stars in the sky, one at a time. "Vega, Altair, Deneb."

Then they let go of my hand to fish for something in their pocket. It's their waterproof marker—fine tip on one end, fat on the other—the one they use to write a note to Bailey at every notice board. We always leave one of the new carnations we made out of pipe cleaners for Eddie among the *MISSING* posters, and I always check the photo of the Girl Scouts to see if there are any pictures of them. There aren't, and I don't know why I keep comparing their faces with the grinning class photos of any girls around their age. Anyone who would be looking for them is long dead, no doubt. And even if they aren't, there's no way I can help them. Cosmo kisses my lips, then neck, and then reaches for the hem of my shirt, thankfully pulling me back into my body.

"Can I?" they say. My pulse feels like it's going to bust the vein right out of my neck and start spraying like an out-of-control fire hose. How can this gesture, this whatever-they're-doing, make me feel like this? I nod. Cosmo puts the pen between their teeth and lifts my shirt over my head. "Lie back."

"The lyre of Orpheus." They make six dots, then trace the shape of the harp the Lyra constellation makes, with a light touch that sends a rippling shudder out in every direction. "Made music so enchanting that even rocks fell under the spell."

I wake with a gasp out of a nightmare where Cosmo and Racer had just left Liv behind, locked her in the bunker from the outside. My sleeping bag is twisted between my legs and my head is fully on the dirt and not on the thin sleeping mat or the stuff-sack-and-spare-clothes pillow I started out with when Soren and Racer took over watch. I am so stiff that I cannot move for a moment. I stare at Cosmo, also on their side, asleep beside me, neatly arranged on their mat and bag, their hands tucked under their cheek. Between the two of us is a line of fat black ants trooping eastward, so neatly in order that they don't freak me out.

Liv isn't in the bunker. We're on our way to get her back, and Cosmo's brother too.

I get up as quietly as I can and go join the boys, who are half-asleep at their post. I kick Soren's boot.

"Up. Up!" I reach for his hand. "I need you."

I lead him away from the others. "Tell me this is okay?"

"You and the junior sharpshooter champion who rocks a mullet better than anyone I've ever seen?" I wait for a real answer. I know it's coming. Soren squeezes my hand. "Why wouldn't it be okay?"

"Because right now everything is about survival. We have to survive so we can get to Liv."

"And Cosmo is surviving so they can get to their brother," Soren says. "So that makes two survivors messing around. Can't two survivors occasionally feel something other than a crippling sense of impending doom?"

"You approve?"

"I do. I also approve of huckleberries. Which Racer and I are going to pick now. Yes?" He raises his eyebrows and really, really looks at me.

"Yes."

"It's okay to feel good." He kisses my forehead. "Racer says we'll run after we get the berries. Your *they*friend better be ready by then."

—

We don't protest Racer's practices anymore. Our running club has graduated to wearing our packs and weapons for practices. We leave the horses in the middle, so we can check on them every time we pass. Our circuits are usually short, with lots of laps.

As I jog, I wonder if Liv is keeping up with her training. She was Racer's most enthusiastic athlete, and the most natural one too. I wonder if they've made her put on shoes, and who got injured in the process of her refusing. I wonder if she's being fed better food than we ever had to offer, and more of it. I wonder if there are milk cows, and milk fresh from them, which is her favorite beverage of all time, even if there is a wall of glass-doored fridges stacked with every soda, iced tea, and energy drink one could choose from. I lose myself in these thoughts so thoroughly that when I tear myself away from them before I can cry, I find that I'm not running anymore. I don't remember stopping, but here we are, all back at camp. The others are packing up while I stare off in the general direction of hope.

We ride along a lake, none of us saying much, until we see a sign for Sandy Beach Resort.

"That's an original name," Cosmo says as we stop at the entrance, where we have a view all the way past the office and the cabins to a wide, sandy beach and a concrete boat launch.

"Empty," Soren says. "Let's check it out."

"*Looks* empty," I say.

We ride in slowly, eyes on the forest that lines the property to the east and west.

It's been picked over more than once, by the looks of what's left—patio furniture, curtains, piles of musty bedding, utensils and cleaning supplies, garden hoses, a ride-on lawn mower, a stack of ladders, and two pallets of concrete blocks parked beside a pile of dirt and a wheelbarrow of mulch that were on their way to being landscaped.

The most interesting find is on the beach: the cold remnants of a very recent campfire, with five empty cans of Dinty Moore Beef Stew strewn on the sand, eaten recently enough that the insides of each can—wiped clean—are still pristine, except for a few ants.

"They must be going west too." I pick up a can and breathe in the smell of the stew, and even though I'm probably making it up, it's an oasis of a taste profile I would kill for, even if I've never actually tried the stuff. "Or else we would've come across them yesterday."

"If Liv was here, she could tell you how many there are." Soren crouches in the sand. He runs his fingers over a distinctive print made of chevrons, heel to toe, and then another with a heel.

"Five people," Racer says. "Five cans."

Halfway through the next day, we spot a group before they spot us. No fake military uniforms, which is a good start. We slow down and watch them picking blackberries on the other side of the overgrown ditch that runs along the highway, which is only two lanes at this point.

"Five people and a dog!" Racer whoops with glee when he hands the binoculars to me. "A dog!"

"We still have to be quiet, Race," Cosmo says. "We don't know if they're safe or not."

"Five," Soren says. "I bet you those are the Dinty Moores."

From this distance, the group looks like two boys and three girls, all around our age or a little older. They have reasonably sized packs with liter water bottles with Sawyer filters attached, one in each side pocket. They wear sun hats and zinc slashes on their cheeks. They each have a small tub they're filling with as many berries as they eat, chatting easily as they do. The dog is a spaniel-ish mutt, by the looks of it. Kind of scrawny. I'm guessing that he belongs to the boy with the wide-brimmed straw hat with a flowered scarf as a band because the dog doesn't leave his side. The scarf tails are long and hang down, dancing in the breeze, making the scene look way sweeter and more pastoral than it is.

We watch long enough that they fill their containers and get back onto the road. Five pairs of matching hiking boots. This makes me think of the Orca Swim Club, when I'd rather think of these five people as friends who came upon an outfitter that had boots in their sizes, sitting there together and helping each other try them on.

"I vote we go say hello." I hand the binoculars to Cosmo.

"I vote hell no." Cosmo watches them for a long minute before lowering the binoculars. "I say we ride right past. Stick to ourselves. Stay focused on getting to Astoria with no more drama."

"I agree with Cosmo," Soren says. "Let's wait. Give them a chance to get ahead. They can run into any zees first."

"Race?" I know he'll be on my side. He has a turn with the binoculars, and when he says yes, it makes it a tie.

"I want to meet that dog," he says.

The dog follows the boy, but with stiff legs that he has to kick out to the side because they don't bend the way they should anymore. His tail is up, and his head is high, eyes alert, waiting for each berry the boy tosses over his shoulder for him. The dog catches every one, without fail.

"If those people look friendly," Cosmo says, "it's because they're friends with each other. Not us."

"Do you all agree that they look . . . normal?" I say. "Like regular people? Maybe even nice people? Not like Tars, or assholes?" I know it's only a matter of time before Soren's curiosity will get the best of him. I just have to keep stringing it along until it kicks in. "Don't you want to meet the pretty boy with the hat? I mean, come on. The hat. That shirt."

The boy wears an orange tank top, with a deep V-neck that offers up a good look at his tight brown pecs, and loose yellow pants.

"He is pretty." Soren has a look through the binoculars, just as the group shrinks in the distance and then disappears entirely around a sharp bend. "Yeah," he says. "Let's go say hi to the Dinty Moores. See if they know anything we don't know."

"The Dinty Moores could kill us," Cosmo says. "And my hat is prettier than his."

"Prettier?" I say. "Is that the word we'd use?"

"Anyone traveling with a lame dog is not going to kill us at first sight." Now Soren sounds the most determined of all of us, which is rarely the case. "Come on, let's catch up."

"We've got time. They're not going anywhere other than west

along the highway," Cosmo says, even as they trot Leus forward. "Unless they take off into the forest."

"So, let's go introduce ourselves." Soren hands the binoculars back to Cosmo, who takes just a moment before nodding. "Before they do that."

"I bet they can't run," Racer says. "I have shirts for all of them. They can join ZARC too."

"That dog definitely can't run," I say.

"Why are we talking like they're our new best friends?" Cosmo says. "I've met a hell of a lot of strangers in the last year. Look how many of them I was still traveling with before we met. This is like *Survivor.* It's all about allegiances. Everyone just chill."

When we've caught up enough that we can see them again, I take a turn with the binoculars. The pretty boy switches his hat for a baseball cap and crouches. The old dog scampers up his back and lies across his pack, steadier than his limp suggests.

"See that?" I hand the binoculars to Cosmo.

"You are all soft. Am I the only one who noticed the weapons?" Cosmo adjusts their belt, as if reassuring themselves that their guns and Alice are still there. "Three guns, two hatchets, and whatever else that isn't easily visible."

"And a bowie knife," I say. "I saw all that. They'd be idiots if they didn't have weapons."

It doesn't matter if we think they're a threat or not, because our option to vet them is taken away when we come out of a sharp curve to find them spread across the two lanes, facing us, the aforementioned weapons drawn and aimed at us. The dog stands in front of them, head lowered, growling. Clearly this is a familiar formation for them, because it looks like a scene out of a movie about this exact situation—one that was rehearsed a lot and has already had many takes. We do the opposite of spreading out. We angle our horses into a tight line, flank to flank.

"Hey!" Racer hollers at them. "Hi! We're the Zombie Apocalypse Running Club! Want to join? I have shirts. I can teach you to run."

"Teach us to run?" the shortest of them shouts. She's Black, with her hair up in a wrap, which adds a few inches in height but doesn't make her taller than any of us, including Racer. "Thanks, but no thanks."

"Shut up!" Cosmo grabs Racer's arms. "Stop!"

"Don't touch him like that," Soren hisses.

"I'd say the same thing to anyone!" Cosmo rests their hands on their guns. "This is so stupid. I knew we should've let them get ahead."

"Don't call him stupid!" Soren yells, which he does so rarely that each time it happens, I just assume that his—or someone else's—life is at risk.

"I didn't . . ." Cosmo sighs. "Fuck. Fine. I'll go talk to them. If they try anything, I'll get them before they get us. Then we'll just have to outrun whatever zombies come out of the mountains."

"No one is shooting anyone else," I say as Cosmo pulls forward on Leus.

"Good. Because I've managed to avoid killing actual people.

So far." They glance down at their guns. I know they want to check how many bullets they have, but won't, so as not to draw attention to the guns. "Do you know how I've done that? By lying *low.* By going it alone."

I'm having a hard time focusing on the immediate threat in front of us, because Cosmo is starting to piss me off. They want to do this right here? Right now? Fine.

"Then why are you even still with us?" I sweep my arm westward. "You sort of know the way. Feel free!"

"I *am* free," Cosmo growls.

"Family problems?" the spokeswoman hollers. I laugh, not because anything is funny; just the opposite. This is such a stupid conversation to be having. The laugh is all nerves, because I don't want Cosmo to leave us, and here I am, basically inviting them to fuck off. "What's so funny, Tall Girl?" When I don't answer, the line of them advances toward us.

"This is ridiculous," Cosmo says. And then, "Wait! Hold up. I'm coming. Just me. Alone. Just to talk."

"Stay right there." The loud girl is flanked on one side by a slightly taller Black girl with mirrored, heart-shaped sunglasses and her hair pulled back into a ponytail, and on the other side by the pretty boy—who switched back to his fancy hat with the scarf. His ball cap hangs off his pack. The group is bookended by what looks to be a brother-and-sister pair, who have matching ash-blond hair long enough to tuck behind their ears. Their hair matches their complexions, which almost match their slightly more tanned cowboy hats, which match their same-same tan T-shirts and khaki shorts, which—if you half close your eyes—

make them look almost matchingly naked. Those two have rifles. The other three have hatchets—seemingly the trendy zombie-apocalypse weapon of choice.

"We just wanted to meet you," I say. "We thought you might be some good to come across, you know? After a whole lot of evil."

"That's sweet," the leader says.

"Or we can do some trading," Soren suggests.

"We don't need anything," Heart Sunglasses says.

"Yes you do," Cosmo says. "Everyone needs something."

"No, actually." The leader. "We don't. Do you?"

"We have salmon jerky," Racer says.

"You don't offer the best—" Cosmo starts to correct him, but then stops when Soren reaches over and punches their arm.

"Patronize him one more time, and I will punch your face."

This is so unlike Soren that I forget what's going on for a moment. When I glance back at the other group, they're in a huddle. The dog hasn't moved. Head still lowered, still dedicated to his growl, he keeps his eyes locked on us. He doesn't even look away when the group breaks up.

"Call my dog to you," the boy with the hat says. "His name is Captain. He only goes to people who he trusts. He's a quick judge of character. He's been right for his entire life. Fifteen years. Get off the horses. Put him to the test."

The four of us gather in front of Odger.

"Captain!" Soren says. "Captain Dog."

"Just *Captain.*"

"Captain!" we all echo, Racer loudest of all.

The dog hobbles over as fast as he can, seemingly getting

younger with each step, because by the time he reaches us, he's practically bouncing, his tail going so fast that he's hitting his own haunches with it.

"Are you seriously that tall?" the one with the hair wrap says as they approach, weapons put away, hands extended for what turn out to be handshakes, which are maybe the first ones I've ever had by way of a greeting. In this informal zombie wonderland, that's not at all what I expected.

CHAPTER 21

They usually have bikes, the pretty boy explains. His name is Navinder. Navi for short. "We ride them till they get flats, and then we find more bikes. But ours got stolen at that lake resort back there."

"We went to sleep and woke up and nothing else was taken," Deedee says. She's the loud, short one, and clearly in charge. She and her cousin Jordan—heart-sunglasses girl—and Navi do most of the talking. The Beige Twins don't say much at all. They don't even introduce themselves. They just glare at us, arms folded.

So, we walk together, none of us wanting to hang around in one spot too long.

"More likely those thieves will ambush us rather than any of the zees," Navi says.

"Probably didn't even need the bikes," Jordan says. She takes off her sunglasses, revealing big brown eyes and very, very long lashes. It takes me a few seconds to realize that they're fake. "Just fucking with us."

"Just wanted to slow us down," Deedee says.

"Could've been Tars," Cosmo says.

"I doubt it." Jordan is slender, with long limbs and a short torso. She doesn't look much like Deedee except for in the face. Take headshots and you'd think they were siblings. But besides being shorter, Deedee is busty and curvy. She's eighteen, the oldest of all of us. The Beige Bookends and Jordan are all seventeen. Navi is sixteen. "They don't do anything quietly. All guns. All the time."

"Idiots," Deedee says.

"Dumbasses," Navi says.

"Well, we didn't see anyone go by with bikes," Cosmo says. "Or any vehicles. So best we can hope is that they're west and out of our way."

I watch Cosmo speak. They're so sure of themselves, with anyone, it seems. It's easy to imagine them sliding into any group. And out of any group. For the very, very first time, it occurs to me that maybe this is an MO. Maybe I'm a piece of that. Something comfortable. Something that makes them feel good. Someone who can make them feel good. Maybe when I kiss Cosmo, it takes place in one universe, but maybe when they kiss me back, it's happening somewhere else. Behind the moment and the kiss in common, it's something entirely different for each of us.

The Beige Wonders walk together, off to one side. The only things they regard with anything other than suspicion are the horses, which they look at with pure adoration, so much so that it occurs to me that they might steal them, if they have the chance.

"What's with the brother and sister?" I ask.

"Brother and sister?" Deedee laughs. "Oh no. Nope. They're a couple." I very pointedly do not take the bait. I just wait for Deedee to keep talking. "We've been traveling with them for a month, maybe? They're tougher than they look. They have the most zee kills. More than all of us combined, anyway. They grew up on farms. Beside each other. They've been together since they were eleven."

I cannot even imagine Liv with a crush, let alone a boyfriend. I'm not sure if it's gross or sweet.

"Where are you going?" I ask.

"Jordan and I are going to find our brothers and sisters," Deedee says. "They're in different Children's Villages. My sisters are in Astoria, and Jordan's brothers and sister are in Newport. Looks like maybe a few days' ride in between, along the coast."

"We're heading for Astoria too. Soren and I are going to get our little sister. Cosmo has a brother. They're both there."

"How much older are you than Soren?"

"We're twins."

"Bullshit."

"We are!" I say. "We're seventeen."

It takes three miles for the group to believe that Soren and I are twins, because what proof do we have except for our story? It's odd to think that Liv is the only one left to attest to us being twins.

—

We set up camp at a Washington State Department of Transportation salt shed. There's just a small pile of salt, but it's enough to hide behind, with a burnt-out WSDOT dump truck making a good barrier on one side and the concrete block wall on the other. The Beige Bookends go to "sleep" right away, setting up in the farthest corner, so they can do last watch, which I'm pretty sure is code for not wanting to hang out with us.

"Homophobes?" I speculate when Soren and I head out with Racer to pee one last time before bed.

"But Navi's queer," Soren says. "Adorably."

"Maybe they don't know?" I put on my best hick voice. "What with bein' country bumpkins and all?"

"We're country bumpkins."

"They know," I say, relenting. "Like it or not, they tolerate him. Probably pray for him all the time, but tolerate him too. Plus, he doesn't have someone to be demonstratively queer with, like Cosmo and I do. I see how they look at us when we hold hands. Or even sit too close to each other."

"It's not too close."

"You know what I mean."

"Yeah. I do. Okay. I'll take homophobia. For now. So long as they're not being weird about Racer, are they?" Soren whispers. "Because if they are, I'll beat the shit out of them."

"I have a hard time picturing that."

"Me too."

"Maybe it's just Cosmo." I realize it at the same time that I say it. "Maybe Cosmo is the poster child for a whole lot of bullshit they were fed in the before times."

"Homophobic *and* transphobic assholes."

When the three of us return to camp, we meet Cosmo, heading to the forest to pee. Soren lays out what we think is happening. Even in the dark, I can see Cosmo's cheeks go red.

"I figured," they say with a catch in their throat. "Doesn't matter. Fuck 'em."

"Let's not travel with them," Soren says. "We can part ways in the morning."

"They're zee-killing machines," Cosmo says. "If they can help us get to the Children's Village without being killed or turned, I don't care. If they stay out of my way, I'll stay out of theirs." With that, Cosmo heads into the dark forest, looking about as small as one does when disappearing into a planetary shag carpet of giant cedars and pines.

The next morning, the others stare at us as we stretch before ZARC practice. They listen to Racer explain.

"Want to join?" he says. "I have shirts for you, and you. And you. And you. And you."

"How the hell do you have shirts?" Jordan says.

Racer pulls the rest of the shirts from his saddlebags and sets them out, in a row from extra-small to XXL, on a low wall made of enormous concrete blocks—after he's brushed it clean.

"I have all the sizes," Racer says. "Please, take one."

"Who says we want to?" Deedee says.

"We should want to," Jordan says.

The Beiges stand off to one side, arms folded.

"I'll do it for a team shirt," Navi says. "I've never been a part of a team. Also, I'm a pretty good runner. I used to go jogging with my dad before school. That was a long time ago, though."

"This is stupid," Deedee says as she takes off her tank top to reveal a tie-dyed sports bra before she pulls on a ZARC shirt. Jordan cuts the sleeves off hers and twists the hem into a little knot above her hip. Navi does the same. The Beige Twins each take a shirt but sit out the practice to keep an eye on the horses and our things. They stand atop the wall, one facing east, the other facing west, guns cradled in their arms.

We all hand our shirts in after practice, except the twins, who leave them in the dirt behind the wall, where they kicked them when Racer wasn't looking. I pick them up and go to find the twins, who are sitting in the shade of the shed, alone. I shake out each shirt in front of them and then make a big production of folding each one into a neat little package. I hold them out.

"Want to give these back to Racer?" They shake their heads in unison. "Fine. I will. You don't deserve them anyway." I try to think of a way to kick up dirt as I turn and walk away, but I just end up stalking off with the shirts under my arm, rehearsing what I'll tell Racer.

There's no way of arranging everyone on the five horses, so we start out walking together again, with most of the packs arranged on the horses. Navi tried to convince Captain to ride on Rune, but he balked, so he's got his pack on, in case Captain needs a rest atop it while en route. We head west, with the sun rising hot on our backs. About an hour later, we see two trucks that stand out from the other abandoned cars, with their dusty windows and deflated tires and rifled-through insides. One has a pile of bikes in the bed. They each fly a black flag, but it's minutes before enough wind picks them up for us to see what's on them. The Tar symbol, stenciled and spray-painted in white. We stop, but when none of us see any movement, from the trucks or the road or the forest beyond, we silently agree to keep going, slowly, and with our eyes locked on the trucks.

The Beige Beloveds go ahead. When Cosmo joins them, hands hovering above their guns, they don't even honor Cosmo with a glance. They just walk a little faster and a little closer together.

We let them go ahead, but when they get to the first truck, they share a few words, and then Cosmo waves me over.

"Zee!" they yell.

"Kill it!" Deedee yells back.

"No!" Cosmo beckons me again. "Eira! We need you."

I get up into the saddle and hurry over. When I get there, I see a fresh zee thrashing in the driver's seat. Both she and the woman in the passenger seat wear the Tars' surplus-store military-ish uniform, but the difference is that the driver zee killed the passenger, whose neck has been mostly chewed away, leaving a slick of congealed blood that makes it look like the pleather upholstery started out crimson red at the factory.

I draw Gertrude from her scabbard. She is sun-warmed in my hands as I approach the driver, who reaches for me, scratching the air, her mouth painted with the passenger's blood. Her eyes are milky and weepy, but she turned so recently that the blue eye shadow on her lids is still in perfect shape. The ooze from her eyes has streaked her mascara, though. She snarls and lunges so far out that it's only the seat belt trapping her there. "I've never had a chance to see one for this long, up close."

"Kill it," Beige Girl says. She and Beige Boy have their daggers drawn but understandably don't want to get anywhere close enough to this excitable mess for her to rip their throats out. A long sword is definitely the weapon of choice here. Second choice would be Alice.

"Oh, hi." I take one hand off Gertrude and extend it in her direction. "I'm Eira. This is Cosmo. Nice to meet you."

"Just kill it," Beige Boy says.

The zee gurgles and growls, clawing at the air between us.

"Ever killed one with anything other than a gun?" Cosmo says.

"That's a dumb question," the boy says. "Guns are just better."

"Guns are dumb—"

"And that's the junior sharpshooter champion saying that," I interrupt.

The Beiges shrug.

"Three years in a row," I add. Cosmo puts their hand on my arm. The zombie clacks her teeth and snarls. But I'm not ready to dispatch her. "So, you shoot, which draws out more. Is that just to add to your count? These aren't fucking squirrel pelts." The driver zee folds over herself in her mad effort to get to me. I reach forward and stab her through the eye, pushing her upright as I do. When I pull Gertrude away, the zee flops onto the steering wheel. More specifically, the horn, which blasts confidently for a good four or five seconds before I can move her off.

"Darn it!" Beige Boy actually says this. This is *actually* what he says.

"Fuck!" Cosmo corrects. They grab my wrists and yank me away. We run back to our group even as the other group runs forward to untangle their bikes and wrestle them out of the back of the truck.

Then several long moments pass, during which we just listen, to the birdsong, the wind through the ash trees, Captain's panting, the river rushing along out of sight at the bottom of the ravine. There is no mistaking the noise that gets louder and louder, even if it sounds like a herd of deer crashing through the bush at first.

Footsteps. A lot of them, running *fast.*

"Go!" Deedee screams.

We take off. But the seconds we wasted in waiting cost us. There are fifteen zees, at least. All men, all dressed in WSDOT uniforms in various states of ruin, clambering up the steep pitch and throwing themselves onto the pavement, reaching for the group on bicycles as they furiously pedal by. The fastest zee launches his ungraceful bearlike shape at Beige Boy and knocks him off his bike. The zee dips his head down and bites into the boy's cheek as he kicks at him and screams. We gallop past the bikes, past the boy, who rolls onto his knees and then onto his feet and starts running after us, like he's trying to catch up rather than infect us.

Several of the zees cut off to the south and start running alongside the group on bikes, seemingly aiming to cut them off from the front, making a sandwich of doom with the group bringing up the rear. Beige Girl lags behind, maybe deciding whether or not she should go back to her other half. Tears course down her face.

"Run!" Soren yells. "Keep going!"

But she doesn't. She stops, plants her feet on either side of the bike, and squeezes her eyes shut while the ten zees fall over each other to take her down. Four get up right away and keep running, while the others smash her head onto the concrete and tear at her abdomen until they're unspooling her intestines and stuffing their faces with her viscera. Beige Boy comes up behind her and doesn't even pause for a nanosecond before running right past her, his eyes newly red-rimmed and trained on the nearest person in his path, Navi, who can't ride as fast because of Captain perched on his pack.

Ahead of me, I see Soren looking over his shoulder at Navi and Captain as they get smaller and smaller behind us until the bicycle group just looks like the leading edge of the troupe of zombies.

"Soren," I say when I realize that he's thinking about turning back. "No!" This is aimed at Cosmo too, who is already turning back. When Racer starts to turn back too, I scream at him. "No! Racer, keep riding! You keep going. We'll get Navi. Stay with Jordan and Deedee when they catch up. We'll catch up too. Go! Go!"

"Okay!" Racer, thank goodness, keeps riding west. Soren, Cosmo, and I ride back, toward the snarling throng.

"I'll slow them down. But we can't keep shooting. There might be more." Cosmo cuts away, cantering along the westbound shoulder, too fast for the zombies. They dart back onto the highway and slice in between the zees and the bicycles. Once on the other side, they draw their guns and start popping the zees in the head, dropping four in as many seconds.

"I'm going to grab Captain!" Soren brings Rune up beside Navi. "Keep pedaling." He leans over and grabs the dog by the scruff of his neck. Captain protests, twisting in midair like a fish on the end of a line. Soren keeps hold of him, though, wedging him under one arm while reaching down again. "Give me your hand. Now!"

"You can't lift me!"

"I can!" Soren takes his foot out of the stirrup. "Use that. Do it!"

Another two shots, and it's four zees left at the rear—five including Beige Boy now—and another five still aiming to get us from the west. As soon as Navi's hands leave the handlebars, the bike wobbles, nearly catching his one foot while he jams his other foot into the stirrup and throws his leg up and over the saddle.

I aim for Deedee, who stands in her seat, pedaling hard but assessing the incline coming up with dread, twisting her face into something unrecognizable. She and Jordan won't be able to get away from the last of the zees if they have to ride uphill.

I kick my right foot out of my stirrup and offer her a hand. With zero hesitation, she throws herself up at me, not even bothering with using the stirrup, not waiting for me to help her up. She grabs my waist and flings her legs up onto Odger, squeezing in between me and my pack. Struggling to hold on, she grabs a knife from her boot and stabs a zee in its cloudy eye just before it can pull her off. The zombie careens backward, knocking the two zees behind him down. This gives Jordan the few seconds she needs to angle her bike in my direction.

Without a word, she lets go of the bike and reaches up, grasping my outstretched hand and letting me swing her up and onto the saddle in front of me.

"Go! Go!" Deedee screams. Jordan gathers herself and then reaches around to grab Deedee's hand. The two of them sob as I kick Odger's flanks and lean into the hill that stretches up ahead of us. I can only hope that the zees get more tired on the incline than Odger will, with the added weight of two other people.

The zees keep running for us, but we put enough distance between us that they soon fall out of sight, which means they'll stop, because they won't be able to figure out where we are. When the incline ends, we stop at a viewpoint with three concrete picnic tables that have fared well in the apocalypse; the burnt remains of an outhouse that hasn't, with the white cylinder toilet melted into grim abstract art in the middle of the concrete floor; and an interpretive sign introducing the view across the gorge of hexagonal columns of rock, which I learn were formed by dacite lava between 110,000 and 20,000 years ago. Soren comes up beside me as I read the sign.

"No such thing as rocks that old," he says in his Dad voice, which was never a very good impression. "And surprise, surprise, no mention of the Great Flood. Now *that* was a truly cataclysmic event."

I open my mouth to reply with my much better impression of Dad, but instead a sob erupts from deep in my body. Some dark, hot corner pushes it up, and I fold over the interpretive sign, racked with tears, looking, I am sure, as if I am grieving this stunning rift in the earth.

I hear more crying from behind me. Deedee, Jordan, and Navi stand in a huddle, arms entwined, heads bent together. More crying comes from behind me; Cosmo and Racer are headed for us, both bawling. The last one to crack is Soren, who fits himself into the puzzle of Cosmo, Racer, and me. We are all crying now, seven mostly strangers halfway up a mountain pass, all with one thing in common: terrible, terrible loss. From the outside—if there is an outside anymore—people might think we were mourning the Beige Twins, but they are only the most recent of the losses, and not much of a loss to me and my people, if I'm being honest. This might sound callous, but it's just me being careful of my peoples' already broken hearts.

Packwood is bigger than Marion Gap, but not by much. The community center has a message board too. It takes over the entire front of the building, but none of us see anyone we recognize. Cosmo flips over a notice for the second coming and writes their note to Bailey with their marker in their fat block letters with exclamation marks and hearts and stars. We leave one of the pipe cleaner carnations and a note for Eddie and keep riding. Soren, Navi, and Captain ride on Rune. Deedee and Jordan ride on Buttercup. Racer is alone on Niki, for two reasons. One, Niki has no intention of sharing Racer, and two, Niki is pretty small.

That leaves me on Odger and Cosmo on Leus. When they're riding just a little ahead of me, I can get a really good look at them, without them knowing. The silver hilt of one of their guns catches the sun. There are three new, deep marks on the holster. At first, I wonder if it's from a zombie, if a zee got that close back there. But then I marvel at the fact that I know those are new marks. That means I've taken a very careful inventory of Cosmo. Cosmo glances back and tips their cowboy hat with a smile, like we're on a trail ride on just about any sunny afternoon.

I love this.

I hustle Odger up a little, so we're riding side by side. I want to take their hand, but the horses' girths make it impossible. And I'm not sure that they'd want to hold my hand. We don't say anything for miles and miles until we see a zee crawling along the pavement, its skin worn away at the elbows and knees as it army crawls down the middle of the road.

"Leave it?" Cosmo says.

"Yeah."

All of us give it a wide berth, even though all it can do is clack its teeth and scratch at the pavement in our general direction.

CHAPTER 22

We bed down for the night in a barn on the outskirts of Randle, just above the Cowlitz River. Close enough that when Jordan and Deedee take over watch and Cosmo and I can go to sleep, the river is a white-noise machine. I lie on my back, totally naked because the heat is not diminished by the proximity to the river, even if the breeze is slightly cooler. Cosmo lies beside me, down to their boxers.

"How can you be totally naked?" they whisper, even though everyone except Racer is still awake.

"You're practically naked," I say. "You take your shirt off all the time."

"Keyword being *practically.*"

"It's the only way I might get some sleep." I roll onto my side, which brings my boobs over too. I draw up my knee and then dip it over my lower leg, in a model pose. I put a hand behind my head and arch my back just a little. "Does my nakedness bother you?" I say with a pout.

"Absolutely."

I roll onto my back, hands straight at my sides. "Oh." *Absolutely.* What does that mean? What does that even *mean*? I'm just about to ask, but then Cosmo sits up.

They stay like that for a second or two and then say, "Turn over. Onto your stomach."

After I do, Cosmo straddles me. Their weight on me is delicious. I feel them slide their hands up my back, lowering themselves until they're lying on top of me. "Absolutely bothers me." They make fists and roll them along my shoulders, then massage their thumbs up my neck. The river gets louder, until I don't hear Racer snoring. I don't hear Jordan and Deedee murmuring outside. I don't hear the hushed giggles of Navi and Soren as they cuddle in the corner, as if they've been dating for months and did not in fact meet for the very first time yesterday. I just hear the river shushing as it rushes by. It sounds sleepier. Slower. Not metaphorically. For *real,* as if the water has actually slowed down so we can all truly rest, even for just one night. First, though, I turn over beneath Cosmo. This surprises them enough that I catch them off guard when I pull them down and kiss them, the river getting louder and faster the longer we make out.

I wake up exactly as we fell asleep, spooning on our right sides. I pay for it with my side being numb and my hips screaming for distraction. Cosmo's head rests on my arm, tilted up so I can see the line where sweat met dirt yesterday. I want to kiss that spot, where their jaw and neck come together, but as much as I'm in pain, I want to enjoy this moment for as long as it can last. I want to hold on to last night.

Navi and Soren come in with two feed buckets half-full with fat, warm blackberries. They're giggling as if they hadn't stopped all night, although I know they did sleep, and they were quiet on their watch so as not to wake us up. Navi leans in and kisses Soren on the lips.

"If you two are going to do that all the time"—Deedee waves a finger at them and scowls—"we're going to send you to ride ahead. You can meet any zees first."

"I agree," I say.

"We have a ship name." Navi plants another kiss on Soren's lips.

"Oh my God," Cosmo says.

"Seriously?" Deedee laughs. "Is it short? With one letter for each hour you've known each other?"

"Queers move fast at the end of the world," Soren says. "Am I right, Eira? Cosmo?"

"What's the name?" Jordan says. "We are all so very much dying to know."

"Savvy," Soren and Navi say in unison. Then Navi adds, "So cute, right?"

Jordan gags.

Cosmo and I glance at each other, and then away immediately.

"Now, eat up, ladies and gentlethems," Navi says.

Each berry bursts with flavor, but it's not enough for a meal, even with the chocolate pudding mix and soy protein powder the Dinty Moores have to share. We need to find more food, to supplement what we took from BATO and are rationing so carefully. I should be eating almost twice as much as everyone else, but that is not happening.

Cue montage of plucky survivors chatting amiably while making their way from property to property over the next few days, going through every cupboard, cellar, attic, barn, and garage and mostly coming up with nothing but half a box of expired granola bars—watch them eat them, oh, so tasty!—and the odd can of the odd thing, until jackpot! Four cans of Spam in one of those weirdly deep corner cupboards, and all we paid for it was Racer's finger in a mousetrap, because he was the one who bravely stuck his arm into the dark. That's okay, brave lad! More Spam for you! *Ha, ha, ha,* some laughter. Navi and Soren—excuse me, *Savvy*—spinning in a field of wildflowers, like they're in an ad for an air freshener. A poignant moment between ransacking homes when everyone brings out photos of their little siblings: Bailey; Liv; Deedee's sisters, Imani and Teyana; and Jordan's brothers, Jayson and Joseph, and sister, Joy. I even pull out the picture of the Girl Scouts and pass it around. But let's not spend too much time on this. It's painful, which is why this is the first time for show-and-tell.

Back to the montage! Oh, look! A zee! Stab it in the eyeball. Nice job, Gertrude. And another one that runs their eye right into Gertrude. Oops, we're bedded down for the night and here come three more zombies. Cosmo—caught completely off guard—shoots them before even thinking about it. But that's okay, no more zees within earshot. Phew! *Hey, hey, look at that, right?* they say. *One bullet each. Hot, right?* And I admit to myself that it is very hot to watch them flex their sharpshooter muscles.

This is how we only move twenty-three miles in three days, but at least we've gathered enough food to last us a week or so. The homesteads are few and far between up here, but they've given us more than we got from the places we searched down in the valley.

"We can get to Astoria before our food runs out." Deedee stabs the coastline on her map. "If we're not stupid."

We have four maps among us: the Sigurdsons' back-roads map book; Cosmo's new AAA map of Washington and Oregon, to replace the one they lost; a western-states map Deedee holds on to; and one of the Children's Villages maps Jordan and Deedee have from when they signed for their siblings to go. That last one only shows a few interstates, with stars marking the five Villages dotting the West Coast and the ten dotting the East Coast.

Mostly, Soren and I know where we're going. But as we get closer, we want to make sure we don't veer off track. Especially if we're rationing food.

"We stay on 12." Soren traces the road we're on. "All the way to I-5. Then south. Then west again."

Navi reaches over him to point to Astoria. "There." He stabs an Oregonian outcrop that points up to Washington, like it's testing the wind. "That's where the Children's Village is."

—

We camp at Riffe Lake that night, laying out our blankets and mats and sleeping bags under the stars, which crowd the sky to get our attention. It's too hot to be under anything. We're all down to our underwear, but still we toss and turn.

Deedee gets up and brushes dirt off her butt. She strips off her underwear and bra and takes a run at the water, going deeper and deeper until she dives right under and, for a moment, is utterly *gone.*

"She's fine," Jordan says. "She's a good swimmer."

A few more seconds pass before she breaks the surface and waves, not daring to whoop or holler for us to join her.

"Anybody else?" Jordan strips down too and strides into the water. She stands there for a minute, the water just below her waist.

"Want to?" Navi says. He blushes instantly, wisely not turning around when Soren answers.

"I absolutely want to." Soren gulps back the last word, his Adam's apple getting stuck halfway. They strip and run in, with Captain bouncing along behind them, suddenly much more spry than he usually is. That leaves me, Cosmo, and Racer, standing around in our underwear, which already feels vulnerable enough. I have never seen so many naked people that I'm not related to.

"Are you going in?" Cosmo asks. They've moved so close that our arms are touching. Hot and sweaty, it's pleasant, and unpleasant too. We all stink so bad that no one complains of body odor, but up this close, Cosmo really stinks. Which means I do too.

"I'm doing it." I strip off my sports bra and boxers and freeze. If I run, there will be so much bounce: butt, boob, belly. I stride like Jordan did. As if I'm powered by confidence and not insecurity.

When I dive under, bliss erupts with the water I displace, and a cold, muted quiet plugs the noise from the others above, who are louder than they should be. I come up and see Cosmo and Racer on the bank, watching us. They both stand with their hands on their hips, legs spread just a little. Classic superhero poses.

But then, suddenly, we're all watching the forest just above them. Something crashes through the huckleberry bushes and new alders. In the time it takes to pray that it's a buck, we see that it's not. It's a zee, arms pinwheeling as she falls off the little bluff above the sand and rights herself.

"Run!" Cosmo grabs their hat and screams at Racer, and all of us scream at them both. "Run!"

Racer takes off, sprinting down the beach and into the blackness so quickly that it's like he disappeared. Cosmo takes off running in the opposite direction, leading the zee away from Racer. The beach is long and moonlit. The water laps at the shore. It is a beautiful night to run for your life. We run as fast as we can out of the water, which is not fast at all. Cosmo keeps running. They have to. They don't have any weapons, and trying to beat the zees off never works. Run, Cosmo. *Run.*

Soren is out of the water first. "Hey! Come get me!" He lunges for his hatchet as the zee spins and lurches for him instead. She runs down the beach after him, until she's close enough to launch at him. We've all got our weapons now, but just as Soren raises his hatchet, Navi steps in and stabs her in the temple with his dagger.

"I got you," he says. To Soren. Not the zombie.

The zee collapses forward onto her knees, planting her face in the sand, her arms tucked under her, like a yoga pose. It's not until Racer and Cosmo are safely back that I punch Soren in the arm. "Aw. So sweet!"

The Children's Village billboards become more frequent once we get to I-5. Mostly people have left them alone, but there is one more spray-painted by the Tars. We don't see any Tars in person, though. Just more zees. Navi has been keeping track since the one at the lake. Thirty-two. But it doesn't feel like as high a number as it might seem. With seven of us, it's a lot easier not to die.

"Racer! Let's go!" I shuffle Odger into a slice of shade while Racer selects a green carnation from the bouquet of exquisite silk ones he found at a florist shop in the last town. He wedges it in among the detritus of messages and photos, in between the note Cosmo left for Bailey—this time on the back of an ad for a utility trailer for trade in exchange for canned goods—and the note we leave for Liv. Every time we stop and leave notes, my hope grows. Even though it's been true all along that with each step, we're getting closer to Liv, it's only starting to feel like that now. If our method of string measuring on the AAA map is accurate, there are about eighty miles between us and Astoria.

Thunder rumbles out of the black clouds that have been building a bank in front of us since we woke up this morning. No one wants to jinx anything by saying it might rain, but all of us keep checking up on that stretch of beautiful, fat storm clouds that promise the first rain since any of us can remember. We follow the clouds all the way into Longview, where there is not a single zee in sight. A fire scorched most of the city, some time ago by the looks of it. Maybe even last year. Every storefront window is smashed, which we haven't seen before. It's like someone made it their personal mission to do it. That is serious commitment to a very personal rage. Or release.

"Or maybe it's just smart," Deedee says. "You'd hear anyone coming."

We weave the horses down the middle of the road, away from the glass. We end up by the banks of the Columbia River, at the backside of a hospital that is entirely burnt out at the front. There is a Children's Village mural, mostly scorched off the wall, by what might've been the main entrance before the fires. Cosmo and I get our horses to pick through the rubble a bit. There's a crumbling bankers box under a metal door with its paint seared off. Most of the papers inside are ash and char, but the very bottom of the pile is only singed at the edges.

CHILDREN'S VILLAGE INTAKE & ASSESSMENT

Name of minor (<16 yo):
Photo:
Family members (living at time of apprehension):
DOB (if known):

Apprehension details:

Preexisting medical conditions, allergies, mental health concerns:

"This was some kind of outpost." I hand out the forms.

"Maybe a place where they assessed them before they took them to the villages?" Jordan says.

"Where is everyone?" Cosmo crumples the paper in their hand. "If this was supposed to be a safe place, why is it destroyed? Who set it on fire?"

"Doesn't mean someone set it on fire," Deedee says. "A lot burns down when there is no one to put out fires and no water to pump on them."

Cosmo and I share a look. "I don't know," Cosmo says. "Something feels wrong."

"We haven't seen any Tar tags for days," Jordan says. "And no Tars since the batshit one in the car."

"It's just the fire," Navi says. "That's why they left."

"The kids are okay," Soren says. "We'll see them soon."

Those two—and Racer—are the optimists of the group. It's always good to end a conversation on something one of them says. So we do.

Jordan and Deedee stay with the horses as they graze in what was a fenced-in off-leash dog park above the river, just out of sight. We have three flare guns now, so we can split up and still summon help if the danger outweighs the risk of the noise. The rest of us hang out on the loading dock, which wasn't touched by the fire but still smells of it. Lightning cracks out of the black clouds, starting a fire on the other side of the river, where the slope is tinder-dry. After a minute or two, there are six small fires eating up the dry brush and threatening to combine.

"Is that where we're going?" Cosmo pushes their hat up to get a better look.

But before anyone can look at a map, a deluge dumps out of the bank of clouds, like God let down a heavy curtain of it, and soaks the hillside.

"Rain!" Racer cries. He runs out into it, and we all join him, holding back the zee-drawing whoops and hollers we all want to offer up to the big, plopping drops hitting our faces and arms and soaking our clothes. Navi and Soren dance around Racer and then reach for him to join them. Captain makes slow circles around them, his arthritic butt wiggling with delight. He snaps at the rain, tail metronome-ing faster than I've ever seen from him. Soren gives me a pointed look when I try to join too. He glances at me, his brow furrowed, and then at Cosmo, then back at me.

Cosmo grabs my hand, and instead of spinning me around, they pull me to them and lift their chin and look at me, blinking through the rain pelting their face. I bend down, and in this one movement, the last few months wash away, and the rain doesn't touch me, and I tilt their head and kiss them. . . . They kiss me back, and I realize why kisses in the rain are a trope in every way of telling a story: songs, poems, movies, books. The rain washes you into another world, where nothing else matters. Not even zombies. Not hunger. Not the terrible pain of loss.

—

Once we're fully soaked and now suffering from a new, terrible damp heat, we retreat to the loading dock and watch the rain.

Navi and Soren go check on Jordan and Deedee, who are comfortable in a picnic shelter near to where the horses are enjoying the rain.

"Someone dragged lawn chairs in there," Soren says when they come back. "They say they want to stay there tonight, but I think that's because they're tired of all of us and not because of a couple of zero-gravity loungers or horse duty. I'm not tiring." Soren hooks his arm around Navi's neck and pulls him in for a kiss on the forehead. "I don't know about the rest of you . . ."

"It's not my business to say." Navi pushes Soren away with a laugh. "But they probably don't want to be around the coupleness. Deedee and Jordan both had boyfriends, back when this started. They were dead before we met, but it's taken them a long time to not hurt out loud every single day. They probably don't have a lot of patience if we're being super cute. So, dull the sparkly edges, people. Okay?"

"Wait." Soren flips his braids over his shoulders. "We're a couple?" He waves a finger at Cosmo and me. "You two are a couple? We're using that word? Specifically?" I want to hug him, I'm so thankful that he's saying it for both of us.

"You have a ship name," I say. "Doesn't that automatically mean that you're a couple?"

"But the word itself," Soren says. "That's new. To us, anyway. And to you two, right?"

Instead of answering, Cosmo covers my face in kisses while Navi dips Soren and gives him one long, lingering kiss.

Racer uses his hatchet to make kindling out of a chunk of dead tree. He starts a fire in an oil barrel that other travelers already set up in an area with a view of the river, complete with a comfy arrangement of waiting room furniture in a circle around it. There are even weather-warped side tables and stacks of books from the hospital auxiliary shop to choose from. Soren and Navi boil water to make tea with the anise from an overgrown tangle of a community garden we passed on the way in. Navi's made a bed for Captain on one of the chairs, using a pile of blankets he and Soren found in a supply closet on the second floor. After Captain's initial excitement and exploration of the loading dock, he mostly just stays curled up, except to go out to pee. Cosmo and I find a supervisor's office. RUTH KEMENICK, her nameplate says. Ruth Kemenick, who, by the looks of the shelf of framed photos, had at least three grown children and twice as many grandkids. Her desk is scattered with news articles printed off the internet. She must've been printing them off madly, in the time before the internet went dark. They're all time-stamped for that day we were driving home, and the next day. On a little whiteboard is the heading *Days Until Retirement!!!* and a frame made of washi tape and the number *13* printed in blue dry-erase marker.

"Almost made it," Cosmo says as we carry the papers back to the loading dock, where we sort them in order of time.

At first, it's all about the progression from Russia to Alaska and then south. *Mass killers.* Then, *Is it infectious violence?* And reams of chat room speculation: *zombies, government secrets, weapons of mass destruction.* And bold ideas of what to do about it: *Nuke 'em. Build a fence!* Flame throwers, citizen militias, antidotes. And then, during that first night, the reliable news sources start calling it Hypertox, a human-made, mutated strain of *Toxoplasma gondii,* which is where we're at now.

Weapon of mass destruction, or nature's accident?

The last article has one giant word for a headline: *HELP?*

The article that follows isn't asking for help. It's suggesting it. Even before the internet went dark, there was a glimmer of hope.

> Work has been ongoing for years in a lab in South Korea, where scientists are developing pyrimethamine with a "seeker" agent, which will interfere with the formation of biomolecules within Hypertox cells. While the origin of this *Toxoplasma gondii* strain has not been determined, this program has been working on antidotes for a weaponized version. This information came to light when the United Nations convened in Melbourne last night.

"Listen to this." Soren and Navi pass a trashy romance novel back and forth, reading the steamiest parts out loud. *"She arches her back, lifting her hips to his manliness."*

"Soren . . ."

"'Take me,' she says. 'Fill me up, like I am your hot rod on empty.'"

Racer finds that part particularly hysterical.

"Guys, read this instead." I hand Soren the paper. He reads it out loud. When he's done, Racer takes the paper, tracing his finger over the words until he finds what he's looking for.

"Cure." He grins as he reads the words leading up to it. *"This is the first hope for a cure."*

"So long as that lab is still working," I say.

"Even if it's not, the work is out there. It's happening!" Soren says. "We'll run this to Jordan and Deedee. They need to come back so we can all celebrate!"

The next morning, we do our running practice together, doing lots of short laps—along the river trail, keeping the dog park with the horses and Captain in the middle. When we're all at the dog park and glugging water, Racer digs in his pack and pulls out a tangle of plastic medals that say *#1 Student* and look like they came from one of the Dollar Generals we've scavenged along the way. The thought of him pocketing those makes me want to grab him in a very sweaty hug.

"Ugh! Gross!" He pulls away. "You need a shower."

"So do you," I counter.

"Now be quiet," he says. "It is time to hand out your medals. Congratulations, Soren Helvig." He drapes a medal over his head. Then one for me, and all the others. "Good work, Zombie Apocalypse Running Club athletes."

"Why are we getting these today?" Jordan asks.

"We all ran together," Racer says. "And we talked. The whole time. That means strong lungs. You can run far. You will be *safe.*"

It's true, I marvel. It took this long to do it, but I can finally carry on a conversation while running. "But wait," I say. "How come Navi and the girls can do that already?"

"They are more fit," Racer says.

"Snap!" Navi kisses his medal and then turns on his heel and gives us a catwalk strut to where Rune is munching on clover. He tosses us a simpering pout and finishes with his best model face: equal parts simmering and elated.

We ride out of Longview, all wearing our medals and feeling pretty good about ourselves. When we come to the bridge we're supposed to cross and it's half-tilting into the Columbia River, we happily take our chances using the dodgy repairs people jerry-rigged before us. We have to coax the horses across the steel plates and gravel patches, but once we're on the other side, we're on our merry way again. We're still pretty cheerful when we get to a pile of burnt bodies in between two cars. They block the whole road and are so charred that we can't tell if they're people or zees, and we can't decide what kind of message whoever set up this tableau is sending. There are no Tar symbols, no Children's Village billboards, no messages of any kind. And no way of going around without taking a big detour. That's when the mood changes.

"The bridge and this," Cosmo says. "This is the Children's Village keeping people away."

"But they want families to come," Soren says.

"Unless they don't," Deedee says.

"Maybe it's just a deterrent," I say. "To keep everyone else away? People who are going to get their kids will put up with a whole lot more than sightseers will."

"Sightseers?" Deedee laughs.

"You know what I mean, though, right? You'd kill for your siblings—"

"*Have* killed." Deedee clicks for Buttercup to head off the road into a dense forest, which ends up taking forever to pick through and which leaves the horses annoyed and exhausted by the time we get back onto Highway 30.

"I don't like this," Soren says after an hour of us plodding along the dirt shoulders to go easy on the horses' shoes. "Something isn't right. Where are the Children's Village signs? Where are *any* signs?"

While the others speculate about what we're riding toward, I cannot form words. Soren is the positive one. When we both sense something is wrong, it always is.

Always.

We ride into Clatskanie, which is just another ghost town. No Tars, no zees, nobody. And here too, all the windows are smashed. We fall silent as we make our way westward, back to the forest-lined highway, with the river rushing ahead of us to the ocean. We only stop when we agree that the horses need a rest. Even though we're so close, we aren't.

CHAPTER 23

There is a subdued calm among us as we get up and get ready just before dawn, when the songbirds are still quiet. We ride in near silence until we finally reach the outskirts of Astoria around midday. It looks no different than any other small city we've passed. Large swaths have burned to the ground, leaving flattened strip malls and car dealerships, and parking lots full of blistered carcasses of cars and trucks and the debris that collects in these charred ruins, swept in on the stiff, salty wind from the ocean—so many plastic bags and paper drink cups. And so much paper, as if every file box blew open, freeing every single invoice and purchase order and patient file and quarterly report to blow across town and decorate the bleak, blackened post-fire mess like confetti.

The highway is cleared, though, which gives us hope. We've slowed down a bit since the city came into view, as if we collectively and silently agreed that we should. I focus on the road in front of me. The asphalt specifically, because I don't want to see the decay pushing in from both sides. Somewhere very soon, we will turn a corner and see the Children's Village. I tell myself there won't be a crescendo of heartening music. There won't suddenly be row after row of brightly colored cottages, where the kids have been staying like it's summer camp. There won't be a pool, a library, or a community center with basketball hoops. But there will be a playground and a mess hall and a crafts station.

"Stop." Soren pulls up beside me. "You can't know. We can't guess."

"I can't stop."

About five minutes later, the wall comes into view.

"That is beautiful," Cosmo says.

"Maybe not beautiful," Deedee says. "But if it's keeping our kids safe, okay." The wall stretches for as far as we can see to the north and all the way to the water on the south. Made of varying heights of sheets of mismatching corrugated metal, it is actually quite ugly.

"Ugly beautiful," Navi says.

"Let's go get Liv Helvig!" Racer says.

We ride faster but slow to a stop when the first billboard with instructions on how to access the Children's Village comes into view. The Tar symbol is stenciled over it in black—that colon-shit shape with legs, although the stencil has the correct number of legs this time: eight. The symbol is stenciled over the next billboard too, but we can still read this one:

WELCOME! Your children will be so excited to see you! Please follow these guidelines to ensure a successful reunion.

Weapons-Free Zone—Register and leave yours at the gate.

Travelers' Concierge—A safe place to leave your means of travel.

Physical Inspection—To keep our children safe from diseases of all kinds.

Family Counselors—Assigned to help with a smooth reunion.

Family Coaches—What's next? Our coaches will help you make a plan.

YOU ARE WELCOME HERE. WE ARE SO GLAD YOU MADE IT.

WORLD CHILDREN'S VILLAGES—
a UNICEF project

"Why is the Tar symbol there?" Racer says. When no one answers, he asks again. "Why is it there? Are there Tars here?"

"We haven't seen any," I say. "For so long."

"What do we do?" Cosmo covers their face with their hands and shakes their head. "What the fuck do we *do*?"

"What are the chances that it's just a tagger?" Soren says. "Just one lone asshole who did this. Or maybe a few, even, but not enough that we have to worry about the village. The wall is solid. It's doing its job, right?"

"We all think it's beautiful because it *is,*" Navi says.

I glance at Deedee, who stares at the place in the wall where a portal is built out. Black flags fly on either side of the entrance, but we're too far away to see what's on them. "Let's go see those flags," she says. "They look like Tar flags to me."

"Yeah," Cosmo says. "If they have the piece of shit on them."

My head pounds with panic as we ride west. The thrum is so loud that it pushes out every thought I try to hold on to in favor of amplifying the ones I don't want. I tell myself the Tars didn't hurt us back in Naches. But then I hear myself screaming from below that. *They're never giving Liv back! You came all this way for nothing! All the kids are DEAD.* When I look at the others, the expressions on their faces are all the same: grim, unchanging, all focused on the wall that is getting bigger and more ominous as we get closer. They're either too numb to react anymore, or they're paralyzed by fear, probably playing out their own worst-case scenarios in their heads. None of us scan for Tars who might be watching the road. We just plod forward, because none of us are willing to go back so long as there is an ounce of possibility that our siblings are in there.

Sure enough, the wind lifts the flags to reveal a Tar symbol on each. We can see the portal now. The guard station is protected by curlicues of razor wire spewing out from either side. There is a narrow road that leads past the guard station to a massive chain-link gate, which opens out to give access to what lies beyond. The chain link is woven through with green plastic strips, though, so we can't see past it.

As we get closer, three Tar soldiers come out of the guard station, with big black guns cradled in their arms.

"This is good," Soren says as they wave. "Better than them aiming their guns at us."

"I don't care if this is a trap." As Deedee says this, I realize that I agree.

"Me too," I say. "I'm going to talk to them. Who's coming?" As a reply, we all drive our horses forward, closer to the wall and the guards. They never lift their guns, even as we get close enough to see each other properly. The guards are one older Latinx woman with what my mom called smokers' wrinkles, one shorter white woman with her uniform pants hiked up high over a big belly, and one scrawny white boy, about our age, whose uniform hangs off him as though he stole it from his dad. They each wear a black baseball hat with an embroidered tardigrade on it: a round white patch depicting a black water bear rimmed in red. Where do you find tardigrade patches to outfit an army? Were they from before? Or is someone out there working a computerized machine with solar power and whatever materials people can scavenge?

"Greetings," the older woman says. "We do not make you surrender your weapons here, but you will unload any guns and secure them out of reach."

Cosmo unloads and puts away their pistols. "This is sounding very familiar," they say under their breath.

The chain-link gate opens just enough to let one person out. An older man, suit pants, suit vest, white dress shirt with tie. He's white, and not as old as the man in Naches, but as he approaches, I see a big ring on his right hand, same as the first old man. This man rocks a salt-and-pepper mullet, with a long, braided rat tail and a neatly trimmed mustache to accessorize.

"You've found the Tars," he says. "*Tars* is short for *tardigrades.* Do you know what tardigrades are?"

"Assholes," Deedee mutters.

"This is almost word for word the same as Naches. Just wait," I say to Deedee, Jordan, and Navi, who haven't had this kind of exchange so far. "They're going to mansplain tardigrades, then offer for us to join them."

"Tardigrades would survive a nuclear winter. They survive in outer space. At the bottom of the ocean. *Anywhere,* under any conditions, no matter how punishing. As do we. As will you, if you join us. Otherwise, you'll perish."

"No thanks." Cosmo knows how this goes too, and doesn't want to wait. "We're here for our kids. We've got names, pictures, and papers showing us as their reunification adults."

"Have a look around." The man flashes his rat tail again as he spins around, arms up, gesturing at all that lies behind him. "Do you see any Children's Village propaganda? Any signs? Any sounds of children playing? No? No. You see our flags. Our people."

"Where are the kids?" The thrumming in my head is gone, replaced by an electric anger that might turn into lightning bolts that explode from my eyes if this dick doesn't tell us where our brothers and sisters are. "Where are they?" I yell.

"I don't know." He shrugs. "They left when we showed up. We offered to live together, but the Children's Village officials rather unpolitely declined. They made such a wonderful, safe community—ocean views!—and we just wanted to join it and help make things run smoothly."

"Shut up!" Jordan screams. "Where are the kids, you fucking asshole!"

"Simmer down there, young lady." He clasps his hands behind his back and makes a *tut-tut* sound. "Do you think you can swear like that in a Children's Village? A *Children's* Village?"

"But this isn't a Children's Village anymore." Deedee squeaks her words past a nearly visible lump in her throat. "Is it?"

We all shuffle, as if ruffling our feathers to puff up before the fight breaks out. Before any of us can make a stupidly under-powered move, and while we're still on this man's good-ish side, Soren takes the lead.

"We know about your screening process and 'assignations,'" he says with finger quotes. "We're not interested. We just want our kids. We have one question. Actually two. And then we'll be on our way. One, are the children hurt or dead? Two, where are they?"

"Once you leave, you will never be allowed another chance to join the organization that is singly responsible for rebuilding the world. The entire world." He holds his arms out, palms up. "I will come back in five minutes for your final answer." With that, he disappears through the gate.

"What the fuck?" Jordan grabs Deedee's arm. "We have to go after him!"

"No, no." Deedee shakes her head. "The kids aren't here. He's not going to help us find them."

"She's right." Cosmo reloads their guns before replacing them in the holsters. "We'll figure this out ourselves."

The three guards stand shoulder to shoulder, watching us, although they don't seem particularly interested in the exchange that just happened. As we ride off, back the way we came, they don't even say goodbye or try to get us to reconsider leaving. When I turn around to get a last look at the guard station, they've all gone inside the little hut and are sitting around a table, playing cards. One of them looks up, but I'm not sure which, because all I see are the hats.

We ride back to the Children's Village billboards, without anyone suggesting that's what we do. Maybe we just want to huddle under the last proof of hope. Maybe there is nothing left to do. Maybe this is where we'll stay forever, seated in a little circle in the slanting light of a beautiful summer evening, with a graciously cool breeze coming off the water. Maybe we'll sit here and starve to death while the horses graze on the clover pushing up amid the rubble. This could be okay to me, if I knew I'd never see Liv again.

"But we don't know that," Soren says. The others glance at the two of us, because they know he's answering some silent statement from me. "We can't give up. Because we don't know."

"You know what I think?" Cosmo stands up. "The kids are fine. Otherwise, any one of those four people would've had a stronger reaction to us asking after them. We're talking about children. Not enemy combatants from the other side. There isn't even an 'other side.' "

"We'll make a plan in the morning," Navi says. "It's getting too dark to go anywhere."

Because we're not hiding, we make a small fire when the

damp air gets chilly. We're all still awake when we see two bicycles coming up the road, headlights bobbing. It's two of the guards—the two women.

The older one pulls right up to the fire but doesn't get off her bike. She holds out a piece of paper. Racer takes it and unfolds it.

"It's a map." He hands it to Jordan, our navigator.

"This is here." Jordan tilts it toward the fire so she can see. "And the coastline, going south. What is this?"

"The kids are fine," the guard says. "They went south, to the next Village."

"How did they get there?" Soren says. "Who went with them?"

"They walked," she says. "I think there was one bus maybe, for the patients in the hospital. Everyone went. No one wanted to stay behind. Not a single person. We don't make people stay, and we don't care if they leave. We're not assholes."

"That guy is," Cosmo says. "For not telling us what you just did."

"And the map?" I say when it's my turn to look at it. "This is where they are? This star? This is so far away! It looks like over a hundred miles! You made little kids walk over a hundred miles? In a zombie apocalypse."

"Children's Village keeps that corridor clear. And they had food. And water—"

Deedee stands up, then the rest of us do too. We face the guards, arms loose at our sides but ready to reach for our weapons.

"Look, it's not on us," the shorter guard says. "We weren't even here then. We gotta go. Our shift finishes in twenty minutes."

"We do a sweep at the end of each shift," the first woman

says. "If you're still here tomorrow, maybe I can arrange a second chance. If that means you've reconsidered."

When we don't see the lights anymore, we kick out the fire and pack the horses again and head for Highway 101 and the ocean. We will not be here tomorrow. With the crashing surf on our right and the moon lighting the way, we're going to get as far away from the Tars as possible, and closer to the kids with each mile.

CHAPTER 24

The Oregon Coast Highway is the most beautiful stretch of road I have ever been on in my entire life, but the beaches and cliffs and sea stacks and tough evergreen forests and even the jaw-dropping sunsets all dull behind the pall of anxiety about what we'll find when we get to Newport, the site of the next closest Village and where the children were marched off to. With or without the horses' approval, we cover the 135 miles in four days. We run out of food on the second day, get chased by a mama bear after startling her and her cubs on the third day, and wake up to rain on the fourth day. It pours down while we pack up, but we don't care. We'll be in Newport by midday, and even if none of us are admitting it, we're all really excited to see our kids and are way more hopeful than is smart.

Jordan squeals when an overgrown golf course comes into view.

"We're close! We're close!"

We coax the horses to go faster, but they're exhausted, and underfed too. Odger sets the pace, and he's refusing to gallop.

We see more houses and businesses lining the seaside highway. All empty, but *just* empty. Not burnt down, not covered in graffiti. No broken windows. Just overgrown lawns and porches being engulfed by blackberries and salal, and wheelbarrows and plastic playhouses and broken tricycles tidied up along the south sides of each building.

"This is all on purpose," Soren says. "Why are they taking care of the houses way out here?"

"I know why." Cosmo beams. "Because they're going to need them. Because they're growing."

"The bridge is coming up," Jordan says. "Hopefully they're taking care of that too."

Before we see the bridge, we see a fence of *MISSING* posters and family photos and notes to loved ones. Above it and spanning the length are big wooden letters, in all the rainbow colors.

♥ CHILDREN'S ★ VILLAGE ★ NEWPORT ★ WELCOME! ♥

"Hey!" Racer leaps off his horse and starts running. He goes straight for something sticking out of the last panel on the left. It's a green silk carnation on a long stem. Racer frees it from the staples and waves it.

"Eddie!" he yells. "Eddie is here! He's here!" He jumps up and down, waving the carnation in the air.

"There's no chance," Soren says. "There can't be. Can there?"

"No." I get off Odger and embrace Racer in a hug. "Let's wait and see, okay? What if another family had the same idea?"

"This is Eddie." Racer clutches the carnation. "He's here."

Beyond the wall of pictures and notes is a guard house that is only different from the one up the coast by its color. This one has clearly been painted by children. It is covered in handprints, and then on top of that is the Children's Village symbol, painted in by someone who was definitely a professional sign maker in the before times.

There are two guards, a few years older than us, rifles in their hands, hatchets on their belts. They look like brothers, but maybe I just want them to be. Their uniform is jeans and a gray T-shirt with the Children's Village logo. One of them wears red Converses. The other one wears hiking boots so beat up they look like they might fall apart if he sneezes.

"Good morning," Converse says, as if it's not strange to receive travelers here on the edge of the world. "Welcome to Children's Village Newport. Who are you here for?"

We all rush forward, talking over each other, reciting names and birthdays in one breath, but then we all stop in unison. We push Racer ahead.

"He goes first," I say. "Tell them who you're looking for."

"Edward—" Racer tries to catch his breath. We gather around him, hugging him from every side. He takes a deep, slow breath and starts over. "I am looking for my big brother, Edward Lee Menendez. His birthday is November 18th, 1995. He is a librarian. He likes green carnations a lot. Like this one." He thrusts it forward. "Like *this* one."

The rest of us squeeze our eyes shut, expecting the guards to consult the laptops on the desk before telling Racer there is no such person here.

"We know Eddie," Converse says. "Everybody knows Eddie."

My body flushes hot and cold in the same instant as we jump up and down, screaming as loud as we think we can get away with, shoving each other like we've just won a football game, the lottery, and a really important bet all at the same time.

"Eddie!" Racer breaks free of the celebrating scrum and starts down the highway on the other side, into downtown Newport. "I'm coming!"

"Racer, wait!" I start to go after him, but the other guard grabs my wrist.

"It's okay," he says. "If someone gets past us, the others know not to worry. Anyone will be happy to help him find the library. Who's next?"

We go in order of who has been separated the longest, starting with Deedee and Jordan. Their siblings are all here, and in good health. Once the paperwork is done, Cosmo is next. They hold my hand so tight my fingers go numb.

"If Deedee's and Jordan's siblings are all alive," Cosmo says, "what does that mean for the odds of ours being okay?"

I don't want to think about it. I just say Liv's name over and over in my head, like a kind of pulse. *Liv. Liv. Liv. Liv. Liv.* Navi hugs Soren tight. Soren has his eyes closed. I know he's doing the same. *Liv. Liv. Liv.*

"Bailey Nicholas Raleigh. September sixth, 2018. Gillette, Wyoming."

"He's here too." Converse gives Cosmo a pen to sign the reunification document. "Congratulations."

"Liv Ingrid Helvig," Soren and I say in unison. "April thirteenth, 2019."

He types. "Check."

"She's here?"

"She is," Converse says. "You'll see her ravens before you see her. And you won't hear her coming. That kid never wears shoes."

The guards radio ahead, so the children can be collected and brought to Reunion Park. They give us a map to the stables, where we can leave the horses first. From the stables to the park is less than five blocks, but it feels like the greatest distance any of us have traveled since the before times. When we're still two blocks away, I spot Liv's ravens perched on a streetlight at the edge of the park. A moment later, we see a small group of kids playing in the playground. I start running. Then we're all running. Even Captain. Liv gets to us first, crashing into Soren and me. The others catch up, and pretty soon we're a ball of tears and hugs and news. The younger kids want to talk about lost teeth, of all things. The older ones start an inventory of friends and alliances. They talk about the kids in their classes, their baseball teams and gymnastic club and what was for dessert last night—mini brownies—and what's for dessert tonight—peach cobbler. I don't know what I expected we'd want to talk about, but all these little colorful details are perfect right now. Huginn and Muninn take off, annoyed by the excitement.

"It's okay," Liv says. "They always come back."

"They kept you safe the whole way here," Soren says. "You're one lucky kid."

"But, Liv." I hold her shoulders tight as all the joyful chatter fades. "Why did you go?"

"We didn't have enough food," Liv said. "And I wasn't even supposed to be with you. I knew it would be easier for you if you didn't have to look after me. I knew you wouldn't just let me go. I knew you'd come find me, and I knew Cosmo was coming for Bailey. And I was right. I was right to go, wasn't I?"

"No, Livie," I whisper into her hair. "We never, ever wanted you to go. But I'm so glad we found you. We were so worried."

"I was never worried," Liv says. "I knew you would come. And now you're here!"

"True." I glance over at Cosmo, who sits on the road, knee to knee with Bailey. If there was a knob I could turn to shrink Cosmo, they'd be twins. Cosmo puts their hands on Bailey's cheeks. They kiss his forehead and run their fingers through his matching cowlick, and then put their hat on his head. They flick the brim up so they can keep gazing at him. He's crying and talking, holding Cosmo's vest in his fists, clearly not intending to ever let go again.

While Deedee's and Jordan's brothers and sisters take them to see their house—they live there with a house parent—Liv takes the rest of us to the library.

"Ta-da!" Liv flings her arms out to show Eddie, seated in a wheelchair, being hugged by Racer, who probably hasn't stopped hugging him since over an hour ago, just after he set off at a run to find him. When Racer finally lets go and stands straight, I see that both of Eddie's legs are gone at the knees.

"He couldn't come home," Racer says. "Because of what happened to him. What happened to his legs."

"I was on my way back to Marion Gap," Eddie explains to me and Soren. "I was trying to get back to Racer. But the bike got a flat, so I was on foot. And then I sprained my ankle and then one of the zees just caught up to me. It was either let it take me down or jump off a cliff." As Eddie keeps talking, that zee with the destroyed foot in Marion Gap flashes across my vision, as clearly as if he's in this library with us. "So I jumped. I just ran off, like some idiot in a comedy. Yelling, arms spinning, eyes wide open. You know what I was thinking about, Race?"

"What?" Racer hugs him again.

"I was thinking about Waffle Wednesday, and how you put mayonnaise and jam on yours and how gross that is." Eddie shakes his head. "There was not one other thought in my head."

Racer laughs so hard he starts to cry.

"But I'm *here*. We're both here!" Eddie peppers Racer's cheeks with kisses. "I lay there for nine days, maybe more. I had my pack, so I had some water. I had a bit of food. I just couldn't move. But then I passed out. That would've been it, but one of the Children's Village convoys stopped. And someone saw me. They brought me here."

—

Eddie lives in what used to be the offices leading off the circulation desk. They're waiting for a bed to be delivered for Racer. There's a room Racer can have for himself, but for now he's sitting on the step outside to make sure he catches the delivery people before they put the bed in that room, because he wants to be in the same room as Eddie.

"It's big enough to put two beds in there and still get around in the chair," Eddie says. "But we'll have to rearrange things a bit."

"We can do that," Soren says.

Eddie glances up at what's left of our group: Soren, Navi. Me and Cosmo, and Bailey, who won't let go of Cosmo's hand. And Liv and Captain, who are both stretched out on a giant stuffed hedgehog in the children's area, under a beam of light from a filthy skylight above.

"Does this compute?" He swishes a finger in the air, adding up Soren and Navi, then Cosmo and me. "Am I doing the math right?"

"Yeah." Soren takes Navi's hand and kisses it. Cosmo and I stand there, neither of us speaking up. We don't move closer to each other, but we don't move apart. I let Soren's answer speak for us. Accurately, I hope.

We're assigned two one-bedroom apartments in a three-story brick building across the alley from Jordan and Deedee and their family. The stairs creak as we climb to the top floor, led by Noriko from Housing, to two doors opposite each other at the end of the hall, with a tall window in between. It overlooks Jordan and Deedee's new backyard.

"They have a trampoline!" Liv spins on a dirty heel and thumps down the stairs and outside, across the gravel alley and into the yard, and flings herself onto the trampoline with Deedee's sisters, who haul her up so they can bounce together. Liv is the littlest, though, so when they jump, she shoots into the air, howling with laughter each time. Noriko hasn't even pulled the keys out yet.

"That is a different kid," Soren says. "And the same kid too."

For the first time, I allow that maybe it all worked out as it should have, and that losing Liv back at BATO was the best thing for her, even if it was the very worst thing at the time.

"Mr. Savvy, may I?" Navi opens his arms.

"Mr. Savvy, you may!"

"Shall we, Mr. Savvy?" Navi picks Soren up and carries him over the threshold of their little place.

"Why yes, we shall, Mr. Savvy!" Soren squeals when he sees the dingy apartment. "It's perfect!"

Captain hates this and barks loud and long enough that Navi has to come right back out and assure Noriko that he doesn't normally bark at all, which we all attest to.

Our apartment faces west but isn't high enough for an ocean view. All the windows are open, airing the place out. I smell the ocean, which is prize enough. Seagulls screech overhead, competing with the absolutely delicious sound of the kids playing in the backyard across the alley. Noriko points out a little alcove off the kitchen.

"This used to be the dining area," Noriko says. "But we put up pony walls to make these into bedrooms. It's the same across the hall." She takes out a small notepad. "I'll put Bailey in here and Liv with Soren and Navi? You can rearrange the occupants any way you want. Just let us know if you do. There's not a lot of housing since the kids came from Astoria. A while ago, you'd have had your own house." She pulls a roll of raffle tickets out of her bag and tears off ten for me and ten for Cosmo. "Housing charges start at the beginning of the month. There's a two-week grace period, so you don't have to worry about that until then. I'll come back to explain how that works another time. Welcome to Newport!" She shakes our hands and leaves.

Cosmo, Bailey, and I stand in the middle of the dim little apartment, which looks like it belonged to a granny before. The couch is overstuffed everywhere except at the corner by the window, where she probably sat every night. Everything looks like it was on its way to being very vintage just before Hypertox broke the world. There's a bunk bed in the alcove, both bunks neatly made up like hotel beds.

"Maybe Liv can sleep over sometimes?" Bailey sits on the edge of the bottom bunk.

"Is that the one you want?" Cosmo says. "Should we go get your stuff?"

"They'll bring it." Bailey lies down and stares at the slats above him and the stickers someone put on them in the before times. "Mostly dinosaurs," he reports. "Some trucks. One unicorn."

"We're going to check out the bedroom," Cosmo says. "You want to go join Liv and the other kids in the yard?"

He shakes his head. "I'll stay here."

There are two single beds in the bedroom, set as far apart as they would be if this was a college dorm.

"It's good that they don't make assumptions, I guess." Cosmo heads to the one set up in the corner along the far wall. It has an orange-and-brown crocheted blanket, tucked in on the sides, circa the same era as the rest of the fifty-year-old stuff in the place. They take their cowboy hat off, undo their belt, and drop their guns and Alice to the floor before sitting on the bed with a bounce. They take the pillow and bury their face in the yellow flower-print pillowcase. "A pillow. My *own* pillow. I get to sleep in this bed every single night."

I sit on the other bed and know immediately that it's not going to work for me. Sure, mattresses are always too short, but I'm used to that. The problem is when there is a footboard. Like this one, with two chunky posts and a tall, arching piece of particle board in between. My pillow is perfect, though, just the right amount of hard and soft. I don't want to put my gross head on it, though. Not before I have a shower. We've been told we can have one hot shower every two weeks. We can have a cold shower weekly, if we want it. We get a hot shower as part of intake, though. While my head swoons at the thought of the first shower—hot or cold—I've had since leaving home, I don't notice Cosmo working away at something across the room. When I look over, they've got their mattress on the floor and are dragging it to the window in the middle of the room, overlooking Deedee and Jordan's house.

"Get up." When I do, Cosmo yanks my mattress off and wrestles it into position beside theirs. "That footboard, right? No good." They pull off the blankets and sheets and the dingy mattress protectors too, until it's two naked mattresses on the floor. "Guaranteed whoever lived here before had a double. At least." They pull open every drawer—all empty—and then start looking in the closet, which is stacked with weathered boxes of Christmas ornaments and fishing gear. Cosmo pulls out two rods. "We can use those." They reach for a wicker hamper. "Bingo." They pull everything out into a heap on the floor. "Towels, face cloths, pillowcases, sheets!" They ball up a fitted sheet and toss it at me. It's pale blue with clouds and green flowers that remind me of Eddie's carnations.

We make the bed up and lie on it. From this angle, we see the tops of the power poles, and a lot of sky, and seagulls. Cosmo rolls onto their side and props their head on their hand. "You okay?"

"A bit stunned."

"Yeah." They sit up and take my hand. "But I'm here. With you. You know that, right?"

"I don't." I shake my head. "Because you don't have to be, now. We got where we were going." I cover my eyes with my other hand. I can't stand this conversation, even if I need it.

"I didn't have to be before," Cosmo says. "This does add up, Eira. *We* add up. Hey, hey." Cosmo takes my hand and wipes away my tears. They pull their sword from the sheath my dad tooled out of leather he tanned himself. "Do you know why I named it Alice?"

"You liked the name?"

"I do. But that's not it."

"I should've asked," I say. "I'm sorry."

"That's okay," Cosmo says. "We were busy. But I'm going to tell you now. Ever heard of Gertrude Stein?"

"No."

"Two American expats in Paris, 1907. Gertrude is a writer.

An avant-garde poet. Alice B. Toklas is a writer too, and a pianist. They fall in love and stay in love against all the odds and two world wars. They're together for almost forty years. Gertrude is big. Alice is little." Cosmo lifts their sword. "Like our Alice and Gertrude."

"Our Alice and Gertrude."

"Like us." Cosmo sets the sword down beside the bed and kisses me, first on my cheek, then my lips. "I named her Alice because I wanted Gertrude and Alice to be together. I want us to be together. Not just when we're fighting zees and trying to stay alive and get back to our siblings, but in times like this too. When we have pillows and there's no rat shit on the floor and we don't have to keep watch all night."

"Cosmo?" Bailey stands in the doorway, face wet with tears. "I fell asleep, and then when I woke up, I didn't know if you were still here."

Liv and Bailey show us where the mess hall is for this part of the village. It's the basement of a church, with tables put end to end to form long rows reminiscent of the feasts at any Renaissance faire. Except the din is not men and mead and wenches and ladies. This is nearly all children. Every table has a head—someone thirteen or older—but mostly it's just kids, being very loud. Liv and Bailey have regular tables, but they lead us to one in the far corner, where Deedee and Jordan and their brothers and sisters are already seated with plates of food.

I'm so glad to have us all together that I don't even glance at the tables down the row. But then something catches my attention. It's a table of all girls, and I know every single one of them. They are the seven Girl Scouts from the picture. Even while I want to run and grab them all up in hugs and cry with relief, I take a seat at our table instead. I sit backward on the bench, facing away from the table, and watch all these children, laughing and eating, talking with their mouths full, shoving each other around. There are Liv and Bailey going to get plates, and Cosmo and Soren and Navi behind them. Captain has found the open door closest to us and waits for scraps with his paws inside and the rest of him in a slice of sunshine coming down the stairs. He only moves when Racer and Eddie come in and he has to move aside for Eddie's chair.

When everyone is back with food, and we are two tables full of our people, I feel something drop. It's not something I can describe with words, because it's deeper than that. It's a kind of contentment that stretches outside of myself to encompass our tables: Cosmo by my side, Liv and Soren, my people, every child in the room, and all of the Village beyond. It takes in the sky and the seagulls and all the Pacific Ocean to the west and the dense forest to the east. And while it does all that and is that vast, it is also small and warm and tiny, as small as this Village is in comparison with our ruined planet.

This is the sweetest spot in the universe.

ACKNOWLEDGMENTS

For Pete's sake, Kelly Delaney, what even? Thank goodness you're such a smarty-pants, because I needed all of your know-how to get through this one. You are an ace editor, my dear, and it shows in this book.

Thank you to Hawk, for being my fellow zombie-apocalypse enthusiast. I will always say yes to watching a zombie movie with you, especially because you're so quick to poke holes in the storyline, only to sew it up with how it should be.

And thank you to Esmé, for fielding so many what-ifs when I was trying to figure out my characters and build the bonkers world they live in. And to the both of you, and Elena too, for helping me sort out the backstory for the zombies. To think this all started with a conversation about eye worms!